By MARINA FORD

Lovesick

Published by DREAMSPINNER PRESS
www.dreamspinnerpress.com

LOVESICK

MARINA FORD

Published by

DREAMSPINNER PRESS

5032 Capital Circle SW, Suite 2, PMB# 279, Tallahassee, FL 32305-7886 USA
www.dreamspinnerpress.com

Lovesick
© 2017 Marina Ford.

Cover Art
© 2017 Alexandria Corza.
http://www.seeingstatic.com
Cover content is for illustrative purposes only and any person depicted on the cover is a model.

ISBN: 978-1-63533-235-3
Digital ISBN: 978-1-63533-236-0
Library of Congress Control Number: 2016915181
Published January 2017
v. 1.0

Printed in the United States of America

This paper meets the requirements of
ANSI/NISO Z39.48-1992 (Permanence of Paper).

To Will.

I'M STARTING a diary.

It's not pathetic. Lots of famous people kept diaries. Lewis Carroll, Dostoyevsky, Samuel Pepys… and diaries are important. As a historian, I should know. I mean, without Pepys, where would we, historians, be? Or without Anne Frank? That being said, I doubt this is going to be that kind of diary. In fact, I doubt it will go past the first entry.

It's pissing it down today. I've watched enough *Battlestar Galactica* to want to die, and I've read every trashy sci-fi novel I have in the house. Well, except for the pile of as-yet-unpacked books on the table by the door. But new novels require a sense of excitement that I can't quite summon at the present. It shows how optimistic I was about today when I spent most of yesterday evening brooding in Waterstones.

I'm bored, and I need something to keep me away from the Internet. Therefore, diary.

I wish I had a better, more exciting job, so I could write about that. Lecturing post-war history at a university does not make a future Ian Fleming, though.

Here's something that happened recently. Two weeks ago the head of my department told me she was going to get her niece to do some web design for our school's website. We're a university. We're literally the place specialists in all manner of knowledge gather in one place to be all experty and specialisty about different subjects. Consequently, we've not just an actual IT department with all level of professionals in web design, but we've got *a special IT team* to deal with our website. However, she is the head of our department, so I approached this diplomatically by asking her, "Is this the niece who decided to forgo her A levels in favour of following Radiohead on tour?"

She said yes but did not think this was related to any argument against her decision. So yesterday (Saturday), she called me up about something and then, circuitously, she asked me about my friend from the

1

IT department. Had he, by any chance, the time to do a discreet spot of work on the School of History website?

"You let your niece have a go at it, didn't you," I said.

"What tipped you off?"

"Well, for starters the website's now called School of Patriarchy. And it plays 'Tears for Animals' in the background. I approve the message, on the whole, but it isn't very inviting, you know."

"She's very passionate."

"Yes, that she is."

Anyway, the school website is now back to its former shape.

This reminds me of the time Jack and I spent a whole evening after a conference in Bristol discussing feminism over whisky—he was trying to provoke me, and I knew it, but I let him because he is Jack, and he seemed to like it when I ranted about basically anything, and seemed amused when I started quoting Wollstonecraft at him and his male privilege.

Jack. Oh well, I suppose it's no use avoiding the subject of Jack. It is what I'm thinking about, after all, so I might as well write about it. He's the reason I'm avoiding the Internet. And the reason I refused all invitations to go out today. Not that anybody would want to be out in this kind of weather.

I don't want to speak to anyone, or see anyone, and I don't want to go on the Internet, where I would inevitably find myself on Facebook and then, equally inevitably, would find news about Him. And I don't want to see any news about Him.

I don't even know where to start writing about Him.

He is Professor Jack Gordon. He's the handsome, debonair celebrity of our department. He's worked with famous people all over the world, even had his own BBC series, which I ended up watching five times because that way I could stare at him to my heart's content.

I remember being intimidated by him when I first joined the department. It was my first post after finishing my research assistant job at Bristol. But then I spoke to him and found that behind the smug exterior hid a great mind. I mean, he wasn't just pomp and glory, he was actually very clever and his interests were far-reaching. For example, when he came to see me in my office one day and saw *Madame Bovary* on my desk, instead of rolling his eyes at me, he actually asked if I ever read Stendhal! I know I'm sounding like a stuck-up git just now, but I don't care. Here was a guy who didn't roll his eyes at me for liking classical literature. Can I honestly be blamed for thinking that he liked me?

I mean, let's gather the evidence: he came to see me in my office. Often. I mean, seriously, he came by a lot! And we talked. There was no end to the things we could talk about! I know that what I've said so far doesn't sound like he was exactly flirting with me, but to my idiotic, moronic, cretinous head, it did. It wasn't precisely *what* he said, but the way he said it. Something in his tone, or maybe the way he looked at me.

And then there was the Christmas party, two years ago.

It took place in the entry hall of our school, and everybody was there, and it was awful and crowded and boring. The sort of affair where you have to stand around the people you work with—or against, as the case may be—and gossip about that annoying brat of a student, or someone's ridiculous publication record, or more often than not, some new administrative decision that in effect puts three times as much paperwork between one thing and another for no other reason but that our university hates trees and free time.

So there was the Christmas "party," and Professor Sinclair decided to make a speech. She's, like, a hundred and a famous bore. She's the star of the first-year undergrad tradition of the nap bet. Basically, the student who can go through a whole semester of all Professor Sinclair's lectures, in any module, without once falling asleep wins the pool of money they collect at the beginning of the year. There were actual years where nobody won.

So when she made a speech, I, veteran that I am, decided to make myself scarce. I took a bottle of wine and a plate of snacks, sneaked under one of the buffet tables, and read *When Worlds Collide*. So I didn't notice immediately when the tablecloth lifted and I heard a male voice near my ear. It startled me.

It was only Jack, his head tilted a little. "Hiding, are we?"

I felt stupid being found like that, but he ducked and came to sit beside me. And there we were, shoulder to shoulder. Professor Sinclair's speech ended eventually, and the party went on, but Jack and I remained under the table, talking and joking and laughing and getting drunk until we became aware that there was no sign left of the party but the cleaning staff.

Four years of this.

For four years I thought this was a slow but sure path to something more. Four years of looks and smiles and what I thought was a secret understanding. At conferences Jack and I would undermine each other's arguments, engaging in witty discussions that were above everybody else's heads—or so I thought. At staff meetings, whenever anybody said anything stupid or typical, we'd immediately look at each other, understanding one another—or so I also thought. Every little moment like that translated into a whole relationship in my head. Probably I sound completely deluded, but I knew we weren't a *couple* or anything like that—I wasn't that far gone. I just thought we were on the same path, were thinking along the same lines, and eventually things would sort of, I don't know, unfold.

But nothing ever happened. I knew he had women, but he never talked of them to me and never seemed serious with anybody, so I thought it was just a front, a mask he wore. I waited.

I hadn't the guts to make a first move. I'm a coward. But I also imagined, absurdly, that this was something that would come about naturally, organically, sort of out of the moment. I know I sound like an idiot—I am an idiot. But I'd had enough of the club scene and the horny, sweaty things that went on there, where you look like meat to others and you look at them the same way. I wanted a connection, an understanding, and I thought this was it.

Then Jack got engaged.

I had no idea he was even dating anybody, and then one day I went to see Sarah, whose office is right next to mine, and who knows everything about everybody, and she told me. I was standing there, hot tea in my hand, not moving or saying anything. It was as if I turned to stone—that was exactly how heavy my heart felt at that moment. I was too shocked to react.

"You all right, pet?" she asked pityingly.

I don't remember what I said or how I got into my office afterwards. I just remember sitting behind my desk, dumbstruck, staring at the monitor of my computer, thoughts tangling themselves in my head. I eventually had it confirmed by Jack himself. Not personally. He sent out a mass email, and then I saw it on Facebook. She's American. They'd had a long-distance thing going on for ages, apparently, and now she is moving to the UK and they're getting married. She's photogenic, the kind of pretty that looks effortless and natural. Like she got out of bed looking goddesslike: a big bright smile, glorious blue eyes, perfect skin. In pictures together they look incandescently happy.

I feel like I've gone insane. Was it really all just in my head? Did this just happen to me? How could I have got so far? What the hell happened to me? I mean, I know I'm in my head a lot, but surely I'm not *literally* delusional, am I?

It was horrible after that. Everybody discussed Jack's wedding. He had brought her to some fancy dinner I didn't go to, and afterwards everybody was full of gossip about her. The reports on her were generally positive—about how beautiful and charming she is. I didn't want to hear it. The rumour ran that he was going to bring her to the Christmas party, so I didn't go. When I was feeling particularly bitter, I went on Facebook to just hate-stare at their pictures and people's congratulations.

And today was going to be different. Today I was not going to hate or feel bitter. I planned to sit in my flat and read or watch something. Play with my dog. Be normal. I was going to stop being a weirdo stalker-creep.

It's not a flattering thing to find yourself doing, let me tell you. But I regret not going out after all. Or having someone over. I insisted I needed the weekend to myself, but while it sounded very reasonable when I was explaining it to my friends over the phone, in hindsight it turns out that just because you know how to be sarcastic better than your opponent, that doesn't mean you're actually right.

I had one mission for this weekend: that I would not go on Facebook. I wouldn't. I won't.

All right, so I had a quick look at Facebook. I just needed to check that everybody was well. There was nothing on my news feed about that bloody wedding. Instead, I received an invitation. From Sarah. An invitation to a funeral, as a matter of fact. To be precise, an invitation to the funeral of Sarah's cat. Her cat's name being, by the by, Mr Bonkers. This is Sarah, and she's awfully fond of me, so I had to accept.

If ever the paranoid government of a dystopian future finds itself in need of proving my insanity so as to arrest me, they will probably use this diary as evidence.

Sunday, 17 January

IN CASE I ever find this diary, some ten years from now, and want to die of shame for how lame I was, I'm making this entry. Today you, Leo Taylor, had a pretty good day. There, how's that? You got up out of bed and you were fine. Nothing remarkable happened at all. You showered, you took your dog for a long walk, you even looked kind of good today—hair went in all the right directions, and you were even checked out by some guy as you waited to cross the street. And not even a lecherous old codger but a man you can think about later on.

Later, when you were at home, Squire—your dog who is probably dead now that you're reading it ten years from now—did that cute thing where he jumped straight onto your lap in an imperious manner, (which you can't resist no matter how many people tell you that you spoil him), totally disregarding the stacks of paper you had balancing there. Despite his nefarious interference, you graded all the essays from your Modern European Economic History class like a champ. And then you had enough time to clean your flat.

You've never been so quick and efficient in your life!

Friday, 22 January

THE CAT funeral.

Yeah, that happened today. I went and participated in—aided and abetted?—a cat funeral. Is that a thing now? I hope not. It was kind of, well, awkward.

That being said, poor Sarah was awfully upset about her cat's death, and she put a lot of work and effort into saying goodbye properly. The cat was buried in her garden. Her husband, Rob—poor soul—looked awkward as he stood there with his hands on the grip of the shovel, waiting for Sarah to finish her speech.

Surprisingly, a lot of people from the department came. I bet it's because Sarah's got dirt on all of them.

It's January, so it was bloody cold, and the burying bit, where Rob put the tiny cat coffin into the pre-dug hole and then shovelled earth on top, was quick. We had to wait in silence as Sarah arranged flowers on top of the pile of earth, while Rob played "I Will Always Love You" from his iPhone.

Yeah, that happened.

There was an awkward moment as Whitney Houston (am I the only one who prefers the Dolly Parton version?) bellowed into the cold, damp air, and we all stood there not knowing what to do next. Sarah and Rob's garden looks really nice in summer, but today it just looked awful: muddy ground, fallen leaves, dry and twiggy bushes lining the fence. Sarah sobbed as she stood at the foot of the grave. Rob's eyes caught mine, and so I went to her, put my arm around her, and slowly, delicately turned her back towards the house.

The gathered crowd let out a relieved sigh as they followed, probably because the wind had picked up, and it had started to drizzle again.

Inside, a large table stood piled with sandwiches and cold snacks and Sarah's excellent cakes. She does make amazing cakes, and I began to suspect that some people came not to say goodbye to Bonkers the Magnificent, but for the baked goods. I mean, even Ralph from the School of East Asian Studies came, and I know he didn't care about Bonkers because he kept referring to Sarah as "Steph." And he ate shitloads of cake. And then he produced a Tesco shopping bag from up his sleeve and started packing some to take home.

In the background, on the TV a slideshow was running featuring Bonkers looking like an annoyed celebrity, tired of having his picture taken. The background music was a compilation of power ballads. Judging from their taste in music, Sarah and Rob's ears must have had a funeral of their own some time ago. I wonder who came to that.

I gravitated towards the bookshelves and examined the huge collection Sarah had of books on anthropology and mythology. There was also a respectable amount of literature on trains—Rob's hobby. I was busy with this when I heard a sort of welcoming noise coming from the gathering behind me. Engrossed by a number of books that formed a series on African mythology, especially the one that talked about Odinani, I didn't turn in time. And then it was too late.

I heard "Hey," and then I turned, and my heart stood still.

I smiled, my face heated up, and I found myself unable to open my mouth. Next to Jack, smiling and looking extremely pretty, stood his fiancée.

I hadn't even bothered to put on my contact lenses. My hair—the blondish mop that passes for my hair—had got wet and tangled in the weather outside. I wore a black sweater and jeans. She, on the other hand, looked as though she was only stopping in on her way to a catwalk show in Milan.

"Leo!" Jack said breezily. "Where have you been hiding?"

He looked smug. My smile stretched wider. Probably like that of a maniac.

"I was ill," I said. My voice sounded shaky even to my own ears.

"You didn't come to the departmental Christmas thing," he said. "You missed some party!"

"Oh yeah," I said with a laugh. "I can guess. I know how wild a bunch of eighty-year-old World War I fanatics can get. They party like it's 1921."

He laughed. How dare he!

"Oh, this is Sasha," he said, finally pointing the wineglass in his hand at the woman standing next to him. "Sasha, darling, this is Leo. Haven't I told you about him?"

Sasha was smiling beautifully, and I waited for some sign of recognition, fooling myself that he had indeed spoken about me. You know, in the evenings, when they were half-naked, and laughing about the gay dweeb who slobbered after him. For better or for worse, there was no sign of recognition in her face.

"I was just looking at these," I said, pointing at the books.

I didn't know what else to say, and Jack kept looking at me expectantly, as though I were a magician he'd paid to see, and I'd come without a hat or a rabbit.

"Oh, I use those too!" Sasha gushed, suddenly quite animated.

"Sorry?" I asked.

"I use those too," she said again. "You know, to practice my balance."

I didn't get it. I looked at her, and then I looked at Jack. And then at her again, and again at Jack. She was beaming a wide smile, but Jack's expression was somewhat pained.

"You use... you use *books* to practice your balance?" I asked, feeling a little prick of amusement, which I knew was bad, but oh God, did I need it. Because I began to suspect that she did not mean "balance an argument" when she said that.

"Oh yeah, I'm a yoga instructor, and sometimes, in tree pose, to make it more difficult, I balance books on my head."

I glanced over at Jack again, and he said, "Sasha, dear—"

But I cut in. "That sounds hard. Do you think this one would be too light for the purpose?"

I took a book at random. I know I was being a dick, but to see Jack's face as she actually began to balance the book on her head, talking about how Jack had "so many books, but they weren't all good for balancing, and they take up so much space!" was priceless.

He got fed up at the end, and shooting an angry glare at me, he snapped the book off her head.

I left them then, under some pretext, and wove my way through the crowd to say goodbye to Sarah and to leave. She hugged me fiercely, which is slightly weird when the huggee is tallish and slim, and the hugger is shorter and rotund. I thanked her for the whole thing and promised to give her a ring tomorrow. Then I shook Rob's hand and went to look for my coat. Somewhere in the corridor, near the front door, Jack caught up with me.

"Oi! Wait up!" he said.

I had just pulled the hood of my coat up—which, in the full-body mirror next to the coat hooks made me look like a delinquent youth, especially in contrast with Jack's rather more respectable look: his elegant suit, the way he kept his hands in his pockets like a *GQ* model, and the fashionably arranged disorder of his brown hair.

"What?" I said. "I've got a bus to catch."

"Yeah? That wasn't nice, what you did there."

"What wasn't nice?" I stopped looking at him because it didn't help my clarity of mind.

I suddenly realised that if he didn't know I was gay or into him, the whole scene back in the sitting room could be interpreted in quite another way. I didn't want a quarrel with him, but I'd be damned if I apologised to him or to her.

"What you did to Sasha, you ape." He didn't sound angry, only a mixture of annoyed and amused.

"What did I do?"

"You know full well—"

9

"I beg your pardon," I said, "we had a civilised discussion about the ideal usage of books."

"You were making fun of her, Leo." He lowered his voice reproachfully. I looked up and saw his eyes alive with amusement. "I wish you'd get to know her better before writing her off like that. She's a nice, sweet person, who only got the wrong end of the stick there."

"Ah, sticks!" I cried, my voice high and my eyelids fluttering in an imitation of Sasha. "I use those too!"

I don't know what possessed me. It was really out of line, but he burst out laughing, and then he said, "You know, men used to call each other out for less."

"All right, then," I said, grabbing an umbrella and pointing it at him in an en garde stance.

"Stop it, you fool." He laughed, swatting the tip of the umbrella away. "How was the cat funeral?"

I said with mock solemnity, "A beautiful ceremony. It did justice to the dignity and determination that characterised the life of Bonkers the cat."

"Well, fuck me," Jack said. "And here I thought they'd just dump the old thing into a ditch."

"That's because you're a barbarian," I said.

He laughed, and it felt so like old times, like he was one of *us* again, that I had to grind my teeth not to say something. Something which would, in the end, be very humiliating, and I am glad I didn't. I left quickly, head ducked under the strength of the rain, and tried not to think about it.

I took the bus home, listening to The Cure on my phone. Out of the windows, the streets were barely visible through the rain. Not that I wanted to see anything—it was bloody gloomy out there: a cement-coloured mass, with here and there a bright umbrella bobbing away into the distance. Tempted to consider where the bright red umbrella was going and who was hiding underneath it, until I realised I didn't give a crap.

The bus kept going with the tempo of an injured snail and kept stopping with a loud squeak. At some point two giggling schoolgirls came up onto the first floor of the double-decker. They fell into their seats, laughing, soaking wet, words and giggles intermingled, their voices the same, their hair different shades of the same colour—a sort of dark blonde—their jeans cut where their bony, white knees were. I was finding myself growing angry at their careless cheerfulness. What were they so giggly about anyway?

Of course, it's easy enough to be angry with womankind for stealing all the men, when actually I should be angry with me and my brain. I suppose, imagining that Shakespeare really meant it to be Romeo and Julio, or that Herbert and Pip in *Great Expectations* were obviously into each other, is not me being cleverer than anybody else; it's just sad and stupid. Jack's straight and he's getting married. This is real. Whatever.

Time to look for job opportunities elsewhere, maybe.

Sunday, 24 January

I GUESS it was to be expected that I shouldn't have a peaceful weekend after meeting the love of my life's fiancée. It wasn't too bad, though.

I spent all of yesterday marking papers and preparing for class, but today I decided I would not repeat my former mistake—no brooding at home and licking my wounds. I wanted to be out of the house. I'd be safe enough with my friends, since I always took really good care not to talk of Jack too much. So imagine my surprise when we finally got down to the pub, and I broke the news as smoothly and suavely as I could. "So, my friend Jack's getting married."

And they all burst out with "What!" and "Noooo!"

So yeah, I might not be as subtle as I think I am.

When I expressed my astonishment at their reaction, Amelia hooted and said, "Oh God, are you *serious*?"

Mark, her husband, shook his head at me. "I'm sorry, mate, but we all thought you were dating him, you know"—and here he did finger quotes—"secretly."

When I indicated I was sure I'd never said a word to make them think there was anything between me and Jack, they burst out laughing.

Lucy said, "You know, you always talked of him with a goofy smile on your face."

"And you kept shushing us that one time his dull show came on the telly!" Amelia added. She was getting loud. She is a large, boisterous woman.

"Yeah, guy looked like a prick," Mark said. "No huge loss there."

"Wow, thanks," I said. "So here's to my evening of not talking or thinking about him."

At this, Lucy hit the table with her pint, spilling half her beer and shouting, "What? Mate, that's not how you get over a guy. You know what they say. The best way to get over someone is to get under someone. You need to get yourself some mangina, love."

"That sounds gross," I said. "I'm pretty sure I was vaccinated against it."

"Lucy's totally right," Amelia said. "No use moping about, like I know you love to do, locking yourself in and reading romantic poetry, and thinking about how... I don't know... *Tristan and Isolde* is really about two men, or something." *How did she know?* "You need to get out there!"

The consensus was clear, but since I didn't just want to get laid, I wanted to drop the subject. I looked to Mark for help. He blinked at me, then at Amelia, who rolled her eyes. Somewhat hesitantly, he began an anecdote about work. Something about a client who didn't keep his part of the contract, and when Mark said he'd sue his arse off, the fellow had the cheek to say, "I didn't think you could afford a lawyer, considering I don't pay you." Amelia, who was very defensive about Mark's affairs, began a tirade on the subject of "that Welsh bastard," and took the heat off me for a few moments.

It's not that I didn't want to discuss the issue with them, but to get love advice from a married couple was like getting advice from your mother. They don't know what the real world's like anymore. They live after the happily ever after—a sort of bubble in which small things don't even exist. Like wondering whether you can be with someone who said they'd never read Asimov.

In Mark and Amelia's case, this was worse, since I introduced them to each other at uni, and they've been together ever since. Their experience of feeling lonely and unloved is basically non-existent. Lucy, on the other hand, is a whole other kettle of fish. She is perpetually, gloriously single and forever on the prowl. So while her experience in dating is extensive, her advice has a certain monotonous quality to it. There was nothing, to her mind, you could not solve with a good roll in the hay.

So, of course, as soon as an opening presented itself, she turned to me and asked, "When's the last time you got jiggy with it?"

"What?" I asked.

"You know, when's the last time someone stuffed your man muffin?"

"Lucy!" I couldn't help laughing.

"Well?" she demanded. "When's the last time you engaged in gland-to-gland combat? When was your last walk in the cabbage field? When—"

By this time, we were all laughing, and she blinked at us and said, "What? What's so funny? Oh, *excuse me*." And then, putting on an accent that I guess she imagined stuffy university lecturers sounded like, she said, "Can you identify, sir, the temporal dimensions of your most recent amorous congress?"

I shook my head. "You don't expect me to actually tell you, do you?"

"Why not?"

"Well, I'm not going to tell you."

"See, that tells me it's been way too long," she said. "Listen, I'm not taking no for an answer. There's this party I'm going to, lots of single people, lots of people to meet. We'll doll you up and you can come with me for the Hunt."

At that point I was wondering why she didn't just call it the Reaping or something equally unpleasant. But the discussion was over. At the back of my mind, I think I realised that she was right—I did need to take my mind off Jack and Sasha. As much as I hated the image of a night out with Lucy, looking for men, I agreed, with a grumble, to go with her.

Either way, they let the topic drop at last. Amelia and Mark told me of this one gay guy they knew, who was also single, but I hope my expression told them precisely how little interest I had in being set up with some random man who also couldn't get laid.

When I got home, I saw a young woman moving into the flat across from me. I said hi; she seemed friendly. I forgot what her name was, though, so I may need to check on her mail when I inevitably get it delivered to my door.

Our postwoman drinks.

Saturday, 30 January

I WOKE up at noon today. That is the absolute latest I've ever got out of bed, ever. Mind you, I only came home at about four in the morning.

Consequently, my mouth tasted like a pub toilet this morning, and my head felt like someone had pulled out all my teeth and hammered them into my brain right through my skull. But the worst of it was that no matter how astonishingly plastered I got last night, I somehow did not manage to erase it from my mind. I'm only glad I didn't pick anybody up after all. In fact, I'm pretty sure I spent much of the night with this Scottish woman, Heather Something, drinking myself stupid.

That is what I remember of the night.

Lucy took me to a bar-club with some of her friends, placing me strategically next to men she thought I might find cute.

I didn't. I'm a one-man sort of guy, and while Jack was on my mind, I was unlikely to find the detritus of London's late-night social scene appealing. None of the men were remotely what could be regarded as "my type." I'm not sure what that is either, but I know when I see someone who isn't it.

There was one bloke who kept trying to engage me on the subject of football, which was just not going to happen; another who looked like he was as high as a kite; and another who was a Tory. One of those horrid, suited, City types whose opinions were sucked in with his mother's milk and who'd never thought to figure out whether they made the remotest sense. When I tried to challenge him on the notion that poor people were so by choice, his response was "You're cute." So that was obviously going nowhere.

Another candidate, upon hearing me tell someone I was a feminist, interrupted my conversation with "Don't say that!" I still don't know what the hell he thought I was saying.

Lucy asked me whether I was insane to talk politics with people in a bar, but what else was I to talk to them about? I didn't know them, and politics is the sort of thing everybody has an opinion on.

Finally, Lucy settled on some guy with whom she spent the rest of the night, and I got drunk with Heather.

Heather was a burly young woman with a very catchy, hoarse laugh, and she had not the least trouble discussing the upcoming election with me. We agreed wholeheartedly on all points.

At four I stumbled back home. Squire was with Daria, the old woman who lives next door and dog-sits for me. The last thing I remember was reaching my door, stumbling, the world whirring around me. And then I woke up on my sofa, covered in an old dog blanket. I've no idea how I even got into the house.

So that was a truly depressing evening, and I'm paying for it now because I've got so much to do this weekend and all I feel like doing is joining Bonkers in his grave.

My parents are coming over tomorrow. I need to clean. And also, I've got to rewrite the paper I submitted for publication two months ago. The reviewers ripped it to shreds, so I need to try and put it back together.

And I need to go shopping—which reminds me, I need to learn to cook.

Sunday, 31 January

MY PARENTS just left, thank the Maker. As much as I love them, they can be tiresome. Though now retired, my dad worked for a well-known liberal think tank, and my mum worked for the European Union. Both see it as their priority to get me as far in my professional life as possible. They saw the PhD as a good start and my decision to remain in academia as a giant failure—compared to my sister, anyway.

When I went down to let them in, that was the first thing they said to me.

"Lena is doing well!" they announced, almost in unison.

I decided to ignore whatever they were implying with that. "Good for her," I said with the sort of cheerfulness you can only put on.

Lena works for the UN and climbs their ranks like some sort of agile gorilla; she's lived all over the world and takes her live-in boyfriend, Yi Chen, everywhere she goes.

It's not that I'm not jealous of Lena. I do envy her success, but at the same time she deserves all she's achieved—I'm okay with that. I'm also okay with what I'm getting for the work I do.

I wish my parents would join us on that level of maturity.

As we were climbing the stairs to my flat and my parents were murmuring to themselves about how I should be making my first steps onto the property ladder, this guy I've never met before walked past us down the stairs and smiled at me.

"How are you doing?" he asked with the sort of concern that implied this wasn't the first time we'd met.

I was very aware of my parents' presence, so I just said, "Fine, and you?" and left with a smile indicating that I wasn't actually interested and neither should he have been.

My parents' visit lasted about four hours, which included dinner and my slow decline into schizophrenia.

"Lena started this fund, and on the opening night, she actually got Michelle Obama to attend!"

"Lena is running a marathon to gather money to cure breast cancer!"

Lena this, Lena that. I was just waiting for them to finally announce she had not only won the Nobel Prize, but that they'd created a separate category for her, the Lena is Excellent Award—you know, like there's a separate prize for maths or economics. Only this one would be just for her.

Once they'd told me everything Lena was up to, they turned on me.

"What do you need to do to become professor?" "What about tenure, is that still a thing?" "When did you last publish something?" "Weren't you going to write a book?" "Whatever happened to that conference you were supposed to chair?" "John Fitzalan's son works at Cambridge... want me to find out if they've got any positions opening?"

It was like a very well-executed trial, the goal of which was not so much to judge you innocent or guilty as to drive you into a frenzied confession of "Fine! I admit it! I am inadequate!" But I composed myself and answered their questions as calmly as I could, with non-answers.

I've learned this much from my life with these people: if you try to actually answer their questions, they commit you to what you said. There will be telephone calls, emails, cross-referenced folders, and meetings set up. My parents should never have retired. They should have started a small country for people who don't know how to organise their own lives. They'd have had a ball.

I cannot put into words how absolutely knackered I am now that they've left. I love them to bits, but at a distance.

I need to go to sleep now. And it's only 9 p.m.

Thursday, 4 February

HAD A rather awful day today. At one of my BA-level lectures, the projector decided to stop working, and I had to pass around an illustration of Walesa at the round-table discussions of the 1980s.

Naturally I got it back in such a state that you'd think someone had had a good go at shagging it. Sometimes I think I work at a zoo.

On the upside, I was asked one intelligent question today. One girl asked me how the members of Solidarity coped in the post-communist world. Unfortunately, although I could provide the answer, nobody else was interested in continuing the discussion, and so I returned to the lecture.

At another class, a seminar, nobody had done the reading I assigned. In fact, that one boy, Craig Something, decided he'd confuse me by dazzling me with his smile to mask that he'd come completely unprepared. Like that would work on me. He should know better than to try and flirt with me—in class no less—with ignorance as a weapon. But what's the use of getting angry? I mean, I can only teach so much. Some of it must come from their own reading.

Anyway, got back late today, still haven't picked up Squire from Daria's, and should look into getting something vaguely food-shaped.

Monday, 8 February

HAD DINNER with Amelia and Mark and the kids. They live out in St Albans, so had to get the train—it's a hassle, I won't lie, but the meal's a tradition, and I didn't dare make an excuse and decline the invitation.

After dinner, Mark took the boys out into the garden to play football or rugby or a weird combination of the two. Amelia and I were sitting in their dining room, watching the boys outside, when she turned to me and said, "I envy you."

This was startling. "Envy me what?" I asked.

"Well, you know, you're alone."

"Yeah, thanks for the reminder."

"Any day could bring something new. Any day you can meet the man of your dreams… any man is a new possibility, any party full of expectations…. That's so exciting."

I laughed. "You're an idiot. The exciting thing you're talking about is the possibility of maybe one day having what you already have."

She smiled. "You don't understand," she said with a sigh.

It worried me. "You're not thinking of leaving, are you?"

"What!" she said. "No! Of course not."

Phew. I was just about to suggest we switch lives for one day, but then I thought one hour would be enough for her to realise how stupid she was being.

"I don't know," she said, "sometimes I miss being single. Sometimes I wish I hadn't met Mark so soon, you know? To have a bit of a playing field, to have fun with you and Lucy as you pick up guys and see where the evening takes you."

"No, you don't," I said. "You miss being alone once in a while, maybe. But you don't want to be single. And childless. Come on. You've no idea what you're talking about."

She sighed and changed the subject.

It was weird to hear the person who had everything talk of being jealous of me, the person who didn't. She was right, I didn't understand. But it did make me think how perhaps it would be wiser to focus on how awesome it is to be free and not settled with kids and husband and mortgage. Maybe I should stop thinking of my situation as pathetic loneliness and think of it as magnificent, luminous, glorious freedom?

Sunday, 14 February

FUCK YOU, Valentine's Day.

Tuesday, 17 February

SO HERE'S something weird that happened today. I had a meeting with Charlie, this PhD candidate whose second supervisor I am, in my office, when there was a knock on my door, and Jack looked in.

I told him I was busy, and he apologised and left. When my meeting with Charlie was over, I was just folding my glasses up to put them away when I realised that someone was standing in the doorway. Jack was still waiting for me. He had waited for half an hour outside my door.

Odd.

He asked whether I had time to grab lunch.

Unprecedented.

I said I had time to go and buy a coffee, something I was going to do anyway, so he followed me down. I tried to be blasé, and as he wasn't talking, I just said any random thing that came into my head. He seemed distracted but followed me all the way down to the rec room, greeting whoever passed us, and waited with me as the kettle came to a boil. Then he walked with me to the reception office, helped me pick out the assessment forms and the thick pile of papers that waited for me in my pigeonhole, and then walked me back up to my door. We've done the coffee walk together before, but never in this weird way—he was never usually quiet.

"Well, was nice catching up with you," I said when we reached my door.

"Yeah, sure."

My hands were full so he helped me with the door. I thought he was gone when the door shut. When I put everything down on my already cluttered desk, I turned to switch the light on. He had come in after me and was standing there, hands in his pockets, waiting silently. "Is everything all right?" I asked.

He just looked at me.

Now, this was very odd. I felt a prickle at the back of my neck. He'd never looked at me like *that* before.

"Are you busy this weekend?" he asked.

"I was going to do some work, I guess."

"I was wondering whether you'd like to go out for drinks, say, Saturday?"

I didn't respond for a while, because my brain needed time to slowly wake up to the realisation that something was happening. Eventually, I said uncertainly, "Yeah, sure. Is Sasha coming too?"

Another moment of silence. Then he smiled. "No, it'd be just us. Like old times."

Old times? I swear there was a flirtatious angle to his smile, but I dare not trust myself on this subject. He told me he'd be in touch, and then he left. And I just stood there.

Then it hit me. I'm going out with Jack! Jack asked me out!

Oh my God! I have no clothes.

Shit.

Friday, 19 February

I WENT out to clothes-shop with Lucy today.

It's not that I don't have dress sense. It's that years of dressing in T-shirts and trousers have translated into a wardrobe that looks like it belongs to an American 1990s sitcom cast member. I don't want to project an "I don't know what I'm doing" vibe. I want something along the lines of "Come to bed with me."

Mind you, I wouldn't if he's still with Sasha. But then, if he were, he wouldn't be going out with me, would he? I meant to find out, but Sarah was off sick this week, so there was no reliable, discreet way of conducting espionage. Facebook tends to deal only in news that rubs shit in your face, not actually useful information, so that wasn't any help. Lucy said I shouldn't worry one way or another—"*You're* not in a relationship, after all. *You* can do whatever the hell you like!"—but I'm not that guy. Or at least I hope I'm not. Either way, it was important to dress for the occasion.

It wasn't easy to come to an agreement with Lucy. Her preferences run along the lines of S & M sex slave, which would not translate well into the sphere inhabited by the Jack Gordons of this world. Finally we settled on a charcoal-grey shirt and black jeans, which were tighter than was comfortable, but Lucy assured me they made me look "sexy as hell."

I wasn't accustomed to thinking of myself in that way, but I was happy enough with what I saw in the mirror.

"Jesus, Leo, you'll break that poor man's straight heart!"

"Do you think so? Will the gay one be the only one remaining, then?"

"Let's hope so," she said.

"Should I wear cufflinks? I've never worn cufflinks in my life. He's the sort of bloke you think you should wear cufflinks for."

She snorted. "Darling, do you want to fumble with cufflinks when you stagger home at night with him? Exactly. No cufflinks, no ties, nothing that will be a bother to take off when you're in a hurry. Or on, for that matter," she said. "That reminds me, you're stocked up on condoms, right? I mean, the last time you had sex, was that in a time when civilisation had invented condoms?" She put her hand to her mouth and her eyes widened comically. "You're not going to try and use lamb intestines on him, are you?"

"Shut up," I said with a laugh. "We're not going to have sex. It's our first date. If it even is a date."

"Oh puh-lease!"

"I'm not like you, okay?"

"Oh puh-lease!" she said again. "You've been puppy-dog-eyeing that guy for four years, Leo. You better rub one off before you go, or else—"

"Lucy! We're in public!"

"Yeah, and so? Nobody's listening. You better heed me, Leo, you don't want to get into a situation—"

"I'm twenty-nine, okay? I know how to take care of things."

"Are you sure?" she asked, raising a dubious eyebrow.

"Yes! I'm not going to sleep with him on our first date, if it is a date. And I'm not going to burst out of excitement. I'm not a fumbling teenager anymore, all right?"

"If you say so," she said without conviction.

"Should I cut my hair?"

"No, it looks cute like that."

It is a trifle long—I have to keep brushing it off my brow and tucking it behind my ears—but I trust Lucy to know what's best. Besides, I realised that despite what I'd told myself, I was getting much too excited about this meeting. After all, this "date" didn't mean he wanted to do anything other than have a drink with a mate from work. I might have read more into his looks and smiles again than was warranted. Okay, so I probably have.

When I got home, I had to take Squire out for a walk, and then I bumped into that man again, the one who spoke to me on the stairs last time my parents were here.

Again he smiled at me, and this time he said, "Fully recovered, then, I see?"

I stopped, because honestly, I didn't know who the hell he was and why he kept speaking to me in this familiar way. While Squire was taking care of the scent department, sniffing the man's boots, I said, "Have we met?"

He started in surprise and then laughed and said, "You don't remember? Well, that explains it. Sorry, we met the other night."

I had no idea what he was talking about. I wondered vaguely if he could be one of my students, but he was too old for that, roughly my own age. Nor do I think I would have forgotten the guy. He was tall and hunky enough that if he hadn't smiled, he would have alarmed me with his insistence on speaking to me. "Are you mistaking me for somebody else?"

"I don't think so," he said. "You tend to remember the people you have to hold up while they vomit."

I wondered whether he was some sort of weird stalker. Or a psycho. I planned my escape route; it involved running upstairs. I sized him up quickly—he was pretty fit, so there was no doubt that he'd be quicker than me. Downstairs would be easier; there'd be people there. Plus, gravity would be on my side. Squire seemed to like him, though. He began to scrabble the guy's leg with his forepaws, eager for attention.

"Oh, hey there!" the stranger said to Squire. "What breed is that? He looks like one of those Lassie dogs, but tiny."

"Er, a sheltie. Shetland sheepdog, that is. I'm sorry, I don't remember vomiting in your presence—Down, Squire, down!—or vomiting at all, for that matter. You must have me confused with somebody else."

He laughed. "I'm Alex," he said, stretching out his hand. It was covered in something white. "Sorry, that's paint. I just moved in opposite you. I should have probably started with that. You were sick in the corridor in front of your door, and I helped you back into your flat. And then you were sick again. And then I put you on the sofa."

"There was no sick on my floor," I said doubtfully.

"I cleaned it up. And then I thought of standing by and making sure you didn't choke on your own vomit through the night, but you seemed to have calmed down. Also, I thought that you probably had nothing left to vomit with. And it would have been strange to stay the night. I'm glad you survived, though." He smiled again. God, this was embarrassing. I wished the ground would open underneath me and just swallow me up. Where's a sinkhole when you need one?

"Wow," I started. "I'm… I don't know what to say… whether to apologise or to thank you first…. I… I… thank you?"

I reached forward to clumsily shake his hand, despite the paint on it. I didn't realise the paint was only half-dry, though, so our hands stuck together and we had to pry ourselves apart, half laughing, half apologising, entirely fucking awkward.

God! He must have thought I'm some sort of drunken hobo idiot. I should have got that "I have a PhD" T-shirt when I had the chance.

He seemed to take it in good humour, but I started babbling. "I assure you this was a one-off…. I've never had anything like this happen before, and I swear it won't happen again! I'm a good neighbour, I promise. Ask Daria… she dog-sits for me sometimes. Or that girl who moved in opposite me—"

"*I* live opposite you," he said.

"Oh, sorry, I mean… the other day I saw this girl…. She'd just moved in, I thought."

"No, that was me moving in. You must have met Thea."

"Oh, maybe. Well, it was lovely to meet you… again. And again, I'm sorry. And thank you…."

We were going to shake hands again but then just waved, laughing once more at the previous handshaking fiasco, and then I walked away. I'm so embarrassed I wish I could fall asleep and not wake up.

Oh hell.

Sunday, 21 February

FIRST DATE with Jack. Or was it?

Well, it wasn't a date, as such. I'm not sure. We went to this upscale bar, which looked awfully trendy and was filled with people who looked like they discussed their son's progress at Eton and the property prices in the Cotswolds. In short, I felt rather out of place and was worried that I looked it. Luckily, I was determined not to drink more than a glass or two of wine—the embarrassment of Friday did not exactly escape my memory.

I've been avoiding Alex the Neighbour since our last encounter.

So, back to the date/not-date. Besides the stifled setting, the evening was actually pleasant. At first, when Jack and I met outside the bar as arranged, he was a little stiff and uncertain, but once we settled down, he relaxed and turned his charm on.

After he had some wine in him, he relaxed out of the charm and into that easy way he had with me, which had made me fall for him so hard. When we talked, though, it was like nothing we've ever had before. I mean, we talked about the same things, we spoke about the same shows we liked and the same books we read. We argued about politics and religion with the same improper fervour as before. So that was like normal.

But there was more. It's like all the things I'd imagined happening between us for the last four years were now happening for real. We spoke of his BBC show.

"If you think about it," he said, "when they show history on TV, it's basically propaganda."

"Do they censor the information you're allowed to talk about?"

"Well, they don't want *new* information. Especially when it comes to the World Wars. There is a very specific narrative dominating the psyche of the nation...."

I said, "I suppose the general image we get, in popular culture, is one that would make the elites look good, if you're talking about a discursively dominated propaganda system à la Foucault."

"Well, yes, exactly!" His eyes were glistening as he reached his hand forward and grabbed mine. "Think about it for just one second! A whole social sphere of entitled people sent young men to die in a fashion nothing short of torturous, and we know that! We celebrate them and sympathise with them post hoc. But!—and here is the crux of the matter—we live in a country that still has a monarchy, and most of our politicians come from the same background as those people who sent us to die so needlessly and torturously. And who will do so again! How is it that we put forward all this information, and we put two and two together, but we never get four?"

Looking back at this conversation, I realise that the other people in the bar must have thought we were insane.

"Maybe because the only 'four' possible is a communist revolution?" I suggested.

"Ah," he said, raising an eyebrow, "but is it? Let me ask you something...."

We spoke like that for hours. Later, we walked to my block of flats. He walked me all the way to my door, and we chatted there for a brief while. It was so easy between us, and though I really did only have two glasses of wine, all my honourable resolve about not sleeping with him melted away.

And so I asked, "Do you want to come in?"

A sort of awareness snapped into his eyes. I was conscious of him scanning me. I felt like a courtesan as I leaned back against the door, smiling at him with my eyes half-closed. He wanted me; I was sure of it. No man looked at another man like that without some serious intentions.

And then he said, in a sort of whisper-growl, "I don't think I should."

He didn't sound as though he really couldn't. It sounded like an affectation, as if he was toying with me. He was leaning in to me, and I thought he was going to kiss me, but by then I had lost my patience with him and said, "Well, see you at work, then."

Luckily, I managed to find the right key and fit it into the lock without much fumbling—now I know why sobriety is such a good thing—and so I managed a very graceful "Bye, Jack" before disappearing indoors.

I saved my dignity, but at what cost? I think I underestimated how fucking horny I am. Well, either way he left, and at least I had the opportunity to hit back at him a little. I mean, hell, what does he mean by fucking with me like that?

Wednesday, 24 February

I HAVE accepted an invitation to a conference in Oslo in two weeks' time. I'm quite excited, as it means I'll be able to see faces I haven't seen since my fieldwork days. I worked on resistance and the Solidarity movement, and I spent nearly a month travelling around Scandinavia interviewing various people who had fled the Soviet bloc in the seventies and eighties.

Anyway, I've a ton of preparations to see to. Need new shoes. Need to speak to Daria about leaving Squire with her. Then I have a massive pile of essays to check, presentations to mark, and then Charlie just sent me yet another version of his methodology chapter, which looks nothing like a chapter or any kind of methodology known to humans of Planet Earth. Oh man, this is going to be a long day.

Friday, 26 February

THE CONFERENCE in Oslo is next week, and I've been in a hectic frenzy, trying to arrange replacements for lectures and placing lecture notes online, and I haven't even begun to prepare for the conference itself. So I've been a bit busy, and as that was the case, I forgot about Jack.

I don't really know how it happened. As I was dealing with emails and preparing Dan to replace me in my lectures, I sort of blanked everybody out. So when Jack knocked on my office door and asked if he could come in, I was genuinely surprised to remember him. I invited him in but told him that I had little time.

"I just wanted to see if I could come over on Friday," he said.

I had been flicking through a thick binder of course timetables, but I stopped mid-motion at that point. "What, to my place?" I asked. He smiled and nodded. "Does Sasha know about this? Does she know you saw me on Saturday?"

"No, she doesn't," he answered.

Considering that he almost kissed me that Saturday, I decided to drop the coy act, since whatever he was, completely straight he certainly was not. "Well, in that case, Jack, I frankly would rather you did not come to see me. I'm not comfortable with this. If you're engaged, then I don't want to do whatever this is."

He came closer, and I was suddenly glad that I was standing behind my desk. I watched his approach warily. It's one thing to say you don't want something, quite another to refuse it once it's upon you.

"And what is that?" he asked.

"I don't know. But I'm not going to be your mistress, if that's what you have in mind."

For a moment I thought I had said too much, crossed a line.

But he nodded. "Of course, Leo, I'm sorry. You're quite right." Then he looked me up and down, quickly. "I will speak to Sasha, and I'll see you tomorrow."

And then he left. Without explaining what on earth that meant.

So today, it being Friday, I spent the afternoon waiting for him like an idiot. I kept looking out of the window, checking my phone, checking my email, even stupid Facebook. I thought that maybe my doorbell was broken, so I went downstairs a couple of times. Figuring that maybe the buzzer was broken, I decided to take my phone, set it to voice record, and then went to try the doorbell outside.

When I came back, I replayed the phone—the doorbell does work. My brain, on the other hand, may need some fine-tuning.

On my way back up from one of the numerous trips downstairs, my neighbour (and source of embarrassment), Alex, poked his head out of his door.

"Hey, is everything all right?"

"Yeah. Why?" I puffed, slightly out of breath.

"I keep hearing the door slam."

"Oh, sorry, won't happen again. I'll settle down now."

He watched as I panted and plucked on my collar a few times to cool down. Running up and down stairs is serious exercise for someone who spends his life sitting behind a desk.

"What happened?" he asked.

"Oh, nothing. I was just waiting for someone."

"A man?" He smiled knowingly.

That caught me off guard, but his expression wasn't that of a raging homophobe. He seemed amused more than anything, and when I said, "No, why?" he laughed.

"Is it the 'I don't think I should' man?" he asked.

He said the "I don't think I should" in the sort of whisper you can imagine Humphrey Bogart putting on—clearly taking the piss.

"Are you listening in on my private conversations?" I asked.

"No, I was sitting in my living room, and you can hear everything that happens out in the corridor." He shrugged. "So sometimes I overhear things. If you ask me, the guy's no good."

27

"What!"

"The guy's no good," he repeated. "He'd have come in with you if he were any good. And now he stood you up, didn't he?"

Being embarrassed and humiliated in front of him was going to be my life now, apparently. But he seemed to be trying to be friendly about it, shrugged in the sort of "what can you do?" way, and then said, "Want to come in? I have wine."

"No, I—I'm waiting for someone," I said feebly.

"Now the way I see it, if he hasn't shown up yet, you better not make it look as though you've been waiting for him the entire time." He tapped his nose knowingly. "Psychology, see?"

"Ps-psychology," I said, hardly believing my ears.

I wondered if he might be gay, but I couldn't honestly tell. It could have gone either way with him. His clothes were kind of rough; he wore an old T-shirt and joggers—but then, if he was renovating, his dress sense couldn't be an arbiter. His figure, as far as it was possible to judge in the baggy clothes, was fit, his shoulders wide, and his arms thick with lean muscle, so that might mean something.

On the other hand, it might not.

"The best thing you can do," he said, "is pretend like you've completely forgotten about him and weren't really expecting him to show up."

He was so cheerful about this that I couldn't help but smile a little and give in.

"You want a pathetic cast-off in your flat, do you?" I asked wryly.

"Nah, mate, you gotta look at it as strategy," he said. "You know, when he comes eventually, you'll say you spent time with your handsome new neighbour instead. And Bob's yer uncle."

"You were closer to luring me in with that wine," I said.

He laughed and opened the door wider. Honestly, by that point, Jack was roughly an hour and a half late. Alex was right; I should not be there when (or if) he did come eventually. *Perhaps he was having a rough final discussion with Sasha*, I thought. But then, he could have called or even texted. So I went in to see who this strange new neighbour of mine was.

His flat is still a work in progress. It's smaller than mine: one bedroom, a bathroom, and a kitchen-sitting room. There is an old sofa in the middle of the sitting room, a TV, loudspeakers, some gaming consoles, the usual thing. Unopened, half-opened, and empty boxes littered whatever free floor space there was.

"So, you're still moving in, huh?" I said, hands in my pockets, trying to forget the image of Jack waiting outside, ringing the bell to my flat, and not hearing any response.

In dire need of a drink, I was glad for the glass of wine Alex handed me, so I disregarded the fact that the wine came out of a box.

Actually, it was really good. I had a second glass before I even sat down.

"Yeah, I painted the bedroom. The couple that was here before me…."

"Oh yes, Anisha and Ameya," I said. "What happened to them?"

"I don't know. But their bedroom walls were entirely crimson. I had a job getting it to look less like the murder studio of a psycho. I'll probably retile the bathroom too. Are you into DIY?"

I laughed, which puzzled him. "Er, no," I said. "I wish I were. My family is, er, of the intellectual sort, if you know what I mean."

"No, I don't know what you mean," he said, pouring out another glass for me and one for himself. "What, they're brain surgeons or something?"

It occurred to me that I might be insulting him, so of course I decided to do that British thing where you're overdeprecating about yourself.

"No, I mean that we don't do things with our hands." Which sounded awful once it came out of my mouth. I sounded like someone called Lord Cecil talking to a man named Gavin who fixed his lordship's Daimler so that he could take Imogen and Gideon to Royal Ascot.

He blinked at me and then said, "It's just a matter of practice." And then he shrugged. "So, what do you do?"

"I teach."

"Oh, a teacher?" he said, as though pleasantly surprised.

"At university. I'm a lecturer, to be precise. In European history, though Cold War Eastern Europe is my specialty."

His face fell. "Oh. You're a lecturer."

Something in his tone sounded as though he didn't believe me. "I am… why?"

"No, I just thought… you look kinda young for a lecturer. Aren't they more like bearded old men with fancy titles before their names?"

"Well, my beard would be a patchy affair if ever I chose to grow one," I said, stroking my chin ruefully, "but as to the rest, I have a PhD."

I don't know why I was saying these things, since I could feel the distance growing between us with every word I uttered, and it was unfortunate. He was nice, and I didn't mean to sound snooty. Suddenly I felt conscious about everything: my accent, my career, my expensive sweater, which I'd only bought to impress Jack.

Jack, who had his own BBC TV series, for heaven's sake.

Desperately trying to move the attention away from me, I said, "What do you do?"

"Oh I'm a personal trainer."

"As in—?"

"As in I train people," he said.

"Oh, for, like—for, like, sports events and stuff? Like the Olympics or something? I've got a friend who—"

"Nah, mate," he said with a laugh, "like in a gym. People book me to find out how to lose weight or bulk up, or how to train so as not to kill their heart, you know?"

"Ah." I didn't know what else to say, but that *ah* sounded stupid enough without my adding anything to it, so it was just as well.

We had finished the wine by then, and he went to his fridge and took out beer.

"Want some?"

I most definitely did. We drank it from the can, and I tried to make it look as though that was exactly how I drank it at home all the time— even though it wasn't.

"So tell me, who is this guy?" he asked.

He meant Jack, of course, and I was a little taken aback by his forwardness. "He's a colleague from work," I said.

"And why is he being such an arse?"

"He's engaged."

I realised that did not make *me* sound like a good person. I'm the arse in this scenario.

"He's… I mean, I had no idea he was engaged… or even that he was seeing someone. I was just… I mean…." I stuttered.

"I'm not judging," he said with a smile that made it all the worse.

"I'm not judging" always means "judging isn't necessary. What you've done is objectively, morally abhorrent."

"*I* am," I said unhappily.

He raised his eyebrows. "Yeah?"

"Yes. Look, let's not talk about him. What games do you have?"

He was happy enough to show me his games, then his CDs—he had a good collection of classic rock albums, which he let me borrow—and then we talked of where all his other stuff would go and how he planned to make shelving and where he would put it…. It was midnight before I knew it, and I felt embarrassed for having taken up all his evening.

On the plus side, in the end, I almost forgot I had been stood up and that he was there to witness it. Once we'd drunk enough, the discomfort had left me entirely. I even told him about Oslo, and he offered to dog-sit Squire, which was nice. He said he loved dogs, asked about the name. I said it was silly but I named my dog after my favourite guitarist. He thought the name was cool and said he also liked the Stone Roses.

I remembered Jack once I returned to my place. I looked at my phone. No missed calls. No texts. I have indeed been stood up.

Great.

Thursday, 4 March

ON PLANE to Oslo. Haven't seen Jack all week. Haven't had any news of him either. He missed a staff meeting on Tuesday, so I'm not sure what's going on. My working theory is that he told Sasha he was leaving her for a bloke and she made him balance books on his head all week as punishment. Or perhaps she ate him. She could use a decent meal.

Oh hell, I'm being cattish again. Truth is, I want to know what happened, and I'm tired of this constant to and fro. If he'd marry her at last or tell me there wasn't going to be anything between us, I think I'd swallow it eventually (ha!), but this never-ending uncertainty is killing me.

31

Anyway, Oslo will do me good. I've brought some good reading with me—*Brigands of the Moon* and *The Glass Bead Game*. I've arranged meetings with some of my friends from my doctoral days, and I'm going to stay at my colleague's house, so I don't have to shell out for a hotel or feel lonely and depressed all week. It's kind of like a holiday for me, really.

As a single man, there's not really anywhere to go without either committing to a party-fuelled visit to a Greek island, courtesy of Lucy, or a family vacation with Amelia and Mark and Co. At which I would inevitably feel like a spare part.

I'm going to try to sleep now.

Saturday, 13 March

OSLO CAME and went too quickly. I hardly had time to properly take in the place, the changes, or to speak to anybody. But I had a good time, and though I don't feel remotely rested, I was glad to land in Heathrow.

Alex picked me up at the airport. It was by prior arrangement, but I was still surprised to find him waiting for me at Arrivals. Alex is a good-humoured sort of person, and you know that's true of a man who keeps a joyful demeanour even after he's just traversed the M25 to pick up his neighbour for no earthly reason but that he'd promised to do so one night after drinking a box of wine and several beers.

In the car, he asked me about my trip. He seemed to think it was a holiday, so he was surprised when I told him my paper, which I presented there, had gone well.

Then he congratulated me on my achievement, which again was a little odd, since my having presented it didn't amount to anything much. It's not like it got automatically published for having been presented or anything like that.

I was mortified to find out that Squire had chewed up Alex's copy of *Lord of the Rings*. I promised to buy him another, but he waved it off as nothing. To make it up to him—because really, he did come through like a champ—I invited him to dine with me that evening. It sounded nice when I said it, and he lit up on hearing it, which would have been gratifying if I had any skills in the kitchen.

The thing I eventually presented to him did not look or taste nearly as good as what I had in mind. It was meant to be spaghetti bolognese, but with the pasta cooked a trifle too long and the sauce from a jar, it was not exactly something you give to a friend as a thank-you. More as a "here, now beat it."

He was polite about it, ate it all, and said it was fine.

"I'm not much of a cook," I said by way of apology.

"I could teach you. I always used to cook for my family."

"You know, it would have been polite to contradict me."

"Oh yeah, no," he said laughing. "You must have misheard me. What I actually said was that you should think of opening up some sort of, er, restaurant."

"If you keep it up, I'll make dessert."

"Are you actually threatening me with dessert?"

We laughed.

"Honestly, though, I can teach you pasta dishes at least," he said. "I mean, they're dead simple, anyway, but I have some family recipes that are real winners."

"Family? You're not Italian, are you?"

"Not entirely," he said. "My dad's American, but his family is originally from Italy. My mum's English."

He told me he was brought up in England, mostly (which would explain the accent), but that his family travelled a lot, all over the world, as he was growing up.

"I'm not your simple, muscled bumpkin," he said. "I've been places, I've seen things."

He looked ridiculously proud of himself as he spoke. It was strange seeing him at my table, but in a good way. He is easy to get on with, and the better I like him, the more handsome I find him. Not that he *isn't* handsome. In fact, he is, in a sort of obvious way, which never normally appeals to me. He's tall, with an upper body shaped like a V—all the more noticeable because he was wearing a nice T-shirt and a pair of jeans that, when surreptitiously examined while he was putting away the dishes, showed off his rather nice legs and arse.

He has that ability to loom and intimidate, so when I met him in the staircase, he'd alarmed me. But now that I know him better, it feels like a ridiculous reaction. He's pretty mellow and easy-going—being around him is such a sweet relief from all the horrible drama that has drained me recently. His hair is lightly curly and dark; his eyes are large, brown and smiling, surrounded by thick black lashes; and because I was watching him, he wrinkled his nose and said, "What? Have I got something stuck in my teeth?"

"No!" I said with a laugh. "No, I'm just tired after the flight."

He apologised and left soon after. I didn't mean him to go, but in the end, it was probably for the best. I really am tired, and with tiredness and some alcohol, all my defences would go, I'd come on to him, and then our acquaintance would go from generally awkward in a friendly way to bloody painful.

Lucy was right, I need to get laid.

Monday, 15 March

I'VE BEEN playing catch-up all day and will be doing so all week. With two catch-up seminars squeezed between a pair of two-hour lecture blocks, I've been running around campus like a demented bull, shoving students aside and trying to get from one end to the other. Added to that I've been talking all day, from nine to six thirty. So now that I have given Fidel Castro's speech at the 1986 Communist Party Congress a run for its money, I'm stuck at home with piles of essays, one PhD thesis draft, two MA dissertation drafts, and the application some aspirant for a PhD submitted last week.

And I haven't even opened my email inbox yet.

Tuesday, 16 March

TOO BUSY to write all, so quick update:

Got a response about my article at last, and they accepted it. I'm over the moon. I'm supposed to be quicker about these things, so after this week's over, I'll be getting on with the next one.

My sister emailed me, saying she'll be in the UK in two weeks, and we arranged to meet.

And finally I bumped into Jack in the hallway of our department. *Literally* bumped, as in I was putting something on the noticeboard and didn't notice him standing right next to me. He was unshaven, which made him look his forty years, and he said he had so much to tell me. Honestly, though, he's not even bothered to ring or text after having stood me up, and I'm beginning to suspect that in a way he sees me as somehow less worthy of proper treatment than if I were a woman. You know, it's like the women in his life are fancy French restaurants for which he will dress up, make an effort, produce a ring, while men are like burgers he will devour with his hands, toy with when the fancy strikes him, and drop like a hot potato when something better comes along.

At least that's the conclusion I've come to, and I just won't put up with it.

I told him I was busy, which was the truth, and left.

Wednesday, 17 March

HAD A very intense sex dream about Jack.

It was kind of weird, though, because we never took our clothes off. Nor do I remember us touching. Odd.

Woke up at three, couldn't get back to sleep. Read a bit, but kept staring at the same page, losing my place all the time, and finally gave up on it. At around half past six, I heard some noise in the corridor. I opened my door to see what was happening and found Alex, covered in sweat, his hair tied back in a tiny ponytail; he'd just returned from jogging, apparently. He had his headphones on, from which the steady beat of some *umtsy-umtsy-umtsy* music could be heard, so he mouthed "Sorry!" and then lifted the hem of his shirt to wipe sweat off his face.

And yes, I could see his well-defined stomach. He went back into his flat while I still stood there, gaping after him.

I am officially a gross pervert.

And I definitely need to get laid.

Thursday, 18 March

THE WEEK from hell continues. I'm tense, stressed, and tired, and I'm beginning to regret that I ever went to Oslo. Also, for some reason, Jack seems to be everywhere.

Today I saw him as I walked to the cafeteria, and then on my way back. Each time he tried to speak to me, but with my schedule this week, I hadn't the time. So at the staff meeting, which involved some of us getting together to discuss the ins and outs of organising a postgraduate seminar for social history of the late twentieth century, he came and sat in. This was odd, of course, because he's a World Wars man, so neither the period nor the subject matter had anything to do with him. But he didn't say anything, just sat there, listening to us bicker about the terrible sandwiches this one catering company had provided last time.

You'd be surprised how passionate people get about the sandwiches and pastries we get at those seminars and conferences.

Finally, on my last lecture of the day, I was about to explain the midseventies to a bunch of undergrads, when the door opened and Jack walked in, silently, and sat in one of the back rows.

"…So if you imagine that suddenly, out of nowhere, Nixon visits China, and then, almost as unexpectedly, Japan and China forge a Joint Statement, you can see that the USSR couldn't help but think…," I was saying before I lost my train of thought.

I looked up at him, because maybe he'd come to tell me something. But he just sat there and listened.

I turned to the students. "Well, what do you think the USSR must have thought?"

"An anti-Soviet alliance was forming?" said one of the kids in the front, the one who looked like a spotty elf.

"Yes, exactly." I looked at the clock. It was still twenty minutes before the end of class. "Let's stop here and discuss the excerpt from Davies in your handouts. Ten minutes," I instructed. "Groups of five. Hassan, have you anyone to read with? No, that is last week's handout—has everybody got the right handout? Yes, that one. Ten minutes, people. Bullet points, and pick a speaker among you."

The students collected in the rows, and that gave me an opportunity to walk up the stairs towards the top back row, where Jack was sitting. "Can I help you with anything?" I asked.

He looked at me with surprise. "I just came to listen in."

"I was under the impression that you already did your degree."

"One can always learn a thing or two. Even in the most unlikely places." He gave me that smirk that means he thinks he's outwitted the room. I used to find it charming. Now I didn't feel impressed at all.

"Well, I suggest an adult education course in a community college. If you ask them to speak slowly, I'm sure you'll manage."

He smiled. Some of the students started listening in, so I turned to them.

"Are we done? Shi Jie, Kacper, can you start?" I returned to the front of the room.

When the lecture finished, I packed my things and walked out as quickly as I could. I don't know what he wants from me, but I'm seriously getting tired of this.

Saturday, 20 March

SARAH INVITED me to have lunch with her today, ostensibly to continue discussing that postgrad seminar, though of course the thing was never mentioned once between us when we got together.

It was pretty apparent that she wanted to gossip. In fact, the moment we sat down, she said, "Well, guess what!"

"What?"

"Apparently they've called off the engagement!" She seemed excited about this. In fact, her tiny blue eyes were twinkling at me from above the menu of Café Rouge.

"They? *They* who?"

"Tsk!" she said impatiently. "Jack and Sasha of course!"

She watched me carefully for a reaction, which was why I was very careful not to show any.

"It's unofficial at the moment, but she moved into a hotel room and it's all going a bit wonky between them, from all I've heard."

My heart sank. He dumped her. He dumped her for me? Could it be? What does this mean? Is that why he's been following me around lately? I didn't ask, of course, because Sarah would have a field day with me, so I schooled myself to say, very properly, "Well, that's very sad. They were a lovely couple."

Naturally she was disappointed in my reaction, expecting tears of joy, maybe, but I didn't feel any. Joy, that is. I felt confused. More than anything, I wanted to talk to Jack. So I distracted her by asking about her new cat, thereby also distracting myself from trying to pry any more information out of her. I told myself I'd let this lie and see what happens, but as soon as I got home, I texted Jack, and a few minutes later, he called me.

"Hey." He sounded unbelievably sexy.

I didn't know what to say, didn't want to sound pathetic by saying something about Sarah telling me about his engagement, so I was silent for a little while.

So he said, "Are you there?"

"Er, yeah. I just thought…. It seemed like you've wanted to talk to me these past few days and I was awfully busy, so I just thought I'd ask if everything's all right with you."

"I'm fine," he said. "I want to see you. Can I come and see you?"

"I don't know."

"Sasha's not here. She's moved out."

"Oh," I said. "Er, maybe tomorrow? Can you come over tomorrow?"

"Your place?"

"Sure." We said goodbye shortly after, and I tried to sit down to work, but honestly, it was like the chair was made out of spikes. I couldn't sit still.

I had this chapter Cate from work wanted me to proofread for her, which I'd promised to do today, but all the words swam in front of my eyes. I had a glass of water and went over to the window. I wondered about taking up smoking. For maybe an hour, I was like this, and then there was a knock on the door.

I knew it was him, knew he had come even though I'd told him to come tomorrow. And yet, when I opened the door and saw him, I thought my heart was going to jump out of my chest. He looked tired and unshaven, and then he stepped in and took me in his arms, just like in an old movie, and he kissed me. He kicked the door shut behind him. Without breaking the kiss, I walked backwards until I fell onto my sofa, and he was on top of me, deepening the kiss, hungrily, and grinding against me….

God knows where this would have ended had I not pushed him back. "Hey, hey!"

"Hm?"

"I can't do this."

"Your first time?" he asked, a little surprised.

"What? No!" We sat up. I patted my hair back into place. "No. I mean, I want to know what's going on."

He straightened his shirt and leaned back a little. "Well?" he said. "I told you, didn't I?"

"No, Jack, you didn't tell me anything. I want to know, is it over between you? I mean, *over* over? Not 'we're taking a break' over; not 'we'll see how things go' over, but did you actually break it off? If you're going to reconcile after you've had your way with me, I want to know. I'm not playing games, Jack."

"She moved out," he said. "And she's going back to the States at the end of the month. We've some things to sort out still, but it's over between us."

I watched him closely as he spoke. He didn't seem upset about the end of the relationship.

"It was a mistake," he said with a sigh, and then he rubbed his eyes. "We've been on and off for years, and I thought… I don't know. I thought it would be neat to finally settle down or something. But then she came to the UK, and it wasn't there… that *thing*, you know, when you connect with someone? I mean, she's great, don't get me wrong. It's just a chemistry thing. We were never really suited, but what with the long distance and everything, it's sometimes hard to tell, you know? It's different with you." He leaned towards me and kissed me again.

"So what," I said, pulling back, "you're going to be gay now? For me?"

"For you?" he sounded surprised. "You're not the first guy I ever…."

"Oh."

"No, I mean, you and I, we connect, don't we? I mean, we talk and there's… I don't know… sparks." He was usually more eloquent than this, and I guessed that he must have been really tired, but it was sweet of him all the same to say it, and I let him off the hook. Besides, he was kissing my neck, and so I asked, "Do you want to stay over?"

"Hm?" he looked up. "Can't. Early morning tomorrow."

He returned to kissing me, punctuating his assault on my lips with words.

"I just wanted to see you for a little bit today. I couldn't wait until tomorrow. I'm flesh and blood, you know."

He said some other things, but I was already plucking at his trousers by then, a little distracted. And then there was a knock on my door. We scrambled to our feet, putting our clothes to rights.

"Who is it?" I asked, tucking my shirt back into my trousers.

"Alex."

Well, this was awkward. Jack lifted an eyebrow at me. "Well?"

"Well, nothing. I'll get rid of him."

"No need," he said. "I should go. I really am knackered, and when I have you, I want to be fully conscious and rested."

So we went to the door together, and I opened it to find Alex standing there with cake on a plate in his hands. So this was more than awkward.

"Oh," he said, looking from me to Jack.

"Er, hi, Alex," I said, then turned to Jack. "This is my neighbour," I explained, and then turned to Alex again. "Er, this is Jack. What's up?"

"I just made some cake," Alex said, looking sheepish as hell. "I thought you'd want some."

"Oh, thanks."

Jack bent over the cake, sniffed it, and said, "Nice. All right, I'll see you tomorrow." And then he pinched my bottom. I jumped. "Nice to meet you, Alex," he threw over his shoulder as he took the stairs down.

Alex and I stood there for a while, listening to him leave the building.

"Oh mate," Alex said ruefully, "I just totally cock-blocked you, didn't I?"

"Er, it's all right. That cake looks good."

"Not as good as sex, I bet."

I let him in.

The cake was fucking delicious, though, so there's that.

Thursday, 25 March

WORK'S BEEN piling up for everyone recently. I see Jack about the department, but when I ask when he's coming over, he says he can't because he's moving Sasha out, or because he has to help with her preparations to get back home. It's not that I don't think it's good he's helping her, considering the trouble he made her go through, but I have a serious case of blue balls, and it's not even funny anymore.

The furthest we got was when he sneaked into my office yesterday and we made out on my chair. He sat in it and I sat astride him, trying to get as close as possible, which was fucking frustrating in those circumstances. It was like we were teenagers, and not in a good way.

On the plus side, Sarah told me I'm being considered for deputy head of department. This was surprising to me, considering that I haven't really done anything administrative often, but I told her I was happy to do it if they asked me. Whatever gene is responsible for ambition, I don't have it. By now, Lena, with her crazy drive, would have been head of school. Which reminds me that I have to clean my place, because she's going to be here soon.

This morning I told Jack of her visit, and he said he could drive me to the airport to pick them up. That was a welcome surprise. What with a potential promotion and a hot boyfriend, I might not look like such a loser next to my super-accomplished sister.

"Let me take you and your sister and her boyfriend to that new French place near Covent Garden," he said.

"Are you sure? That's pretty boyfriend-like behaviour, you know."

"Fuck it, let's get married," he said, nibbling on my neck.

The man's driving me crazy. I told him to come and see me tonight, but he said he had this meet-and-greet with some people with whom he was organising a reception for the Japanese ambassador, who was going to speak about British POWs at the town hall. He told me this with his hand in my trousers, and assured my ear that he would think of me the entire time. It was quite fitting, what with the underlying theme of torture and all.

Saturday, 27 March

URGH.

I don't know why I'm even surprised anymore. At half past three, Jack was going to come and pick me up in his car, and we were going to the airport to pick up Lena. I had told her ahead of time to not book any taxis or anything, that I'd be there with my boyfriend (yeah, I'm an idiot, sue me), and then we'd go to her hotel and on to the restaurant, at which I had booked us a table for four. Half past three arrived, but Jack did not. I had to call him three times before he picked up, sounding distracted. He apologised half-heartedly and said he was really swamped today and he'd have to cry off. I was too angry to say anything, so I just hung up on him, mid feeble apology.

Instead I tried feverishly to calculate how I could best get to the airport on time. Then I remembered Alex.

I felt like a prick imposing on him again, but went anyway and banged on his door. Luckily I found him at home. He had been napping, evidently— he was in a T-shirt and boxers, his hair standing on end, and he was unshaven. But when I explained, in my blubbering manner, that I needed a ride to the airport to pick up my sister, he shrugged and said, "Okay."

"So, what happened?" he asked once we were in the car.

"Nothing. I got distracted with work and—"

"Aw, Christ, don't tell me that man stood you up again!" he said. "Nah, don't glare at me, mate. The guy's no good, and I told you so before. I get bad vibes from him, I tell you."

"Well, thanks," I said. "It doesn't matter right now, anyway."

He shook his head at me but didn't comment further. "So, where's your sister coming from?"

So I told him about my sister and her boyfriend and her UN job, and he didn't mention Jack again, which allowed me to focus on the thing at hand.

Lena and Yi Chen were already waiting for us when we arrived. She called me from Arrivals while we were still negotiating the M25, but once I saw her, all thoughts about the circumstances of this meeting left me because Lena had a rounded stomach! As in, she is pregnant. So it was some ten minutes before either of us was able to do anything other than hug and congratulate/accept gushing congratulations.

"My God, woman! Tell me it's what I think it is!"

"Well, you're not so gay that you forgot how humans reproduce, Leo," she said in her usual dry way. "It's a baby, you numpty!"

"You're huge! How far along are you?"

"Five months," Yi, who was dragging several large bags for the both of them, looked tired. "Four to go."

"He sounds like *he's* having to carry the thing," Lena said. "Let me tell you, it's a lot harder than it looks."

"Don't ask her to demonstrate," Yi said to me. "She will."

I introduced them to Alex. Though Lena and Yi had just completed a six-hour flight, they were both dressed in suits. Alex, who had been sleeping only moments before we left, was still in his slacks.

I could see Lena frowning a little. "*You're* Professor Jack Gordon?" she said, astonished.

"Eh?" Alex said. "Oh no, don't worry, I'm just—" He glanced at me, apparently reading my expression. "Something sprung up, and I came instead. I'm Leo's neighbour."

Lena looked at me, took it all in at a glance, and decided not to mention it again. By way of smoothing over this little hiccup, she said, "I wish I had neighbours that kind. Mine just wrestle with each other and have armies of lawyers attending their big loud parties to which they do not even invite me, the bastards." Then she put her hands together. "Right, well, shall we?"

Alex and I helped Yi with the bags. Lena assured us that she was not transporting her fossil collection, but even among the three of us, the baggage was hard to carry through to the parking lot. Alex was able to carry two bags by himself while Yi and I dragged the third, giant one together.

Despite the initial awkwardness, the ride into town was all right. Lena sat up front, and I sat in the back with Yi Chen, and though I couldn't exactly hear what Lena was talking to Alex about, they *were* talking and seemed to get on well.

Yi leaned his head against the headrest and closed his eyes. "No offence," he said to me, "but you're so lucky you will never get a woman pregnant."

"Why would I take offence?" I said. "Besides, the thing that's paining you is that you got my sister pregnant, which I'll never have to suffer, even if I weren't gay."

"True," he said with a sigh. "Hey, be a pal and wake me in, like, eighteen years or so, eh?"

He napped for most of the drive. Alex dropped them off at their hotel, and then I told them I'd pick them up for the meal later tonight. Once Alex and I returned to our building, I thanked him for his help, but he shrugged it off.

"Hey, it was nothing, don't worry about it."

"No, you've come through for me, and I owe you a big one, honestly. I'll take you out for a drink or something. In fact, why don't you come to dinner with us? It's a nice restaurant, French."

"Nah, it's all right. You catch up with your sister. She's really cool," he said, patting me on the shoulder. "Have fun tonight. Do you want me to take Squire?"

I told him I couldn't impose with my dog on top of everything else, but he said it would be no problem, that he was going to go out running this evening, and he could take Squire with him, so I ended up acquiescing.

Dinner with Lena and Yi went well. They were both refreshed and rested, and we talked of the wedding they were planning. They've been talking about getting married for years now, but I wondered if now, with the baby on the way, they might actually do it.

"It's the timing," Lena said when I asked her. "What with work, and travel, and now the baby, I haven't the time to think of these things. I mean, yeah, we could just nip out to Vegas, but then Mummy and Daddy would probably electrocute us through the nipples."

Yi laughed. "Yeah, if we don't invite the Fitzalans and the Montgomerys and the Herberts…."

"They'll throw a fit!" Lena said. "So, if we do it, it's got to be done properly. And I just can't see how."

It was amusing to me that they'd worry so much about pleasing Mum and Dad, considering that our parents had a little shrine in their honour in their house in Sussex.

I suppose keeping up with their expectations must be as hard as failing them constantly.

"Well, if you let me know in advance," I said, "you could go to Vegas while I drop my lacklustre career and decide to join a cult. They'll be so busy being disappointed with me, they won't notice the wedding."

"Deal!" said Yi at once, stretching out his hand to me.

On the whole it was great to catch up with them. When I got home, I wondered whether to ring Jack, but frankly I was too angry with him to predict a happy conversation. And I don't like to quarrel.

Screw him, I'm going to bed.

Thursday, 1 April

LENA'S ON the plane back to the States. She's not met Jack after all, and he became that thing we didn't talk about, which kind of spoiled her visit for me.

So when I saw him around the department, I was angry enough to want to punch him, and I avoided him. Not that I saw much of him. I did, however, see on Facebook that his status still proclaimed that he was engaged to Sasha Williams. Now, I don't expect him to change this to "Madly in luuurv with Leo Taylor" or anything like that, but honestly, this game of charades he's playing is starting to piss me off.

He can go and hang. I'm calling Lucy to see if she'll get drunk with me.

Sunday, 4 April. The Lake District

LUCY, AMELIA, Mark, Tom, Pete, Laura, and I went camping for the long weekend. We took tents and hiking boots and kicked it up at the Lakes. As could be expected, the weather was shitty, so we were mostly wet and cold throughout, but it was good to be out of London all the same. We've been hoping to do something like this for a while now, especially since Tom and Pete moved out of London when Tom got a job in Leeds. When I was doing my MA, Tom used to be at the centre of my group of gay friends, but ever since Pete came along and the two moved out, I've sort of dropped out of that circle. It became all about hooking up with as many people as possible, and it really wasn't for me.

Unfortunately one of the reasons for my eventual decision to retire from the gay meat market was at the Lakes with us as well: Laura.

Amelia was constantly making efforts to reconcile the two of us, mostly because she couldn't drop me as a friend and Laura was a good work contact.

Frankly I couldn't blame Laura for despising me.

It all dates back to my PhD days. I'd just returned to the UK after a year of fieldwork all over Europe. My last month had been spent in the summer in Scandinavia, and as I spent a lot of time on my interview subject's yacht, fishing with him, I came back looking tanned and feeling quite happy. With my new confidence in my thesis, the wealth of contacts I'd managed to establish, the tan that made me look like a golden-haired god, I felt good.

So when I went to the pub we used to hang out in back then, to see all my friends, I wasn't exactly familiar with everybody. New people had joined and some of the old ones had left while I was gone. I fell into conversation with this one guy who'd caught my eye. He was adorably shy, and so when everybody was leaving and he asked me if he could come back to my place, I was flattered.

He seemed nervous; I suspected I was the first guy he'd ever picked up. In my new, self-assured, "I know what I'm doing" persona, I agreed. He was kind of cute, and he seemed completely into me. And I was into me, so there was something we had in common! It wasn't just that he had never been with a guy before. He went at it as though he were on death row and had to try *everything* before he breathed his last. We literally spent the entire weekend fucking and doing everything two young, functional men could do with one another short of throwing themselves out of the window.

So imagine my chagrin when I emerged into the light of day after this exhausting escapade, feeling proud of myself for having initiated a new (and very enthusiastic) member of gaydom into the ways of the gays, and got a call from Amelia.

"Leo, do you know what happened to Stephen after we left the pub? Nobody's heard from him all weekend long. His parents are freaking out. They want to call the cops! Laura is beside herself with worry."

I told her at once that he'd been with me, and that he was fine—hell, better than fine!

"You *what*!" she screeched into my ear. "Leo, you're not serious! You didn't seduce Laura's husband. *Tell me* you didn't!"

It would have been okay, even, if he had just kept his mouth shut, but I think that despite whatever closet door he had been holding shut until then, I fucked him right out of there. Either way, Laura blamed me, claiming that I seduced him or warped his mind or something.

Honestly, *he* had been the one who asked to come to my place, *he* had been the one who wanted to do everything on the gay bucket list, and had I known he had a wife I would never have done any of it! I mean, for heaven's sake, he had no ring on his finger! How the hell was I supposed to know?

Amelia was furious but forgave me since she believed me that I'd been ignorant of the guy's relationship status. But her friendship with Laura suffered, and she had been at pains to sort of slide me into gatherings where Laura was going to be, maybe hoping that sufficient exposure would eventually immunise her to me. So far, the effect was not very noticeable.

When she saw me get out of Mark's car at Low Wray, she actually sneered. "So, I hear you broke up an engagement. Well done, you!"

I hardly knew what to say and threw an accusing glare at Amelia, but she looked as surprised as I was by that direct hit. Tom and Pete, who heard the exchange, were at once amused and interested. They would be, of course. Living as they did now, they'd probably had no gay drama to feast on for years. Indeed, they latched on to me as Amelia and Lucy did their best to draw Laura away from me.

Pete is incredibly camp and rejoices in turning it up to eleven when he is amongst his closest friends. "So! Tell me *everything*!"

"Yeah, Pete, I won't," I said. "There's nothing to tell."

"So you didn't just break up another straight couple?" Tom sounded exquisitely amused. He is sporting a rather impressive beard these days, and with that, thick-rimmed glasses, a chequered red shirt, and tight jeans, he looks like a hipster lumberjack. "Because word on the street is—"

"Right, where did you hear it from?" I asked. "Seriously, who's spreading all this stuff around?"

"I heard it from Mark," said Tom. "But he kind of assumed I already knew, and anyway, before you get pissed off at him, his agenda was to warn us *not* to talk of your lover because things hadn't exactly panned out. What happened?"

"Nothing happened," I said. "I didn't break them up. He came on to me, and when he did, I said I wouldn't do anything until he was single. Which I did to be decent, by the way."

"Sure," said Pete. "So, once you thanked him on your knees, then what happened?"

"I did not go down on him," I said. "We didn't have sex at all, all right? Like I said, nothing happened."

"That's strange, surely," said Tom. "When was the last time you—"

"Aaaall right," I said. "My dog needs to poo. Out of the way."

And I marched ahead of them, with Squire on the lead, realising that I had got myself into an uncomfortable situation. Wasn't that just typical of me?

But the weekend went as well as could be expected—that is to say, it didn't go altogether terribly. Laura avoided me, which was kind of her, as it aided my own efforts to avoid her. For her sake, everybody avoided talking of Jack, which was a huge relief.

Lucy and I shared a tent, and Squire slept at our feet. We walked and got drunk in the many charming pubs along the way, and we took out boats, and had a good time overall.

I don't feel like going back home to my little flat, where there's just me.

Monday, 5 April

SO LUCY'S staying at mine.

It just sort of happened. On the last night of our trip to the Lakes, she sneaked into my sleeping bag for warmth, clung to me like a koala on a eucalyptus tree, and I blurted out, "Lucy, come and stay with me."

"Huh? What do you mean?"

"Just, I don't know, come and stay with me. One night. Can't you?"

"Darling, I know you turn men gay left, right, and centre, but I like you as gay as you are, you know, and I don't think even *I* could turn *you*."

"I don't mean that, you freak," I said. "I mean, I don't want to be alone. It's depressing."

"Okay." She kissed my cheek. "I'll stay with you."

So after a long day at work today, where I had the pleasure of disciplining a student for using racist slurs against another student—which just fucking kills your faith in humanity—I was kind of surprised to hear noises coming from my flat. I dreaded that Lucy had somehow managed to pick someone up and decided to perform (yes, *perform*) her one-night stand in my flat. Considering the day I'd had, I think I shouldn't be blamed for being angry about that.

And so I came in rather abruptly, catching Lucy and Alex, of all people, in the middle of what looked suspiciously like… cooking. Alex was chopping mushrooms, and Lucy was whisking some cream-like substance in my measuring jug. I didn't know I had one.

"What the—?" I began.

"Oh, Leo! You're home!" said Lucy, as though she and I had travelled back in time to the fifties, where gays weren't people and she and I somehow ended up married.

"What's going on?"

"I met your neighbour." She batted her lashes at me. "He's helping me make dinner for you. We've decided you need to start eating like an adult. So we're making sausages. Aren't you just *dying* to try Alex's sausage?"

Alex's head snapped up and he looked at me, quite horrified.

I was used to Lucy, so I only rolled my eyes. "Good luck with that," I said.

When I came out of my bedroom, having washed and changed, they were again companionably engaged in frying onions and mushrooms and stirring sauces and jabbing at boiling potatoes. I'd forgotten how good home-cooked food smelled. Even once they'd dished up, Lucy continued to flirt with Alex in her usual way. I have to give him that, though: he took it with good grace. Her statement that she liked a man who could handle his sausage and her guess as to how much he could bench-press got a smile from him.

"So, you and Leo are good friends, then?" she said at one point.

I was worried that she was going to make insinuations, which would make Alex uncomfortable being friends with a gay man, but he responded to her affirmatively without even looking up from his plate.

"So, I guess you've met Jack?" she asked.

I threw her a warning glare.

Either Alex didn't see it, or he ignored it. "Oh yeah," he said. "Leo's boyfriend, right? I've seen him around."

"He's not my boyfriend," I grumbled.

"Yeah," Lucy continued, ignoring me. "He's a bit of a flake, actually. What did you make of him? Because I can't quite like him, but then, I've never met him."

"Oh." Alex sounded a little flustered. "I don't know that I can say I like him, precisely. I don't really know him."

"Don't let that stop you from ripping my personal life to shreds," I told him. "As you can see, it doesn't deter my other friends."

Lucy shrugged. "I just want to help you, love."

"I don't need any help. The man's history. He won't come back, and we might as well forget him."

Alex frowned and even seemed a little concerned. "He stood you up again?"

I couldn't really be angry with him, worried as he looked. There was no judgement in his face, nothing but kindness and alarm at my being hurt. He should teach my other friends lessons in manners.

Maybe that made it easy to confide in him. I told him about Jack's annoying elusiveness and what happened with Sasha.

"He's a tease," Lucy said.

Alex contemplated this and then said, "Hm. Reminds me of my sister."

"Oh?" I said.

"Yeah, she's like that. She constantly pines after guys who are married or in relationships or have just got out of this major relationship or—well, people who are in some way, I don't know, damaged? Either way, it's clear to any sane person that nothing would ever come of it, which is what attracts her. I reckon she's into impossible relationships. Your Jack sounds the same."

"How astute!" Lucy said, quite delighted. "That is precisely what he's like, Leo! Look, it all falls into place: He fancies that American bird because she's in the States and there's no danger of an actual relationship happening. Meanwhile, he can tease you, knowing that nothing can happen while he's in a 'relationship' with Team USA. But then the woman has the temerity to come over here with matrimonial intentions. What does he do? He sabotages his relationship with her and decides to go for it with you. But then you want to play house with him too, and so he flees back to his fiancée, who no doubt made an impression on him by throwing a fit and threatening never to see him again."

"Yes," Alex said, "that sounds about right. As soon as you become unavailable, he'll be drooling at your feet again."

It sounded convincing but didn't exactly make me hopeful about my future. Do I even want a future with Jack? Truthfully, my feelings are mixed. A part of me is still a little infatuated with him, let's be honest, but another part has really had enough of his bullshit.

"I should probably give up on men altogether," I said. "As soon as sex is involved, I fuck up any relationship I have."

"Oh pooh," Lucy said. "Sex makes things better, not worse, trust me. How about you, Alex?"

He startled. "Me?"

"Yeah," she said. "Are you sleeping with anyone?"

"Right this minute? No." He adopted an expression of complete innocence, which I didn't trust.

Lucy waved her fork in the air. "Don't you joke around with me, mister. Out with it. Whose bones are you humping?"

I wanted to take that fork and stab her in the eye. Alex seemed to take it in his usual laid-back way, though. He shrugged. "No one's."

"No one?" Lucy sounded outraged.

"Well, you've to meet someone first, get to know them," Alex said. "That sort of thing takes time. I've only just moved to London."

I frowned. "What about that woman I saw? The one who helped you move in? I thought—"

"Thea? Thea's my sister."

"The one who likes damaged people?" Lucy asked.

"Yep."

Lucy leaned forward and smiled ingratiatingly at him. "So you're single."

"Yes."

She persisted. "So, what are you into?"

"Lucy," I said firmly, "can we leave the sex inquisition for a single day?"

I changed the subject then. We ended up having a good meal. I washed up, and we had a few glasses of wine, and then Alex left.

No sooner did the door close behind him but Lucy melted to the floor, quite literally, as though her bones had turned to liquid. She rolled onto her back and said, "Oh. My. God. He is *so* hot!"

"Yeah, louder, Luce. He's only my fucking neighbour." I don't know why I was so irritated, but her flirting with Alex all evening long and her evident intention to go on about how hot he was for the rest of the night did not fill me with joy.

"How can you live next to this guy and not try to sneak into his bed!" She was positively sparkling with, er, enthusiasm.

"Because I'm not a crazed rapist?"

"Oh puh-lease!" she drawled. "He's *so* into you! All that's missing is him just flat-out declaring himself! Which he would, if you didn't send out your 'I don't notice anything that's around me' vibe."

"What are you talking about?"

"The way he *looked* at you, like a puppy wanting a hug! The way he kept handing you the ketchup because he knew you only eat things when they are drenched in ketchup-flavoured soup, you uncultured animal! Darling, *trust me*, he has the hots for you, and I think you've a moral—nay, *sexual*—obligation to jump him. Because a) it cannot be healthy for you to keep yourself as chaste as a plague-ridden corpse, and b) if you don't do it, someone else will, and then it will be too late. And soon you'll walk around snapping at everybody because you're a sexually frustrated grouch who thinks himself a great romantic only because he never dares to actually like people and prefers the constructs in his head instead."

I stared at her, dumbfounded. "Is that how you see me?"

"Yes, but that's because I know you. And now that I've demonstrated I know you"—she was saying this while still lying on her back on my floor—"will you please take my advice and ride that man like a cowboy?"

"I don't think he's gay, Lucy."

"I already told you, you haven't the least sense when it comes to picking up signals."

Luckily Squire, who is always interested in people lying on the floor, distracted her by licking her face.

When Lucy rose at last, she said, "I'm going to bed. May I remind you that I'm here because you're so lonely? There's a bloke a couple of metres that way who's also lonely. He's nice, he's sweet, and he's into you. I know that for you these are all signs to raise your defences, but you're not an idiot, so tell that stupid part of your brain to stop being so stupid and go for it."

"All right, remind me next time to water your wine," I said.

And yet once she was in bed next to me, snoring lightly, I couldn't help thinking about what she'd said. Which is why I'm up now, writing this down. I need to sort my thoughts, and it's not easy with her yelling at me all the time for being an idiot who needs to get laid.

I suppose I *could* ask Alex out. Even if he is straight, which he probably is—now that I think about it, I think that the more inclined I grow to actually go for it, the straighter he becomes, like some sort of twisted reverse magic—if I just ask him out, that's a compliment, right? I mean, I know he's not one of those straight men who's grossed out by gays. Mind you, having to meet him in the hallway and such after he inevitably shoots me down would be awkward.

Then again, I did vomit in front of him, and he's not too disgusted to eat with me, so the man's resilient when it comes to awkwardness. And he's cute. He's got a good smile and a pleasant attitude, and nice eyes and hands, which I have a thing for. When I try to think back on our interactions for signs that he might like me, all I can think of is he's been pretty obliging when it comes to lending a hand and pulling me out of tight spots. But then, he's a friendly sort of chap. I wouldn't put it past him to do that for anyone.

In fact, I'm pretty sure Daria from next door told me that he fixed her toilet, leaked her radiators, and took out her rubbish on several occasions.

Oh bloody hell, I'll just do it. What have I got to lose, exactly? If I dwell on it, it'll grow into this giant Thing, when really there's no need for that.

Tuesday, 6 April

GOT AN email from my parents' friend about a potential job in Cambridge. As a research assistant.

Yeah, that just goes to show what my parents think of my current position. I'm senior lecturer here, but apparently, to my parents that's like being a BA in Cambridge.

Somehow have to squeeze three lectures into a day full of meetings tomorrow. Oh, and stupid Phil spilled half his coffee on me this morning, so for most of the day I looked like a giant poo-monster had vomited on my shirt.

Wednesday, 7 April

SAW ALEX in the hallway this morning, coming back from a jog just as I was heading out. Is it just me, or does he literally look like the straightest man who ever lived?

Wasn't the time to ask him out anyway, what with my having to go to work and him probably thinking about pussy all day.

On the upside, our departmental postgraduate seminar about the immediate post-war years was the subject of three meetings today, each of them chaired by Professor Jack Gordon. Which meant I had to look at him all day and wonder how I can hate his sexy arse so damn much.

Lucy really is right about that needing-to-get-laid business.

The meetings went well, on the whole. We settled pretty much everything, and I had occasion to observe that Jack was as cocky and self-assured as he'd ever been. By now, you'd think he'd have the grace to leave me alone, but no, he must needs follow me out of the last meeting when I was heading home.

"Go to hell," I told him before he could even open his mouth.

"Leo!" he said reproachfully. "Leo, please stop for one moment. What's the matter?"

"Nothing," I said. "I'm going home."

He fell into step beside me. "Leo—" He used his low, confiding tone. "Leo, do stop. I'm sorry, okay? I really am. I've been through hell and back...."

"Good!" I said emphatically.

"It's been a difficult time for me. I thought you'd be more understanding."

I stopped, because I could no longer contain my anger. I wanted to say a wealth of things which would have to be bleeped out in the future biopic based on my life—starring Alexander Skarsgård—but I didn't. For one, we still hadn't left campus, and I didn't want to be heard quarrelling with him.

And for another, it really wasn't worth it. I mean, what do you say to a guy like that? He had no shame, clearly felt no guilt for how he'd treated me, and thought only of himself and his own comfort and happiness.

"Look," I said, trying to be as patient as I could. "I don't know what you've been through, but I'm damn sure that it was within your power to call or text me while you were being put through it. You didn't. You make promises and you don't keep them. It's like you forget me the moment I'm out of your sight. Which is fine. I don't care. Just stop messing with me, all right?"

"Leo, dear," he said, taking a step closer and sounding as though I had wounded him, "don't say things like that. It's not like you to be so cold to me. I'm telling you, it's just difficult at the moment."

My anger was growing. "How difficult can picking up your phone or dropping an email be? Honestly, Jack, do you find these things generally difficult to do? If so, I think you should notify the bodies that awarded you a degree."

"Let me make it up to you," he said. "Let me take you out to dinner. Are you free tonight?"

"No. I don't want to eat dinner with you. Goodbye, sir."

And with that, I turned and left.

Thursday, 8 April

AMELIA CALLED. "Leo, do you think I'm sexy?"

"Er, yes?" A shot in the dark. I had not the least notion whether she was. She has big boobs, and I think straight men like those, for some reason, so I must have been on the right track. Besides, it wouldn't have done to say no.

"Thanks," she sighed. "I just don't think Mark thinks I'm sexy anymore."

"Oh. Well, I'm sure that's not true. When you guys first got together, he could do nothing but grin. We thought he'd had a brain seizure or something."

"Yes, but that was over ten years ago," she said. "Two kids later and things aren't the same as they used to be, you know?"

"Well, I'm pretty sure Mark's entirely Amelia-sexual, if you know what I mean. He's completely into you and nobody else. So I wouldn't worry about it."

"You don't understand…. Neither you nor Lucy have the least sympathy for me!"

"You asked Lucy whether she thought you were sexy?"

"No, you idiot. I asked her how to spice up my sex life."

"And what did she say?"

"She told me to wear a French maid's uniform, spank myself in front of him, ask him to call me Celeste, and beg him to take my virginity."

"Sounds about right."

"So naturally I can't listen to her, since she's insane. I thought you'd know something. I mean, you're gay, you know what men like, right?"

"Theoretically, I know what *gay* men like. Or, to be more precise, I know fuck all, love. Every man is different. You know Mark better than anybody, and you know what he likes."

"It's just been so lacklustre, recently, you know?"

"You've been busy. You're tired and distracted with the kids. Call his mother, have her take the kids for a bit, and go away together. Once you're alone with him, you'll know what to do. Come now, you're the least insecure person I know. You won't let a little dry spell get you down, will you?"

"No, you're right," she said resignedly. "I'm probably making it a bigger issue than it is. I mean, you've no idea what it's like! I haven't had sex for a *month*!"

"Cow," I said.

She laughed.

"No, really!" I said indignantly. "Asking him to take your virginity is very apt, now that I think about it, since your hymen has probably grown back."

"Idiot," she said, but my bitter outburst cheered her up.

Apparently my lack of a love life has that use, at least.

Friday, 9 April

I RECEIVED a copy of my friend Dawn's new book about the Crusades. It's a draft copy she wants me to proofread for her.

It's a tedious read. I mean, it's written in the present tense. An historical, factual book about the Crusades *in the present tense*. I can just imagine her editor telling her, "You've got to spice it up, make it more *now*, make it more *urgent!*" I don't know why I imagine her editor with a Salvador Dali moustache and a toy poodle under his arm. Anyway, it's the Crusades, for God's sake. They're about as exciting as they're going to get.

As to the dating front: in my effort to pluck up the nerve to ask Alex out, I've gone so far as to decide what I'm going to wear when the time comes.

Now that I read that sentence, I feel extremely pathetic. I'm going to go out with Squire and try to remember what it was like to be normal.

Saturday, 10 April

I DID it. I approached Alex.

Yesterday I saw him as I was coming back from my walk with Squire, just as he was heading out for the evening, looking really cute in a leather jacket I hadn't seen him wear before.

His face lit up when he saw me, he waved when I crossed the street over to his side, and he told me he was going shopping. He needed new trainers. I made a lame joke about a trainer needing trainers. I know—I should just shoot myself and spare everybody else the effort. But he laughed anyway, so when we parted I thought, *Fuck it, I'll do it. I'll just ask him out.*

I felt good about my decision. If I tried very hard not to imagine him naked, it'd be easy enough.

So this morning I dressed in the blue shirt that Lucy says makes my eyes pop—which sounds gross, but apparently is a good thing—and the jeans she says make my butt look appealing, which made me think of baboons. But anyway, I didn't get to show him my butt. And so I marched across the hall.

It's funny how I'd rather have rescued children out of burning buildings at that moment than face knocking on Alex's door. It takes less courage to bloody spy on the Russians than it does to ask another man out, I swear.

I knocked on his door and waited for him to answer. It took him a while.

That was because he was on the phone, and through the paper-thin wood of the door to his flat, I heard him say, "Yep, all right, love. Speak to you later."

I don't know why, but his referring to someone as *love*, and looking really, really good unshaven and in his dressing gown (presumably naked underneath), showing off a triangular part of his phenomenal chest made it very hard to choke out any sort of human sound that wasn't a *phwoarrr*.

"Hey, Leo, what's up!" He smiled at me. He kind of looked like Leonidas from *300*, except kind and gentle. Still, no less scary to me!

"Ah, I—I was wondering…." I began, smooth as usual. "I wanted to ask you something, actually."

"Oh yeah? Come in. Sorry about the mess."

So I stepped in. I didn't see whether it was messy or not because I felt a little dizzy. And sweaty. Why is asking someone out such a sweaty business?

He leaned against the counter that separated his kitchen from his sitting room and watched me as I walked around.

I didn't know what I was walking around for, except that it was something to do. "Hey, you put your shelves up," I observed, blindly patting the backs of some books.

"Yeah. So, what's up? You said you wanted to ask something?"

"Oh, yes," I said. "Yes, indeed. I—I have a question for you."

"All right, shoot."

I won't quote myself on what happened next, since I think Gay Cupid has recorded me verbatim for the *Gay Book of Shame* on enough occasions that he follows me around everywhere and makes a record of all I do and say. Suffice to say that I didn't spit it out. I couldn't.

He looked so handsome and manly, and I realised that I couldn't bear it if he shot me down, and I became convinced that he would. So instead, with heat in my face and rather incoherently, I asked him whether he would work out with me.

To be fair, that's pretty gay.

He said "Sure," with the sort of eagerness that suggested his professional standards were offended by how out of shape I was, and he needed to rectify that state of affairs—and soon.

We're going running tomorrow. Punishment fits the crime.

Sunday, 11 April

I CAN barely move my arms.

Alex had to literally carry me back upstairs because I couldn't feel my legs. The whole experience was like *Chariots of Fire*—if behind that group of athletic young men running on the beach to a pretty, uplifting soundtrack, there was the bent-in half figure of a man who had the fitness of an eighty-year-old asthmatic orangutan.

I knew I was out of shape, but *that* came as a shock to me. I'm not joking when I say that by the end I was quite close to staggering home on all fours.

Alex was kind about it, said the first steps were always the hardest, promised we'd take it light next time. I'm trying not to faint at the notion of a next time.

Wednesday, 14 April

ALEX PROMISES me that runner's high is an actual thing.

I think you've *got* to be high to run every day. Humans were not made for running. There's a reason we invented chairs.

Friday, 16 April

ALEX IS making me drink this protein shake, which he promises will help me build muscle. We went running together three times this week. He wants me to come and join his gym, where he'd help me build up my chest and arms.

At work I received an email from Jack today, requesting a meeting. It was all official, in that tongue-in-cheek way of his.

> *Dear colleague,*
> *I am writing to enquire whether it would be possible*
> *to arrange a meeting at a mutually agreeable time.*

You look hot in that polo neck.
Jack

I didn't engage in what was clearly meant to be the beginning of a flirtatious email exchange. As I was leaving for home, I told him I didn't have time to meet him.

Sunday, 18 April

ALEX HAS made me lasagne. He said I deserved a rest, and besides, the weather was shitty, so we couldn't go running outside. Something told me that Alex would have gone if it weren't for me—I've seen him come back from a run drenched before—but I really appreciated the lasagne treat. His lasagne is probably the best thing I've ever eaten. He laughed at my asking for third helpings, but honestly, I haven't eaten lasagne that good in… well, ever!

Then we had drinks. Lots of drinks. Before anybody asks—I did not try to make him drunk to seduce him. I'm not that desperate, and I'm not that creepy. That being said, we got so plastered that neither of us was up for any seducing, even had that been a possibility, which it isn't.

Anyway, we played a drinking game. We would each tell a story, and the other would have to guess if it was made-up or true. If the listener guesses correctly, the teller drinks. Incorrectly, the listener drinks.

I started. "All right, all right, here's one. When I was five, I pushed my sister into a pond, and so she took revenge on me by training her cat to attack me every time it saw me. My parents actually had to get rid of the cat. And that's why I hate cats."

"Wow, you're making it difficult," he said dryly. "Of course it's true. I've met your sister. I wouldn't push her into a pond for anything. What, did you have a death wish or something?"

I laughed drunkenly. "No! But okay, you're right, it's true."

"Okay, so here's mine. I once ran—"

"Oh no, no, no, no! Come on, mate, nothing about cross-country records or anything like that! First, I'll know nothing about it, and second, this is not the time to brag!"

"Brag? Well, I suppose…."

"I want it to be *personal*, and I want it to be *embarrassing*. Go!"

He laughed. "All right, Hauptmann. Give me a minute. I don't have that many embarrassing stories to tell."

"Well, too bad. I wish I could give you some of mine, but that treasure trove is for private use only."

"Like that time you vomited all over—"

"Stories that are embarrassing to *you*, goddammit!" I said indignantly. "Play by the rules!"

"I was kind of embarrassed by that."

"You and me both, mate. Well?"

"Okay, okay, I've got one. See if you can guess if this is true. When I was still serving—"

"Serving where?"

"Oh, I was in the RAF."

"Seriously?"

Alex assured me he was not joking.

"What happened?" I asked.

"I resigned."

"Why?"

"Long story, and sort of depressing. You want my embarrassing story or not?"

I really wanted both, but I reckoned I wouldn't push my luck, so I let him tell me the embarrassing one.

"So, to begin with, my dad was against my joining the RAF. That's to say, he wanted me to serve in the US, the greatest country on earth, yada-yada. And also, he used to be a Marine, way back when, so this was like a betrayal to him. When I joined, he refused to think of my job as real military.

"But then he came to visit me one day in the Mess on base. He's a sort of military-looking guy, or was at the time anyway. He definitely has a commanding presence. And so when he walked out of the base, past the gate, the young officer who stood guard thought Dad was some sort of general or something and promptly saluted him. I saw this happen from the window of my block, and I laughed to myself and thought he'd tell me off later for how our officers salute just anybody for no reason, and whether we were so poorly trained that we couldn't distinguish between a civilian and a general. But then I kept looking out of the window, and my dad was walking back in through the gate, towards the barracks. And again the young officer saluted him."—here Alex demonstrated a beautiful salute—"I wondered what my dad wanted, but he never reached the block, only turned to go back out the gate. And again, another salute. I think he went in and out like that three or four times before I realised that he was actually just really missing being saluted."

"Okay, it's got to be true, but I can't see how it's embarrassing for you. It's kind of adorable."

"It's embarrassing when it happens to you, let me tell you. After a while I wasn't the only one at that window, watching what was going on!"

I scoffed. "Pfft, that's nothing! Once, the postwoman rang as I got out of the shower, and I ran to the door forgetting I was undressed. So I opened the door, saw the postwoman, realised I was naked and then lifted Squire up to hide my groin. So there I was, standing completely starker with a panting dog at my waist, trying to collect my parcel."

Alex, enormously pleased with this story, said, "God, I hope it's true!"

It was, so we both drank. By this time, the rules of the game had become a trifle fuzzy. That was as coherent as the evening got.

I woke up with a head-splitting hangover this morning.

Tuesday, 20 April

UGH, THINGS I hate about most essays I have to read: irrational structuring, lack of argumentation, the use of the personal pronoun, the repetition of the same word over, and over, and over again (and over), and sloppy grammar. But what I really don't like is when I read something that begins to sound eerily familiar.

Today I was reading one such essay, and everything about it sounded strangely like I'd read it before. After putting that essay through the plagiarism program, I found my instincts were correct. I then spent two hours tracking down the source from which it was plagiarised.

I'm going to come down on the fucker like a ton of bricks.

Wednesday, 21 April

JACK HAS been stalking me today. Nothing major, but I think he believes that if he puts on the wounded-puppy act, I'm going to forgive him. And I do feel a little sorry for him, but when I think back on his behaviour over the past couple of months, I really can't see how any of this is my fault—or, more to the point, what prevented him from behaving like a decent human being to begin with. I mean honestly, why didn't he phone me? He didn't phone me once. Or text me. I have to assume that what Alex and Lucy said was right: he wants me now because he can't have me. The moment I start drooling after him again, he'll start finding reasons to disappear. Well, tough. I'm not falling for that trick again.

Sarah cornered me in the rec room today.

"So, the big three-oh coming up, eh? Feeling the jitters?"

"Do you know, I almost forgot I'm turning thirty," I said, quite honestly.

"Oh, I remember when I turned fifty." She sighed heavily. "Rob took me out for a meal, and I put on so much make-up, he actually jumped when he saw me in full light."

I laughed. "That's not a danger I'm facing."

"No, you men can grow older and older and more distinguished as you do it. Even grey hair looks good on you!"

Self-consciously, I put my hand to my hair.

"You don't have any, you daft sod," she scoffed. "And I wasn't speaking of you but men in general. Not that it would be visible on you, anyway, blond as you are."

"And young as he is," Jack said, startling me.

I don't know how long he'd been standing there. He was with Professor Finkley, an old departmental arsehole.

"Little whippersnapper," Finkley said. "In fact, now that I think about it, you look like a little boy still. One could mix you up with one of the students. Certainly you've the same publication record."

He chuckled at his own joke. He is a gross old man, but well connected and a funding magnet, for some unfathomable reason. Which is obviously why Jack is his closest friend in the department. Trust Jack to sniff out the best-connected person in a room and ingratiate himself with them.

Sarah teased me about my age some more, to Jack's sneering amusement and to Finkley's insinuations that I was little better than a baby.

Ugh, sometimes I really hate my job.

Thursday, 22 April

IT'S REALLY fucking hard to run behind Alex. I mean, seriously, how am I supposed to focus on breathing and rhythm and all that, when his arse is just in front of me, the muscles in his legs tensing as they hit the ground, his wide shoulders—argh! One of these days it will be like that scene in *Madagascar*, when the lion realises he is a real lion and his romp through the meadow with his old pal zebra turns into a hunt.

Friday, 23 April

AMELIA CALLED me today to discuss my birthday. It's on the 8th of May, so there's still plenty of time, but she insisted we must plan the thing. I told her I didn't want to do anything fancy, and she agreed—eventually—that a pint down at the pub would be a "fun way to spend your thirtieth birthday, grandad."

It was sweet of her to call, but I'd rather nobody talked of my birthday, but just kind of forgot. I don't know, I feel kind of weird about it. I guess I could be doing more with my life. Perhaps that's it.

When I think about the ambitions I had before I started on my PhD... I wanted to do some outside university work. Maybe for some think tanks, or some multinational organisations. But after I finished all my PhD and post-PhD work, it turned out I'm pretty much only qualified to tell people about my PhD and post-PhD work.

Which turns out to be only interesting to about three people on the planet, and that includes me. And my PhD supervisor. And my mother.

And I think half the time she's just being polite.

Sunday, 25 April

THIS MORNING, Alex and I went to the gym together.

I hate gyms. The running at least feels natural and is out in the open, but gyms smell of stale sweat, and I hate the music. That being said, I could watch Alex lift weights on repeat until I die. God, he's got nice arms. And he's strong! The park where we run—no way would I ever dare go there by myself, especially late in the evening. But with Alex it's hard to feel afraid. It's like you're training with Rocky Balboa, except he's got a cute face. Also, I'm not surprised he's a personal trainer. Honestly, even training—which is, after all, only marginally better than death—is bearable when you've got him coaching you. He's not in the least like those Army drill sergeants from American movies, which is kind of what I feared he'd be. He smiles at you when you do well and immediately changes tack when he sees you can't do something. There's no macho posturing or anything like that.

After he made me lift some weights, which was a chore, he told me to hop on the treadmill, and as he did so, he gave me a pat on my bum. A friendly pat. A chummy sort of pat.

I'm not going to put more meaning into it than I must. Future Leo will be pleased to read I didn't stand there waiting for a repeat but actually went on the treadmill like a good boy, feeling the pat on my bum the entire time I was running.

Monday, 26 April

SO THIS happened.

This morning, as I was leaving for work, Alex opened his door, apparently leaving for the gym. He was wearing his slacks and carried his gym bag. He saw me fumble with my keys and said, "Oh hey, are you busy this weekend?"

"No, why?"

"Do you want to go out with me?"

I froze. Then I turned slowly to look at him, fascinated.

He cleared his throat and scratched the back of his neck and couldn't really meet my eyes. That's how I knew.

"Or not, whatever, I don't—"

"What? No, no, I'd love to go out with you! You mean a date, right?" I said at once, because even though I'm an idiot, I'm not actually self-destructive. He was blushing, and so I said, "Please say it's a date you mean. I've been meaning to ask you ages ago, but I was too shy."

"Oh?" He exhaled in relief and then laughed. "Well, that's—that's nice. I guess I did mean a date." Then, after a pause during which I saw an interlude with us floating in the sky, and gay-arse Cupid pissing rainbows around us, he said, "You were shy?"

"Yeah," I said. "This weekend, huh? Where do you want to go?"

"I don't know. I'll think of something."

"All right, anything is fine with me."

We laughed awkwardly, and then we had to go downstairs together, which was also awkward because, though extremely happy at last to be on the same page, and though my heart was doing leaps and bounds in my chest that would interest a cardiologist, we were both kind of surprised.

Downstairs we parted with a lot of smiles and "see yous." I didn't dance as I walked to the Tube station, but I might as well have done. I've got a date with Alex! Har har har!

Oh God, I've got to turn down the dork in me if I'm ever to get lucky with him.

Wednesday, 28 April

HAD AN undergrad in my office today. He was trying to get me to tell him exactly what to read for his essay. Had to explain to him that finding the right literature is part of the process of research. And that being able to deal with your shit by yourself is part of life.

Youth today!

Dear God, I'm turning into my dad. That isn't good.

Met Lucy, Amelia, and Mark outside Lucy's to help her carry some furniture she'd ordered online. While Amelia and I were busy putting the cabinets together, I casually mentioned that I had a date with Alex. You know, because they're my friends and it seemed like a natural thing to share with them. Immediately, Lucy began a victory dance, while Amelia "accidentally" dropped the screwdriver on my foot.

"What! Why? And you refused to meet my Stuart!" she said.

"Oh, leave him alone," Lucy said. "I told you this was going to happen, didn't I? Oh my God, where is my medal?"

"Who is this Alex person, anyway?" Amelia said pettishly. "I don't like him. I haven't met him, but I'm sure I don't like him."

"That's what I love about you. You're not prejudiced," I murmured.

Apparently, my having scored a date with Alex is a personal offence to Amelia and a personal victory to Lucy. Mark gave me that look that said, "You keep me out of this, mate."

Although, as we were getting ready to go out, he caught me when we were alone and asked, "You like that man?"

"Yeah, he's amazing."

"Good luck."

Luck. *Huh.* It suddenly occurs to me that one of the disadvantages of having so loftily taken myself out of the gay dating scene is that I haven't really had a lot of practice. Four years I've been pining after this one man, who turns out to be a huge disappointment. And now what? I mean, witness how rubbish I was at even asking Alex out!

Lucy was right about the horniness: it doesn't help to be desperate when you want to make a good impression.

Saturday, 31 April

REPORT FROM the front.

I was nervous before the date. Honestly, I don't think I've ever been this nervous before, going out with someone. And it was weird, because I've already spent time with him and we get along. Maybe that's why I was nervous. Maybe I was afraid that the bond we had would spoil when he takes a serious, good look at me. I mean, he's all brawn and masculine energy, and I'm kind of... I don't even know what I am.

He picked me up at half past seven, which was something we'd agreed to in the corridor between our flats. While previously we'd go out of our way to spend time together like normal people, we've suddenly grown bashful. This past week we only talked when we happened to bump into each other in the corridor, as though we were trying to save our best material for the date. Each time this happened, I saw him blushing. Judging by how sweaty my palms felt, I was probably not giving any more self-assured signals myself.

Anyway, he came to pick me up very punctually, which was unfortunate because I wasn't ready. I'd mislaid the shirt I meant to wear, found the only other acceptable one completely crumpled, and when he knocked on my door, I was running around in my boxers, chasing Squire around the flat—he'd decided to take one of my socks and run away by way of a fun game, for which I had no patience. So I had to shout through the door that I needed a few more minutes, which *really* is not a good start.

Worse was to come.

Alex didn't bother to book a table at the restaurant he chose. It had been recommended to him by some friend, who had told him that booking a table wasn't necessary. Alex is new to London, so I must forgive him not knowing that any restaurant that doesn't need a table booked on a Saturday evening is probably not worth going to, but as it turned out, we found that out by ourselves.

When we reached the restaurant, we found that it had shut down. So there we were, in the middle of London, without a table. Alex was disappointed, so I said, "Hey, don't worry. I bet we can find a table somewhere in Chinatown. Maybe we'll have to wait a few minutes, but that's all right."

I really wanted to put a good spin on this, and when he saw me act so nonchalantly about this business, he perked up too, and so we walked through the dense crowds, over the wet pavements in the direction of Leicester Square. The busy streets were not conducive to conversation, though at one point, as we were squeezing our way through a throng of people just emerged from the Tube, he grabbed my hand so we weren't separated.

Once we arrived in Chinatown, after some twenty minutes of running across streets and dodging cabs, our hands somehow still clasped together, we were faced with a plethora of choices.

The trouble with Chinatown is that not all restaurants there are good. Some are marvellous, others not so much, and it's almost impossible to tell which is which unless you check in advance. Or you frequent there often, which I don't. Either way, on Saturday there was one easy way to tell—some of the restaurants had long queues coming out of the door, and others didn't.

Yi Chen once told me to direct myself by the amount of Chinese people frequenting a place, so we eventually decided on one that had a shorter queue than the others. But it still meant we had to wait for forty minutes, and in the meantime, it began to drizzle.

Alex was apologetic about this turn of events, but I wasn't going to let it ruin our date. I maintained that an evening out in London must necessarily involve queues and rain, and by way of making him feel better—and myself too, let's not fool ourselves—I stepped close to him, so that he could put an arm around me, ostensibly for warmth and protection from rain, but also because it felt fucking amazing.

An elderly couple queued in front of us, who must have mistaken me for a girl, what with my hood up and my slighter physique compared to Alex. The woman said, "Aw, how sweet!"

Alex looked down at me, amusement shining in his eyes.

When at last we were let inside, we received a table at the very end of the restaurant, which meant it took the waiter three years to take our order, to bring us water and beer, and finally to bring us our food. It wasn't the best Chinese food I've ever eaten, to be perfectly frank, but I hardly tasted any of it anyway, absorbed as I was in Alex.

At first we talked as we always did, perhaps a little constrained by being on an actual date and by my having serious trouble not gazing at him longingly across the table, admiring the way his eyelashes were stuck together from the rain outside and how his shoulders looked in his shirt. Honestly, I would have been almost too distracted to hear him, when he shifted a little in his seat and said, "I was so nervous about tonight, but it's going all right, right? So far?"

I laughed. "Of course it is. Even if we hadn't found this place, we could have ordered food in and eaten at yours or mine. I don't think I've ever had such a formal date before!"

"No, me neither," he said. Then, recalling himself, "Well, not with a man, anyway."

I laughed distractedly, not really listening. Then what he said reached my stupid brain at last. "Wait, what do you mean? You've dated women?"

"Yes," he said, leaning forward confidingly. "I've not been with a man before you."

I almost choked on my beer. I had to put it down and cough into my napkin. "Wh-what!"

"Oh, you didn't know?"

"You're *straight*?" I said it in perhaps a higher pitch than was strictly necessary.

"Er, no. I don't think you can call a bloke dating another bloke precisely straight," he said uneasily. "Christ, should I have told you before? I thought you knew."

"How should I have known?" I said. "You asked me out, for God's sake."

"Yeah, I know." He blushed and asked shyly, "Is this a deal-breaker?"

"Wait, hold on a moment. Just—just let's take a break for one second and straighten this out. What are you?"

"I'm a human male," he said, blinking at me in confusion.

"Yes, thank you, that's not what I meant. You're straight? Gay? Bi? What?"

"Yeah, I think I'm that last one," he said. "Or I was. Lately, I don't know. I was never completely straight, if that helps."

"Meaning?"

"Well, I liked women, I think I still like women generally, but I like men too. When I was younger, it was just easier to go with the flow and sort of fancy girls, you know? Then, well, I told you about the RAF, didn't I? There was a friend... I liked him. But we were both professionals, and it wouldn't have been appropriate to ask or do anything about it, and then it became tense. Finally I couldn't stand it any longer, and I just left. Since then, I thought I'd try it with a woman again. You know, to just—just try and be normal, whatever that is. But the next person I was attracted to was you."

"Oh. I see."

"Is it going to be a problem?"

"No. No, that's fine. I didn't know, that's all. I assumed—but that's silly. No, of course it's not a problem."

"It's no fun dating a virgin, is it?" he said, smiling wryly.

"Nonsense," I said quickly, trying to make up for my earlier hesitation and confusion. "Honestly, it makes no difference; we'll take it slowly, see how it goes. Only…."

"Yes?"

"Look, I've got to know, this isn't some sort of experimental phase you're going through, is it? There's no girlfriend, fiancée, wife somewhere in the background?"

"No, of course not," he said earnestly. "You don't think I would— I'd never do that!"

"Okay, okay, fine," I said, though frankly my nerves were a little frayed. I had seriously planned to go all the way with him tonight, but now I was concerned about his feelings, anxieties, and fears, and I would have to deal with each of them in turn before we could do anything serious.

Which is fine, I don't mind. It's just not what I expected.

He watched me intently as we were talking of this, as though to gauge my reactions. But though I smiled, I think it came off a trifle strained, because we couldn't be as easy as before after that. We split the bill, which was preceded by some awkward haggling over who should handle it, and then walked back to the Tube station and took the train home.

Alex asked whether I'd come in for a drink at his flat, and I quickly said yes, not wishing to seem as though I had a problem with his confession earlier. But it came out too eager, and he had a bit of a worried expression on him when I did step inside. I sat on the sofa while he took the beers out of the fridge. He handed me one cold bottle and then leaned against the counter, rather than come and sit next to me. This wasn't going well. Several times we tried to speak of something innocuous, but no conversational gambit would stick, and the whole date was dying right in front of my eyes.

I don't know if it was the beer or what, but I decided that I wasn't going to let it die. So I stood and went over to him. "This is stupid. We're adults. We can talk about this, can't we?"

"Yes," he said a little warily.

So I took charge. "I like you, Alex. Not just as a friend or neighbour, but everything." Here I made a vague gesture encompassing his whole body. He smiled and rolled his eyes in embarrassment. "So I'd like to see you again. I don't know, as a boyfriend or something. Whatever you're comfortable with. Do you understand?"

"Okay, yeah, like a boyfriend," he said, perking up.

"Okay. We can just… date and see how things go. You can simply tell me when you're ready… you know, and then we'll take it slowly, and I'll show you everything. If you don't like something, we don't do it. And if you change your mind about this"—I pointed between us—"then we'll just decide to be friends again and pretend this never happened."

"Okay," he said. "Can I have a hug?"

I let out a laugh, because he looked ridiculously pleased for having asked for it, and because the tension between us suddenly evaporated, and I was relieved.

I went into his arms.

He embraced me and… well, that lion thing I was writing about some days ago happened, where suddenly all my instincts went from being "that nice bloke who wants to date him" to "that gay bloke who wants to know how big he is, and what shape and colour, and what his come tasted like." I contained it, however, because I'm a saint, and also because the hug was really nice.

He smelled of the rain and soy sauce and some really nice aftershave. His arms were strong around me, his shoulders broad, and his pectorals hard. I tried to think of unsexy things, like that time when I was seven and my mother made a strawberry jelly in the shape of my sister to celebrate her fifth birthday, and it didn't come out and the thing looked like a giant, gelatinous, vaguely female-shaped blob that I was then forced to eat as tears ran down my cheeks.

My thoughts were as chaste as anybody could have wished, and I leaned further into the hug. It was nice. And then I looked up and saw his face so close I could see the shadow of his recently shaved beard on his cheeks and the tiny mole that disappeared in the dimple of his smile.

He leaned in and kissed me. There was nothing shy about that kiss. His lips pressed eagerly against mine and opened quickly, our tongues met and tangled, and he let out a noise at the back of his throat: a deep sort of moan as he hugged me tighter. He put up one of his hands to cup my cheek and then slid it to the back of my neck to support my head while he plunged deeper into my mouth. In fact, I'm surprised that my clothes didn't melt right off my body.

When he let go, he was grinning. "See? *That* you won't have to teach me!" he said.

"Uh-huh," I said, catching my breath. "That was… that was really nice."

"Yeah?" he asked, his chest swelling with pride.

"Mm-hmm." I leaned in for more but didn't press for anything else, though I don't doubt he noticed the tightness in my jeans pressing against his thigh.

I wanted to end the evening on a good note, so after we snogged for a glorious moment, we said goodnight, and then I went back to my flat.

Monday, 3 May

I'VE GOT to say, I'd quite forgotten how impatient one can get to be home when there's something to come home to. Or, to be more precise, someone.

It's a strange situation, him living right across from me. It's convenient, I won't lie, but it forces a closeness that generally doesn't happen until later in a relationship. Or so I'm told. I've never got that far with anyone. The closest I got was Jamie, at uni, whom I was with for two years before it all sort of fizzled out; he wanted to travel, and I had just won a scholarship to start my PhD. But university relationships aren't like real-life relationships.

I'm turning thirty soon, and things have changed. It's no use pretending that this upcoming decade of my life won't be different. I mean, it's not as though I'm a woman and have to count my remaining childbearing years, or anything like that, but as you mature, I find that you generally become less interested in hopping from flower to flower, as one does in one's youth.

In my case, the experience with Laura's then-husband and a nasty health scare that thankfully turned out to be nothing made that decision for me. I wanted to settle down. I wanted a boyfriend, a partner, someone to live with, even, if it should come to that. The only thing was I wanted to date someone for a bit first before deciding that's where we're heading. With Alex, we haven't slept together yet, and we're basically almost living together already!

After all, what's a corridor for separation? After our date on Saturday, I went to my flat. But on Sunday morning he knocked on my door to force me to go jogging with him, and then afterwards we went out for a coffee, and then I had some papers to grade and a few journal articles to read. I did so, while he played with my dog and took part in a bidding war online for some box set of C-movies. He explained to me why they were important, but for the life of me I didn't understand. Then he went out to fetch the ingredients for lunch and prepared it at mine, and then we ate it. Some of this time we did spend snogging on my sofa, but I think it's quite evident the boundaries are very much marred and fading. I mean, we've only just agreed to date!

That being said, when I came home today and smelled what he was cooking, I was not in the least opposed to knocking on his door right away and spending the rest of the evening at his flat, right after I fetched Squire from Daria's.

We walked the dog together, we ate, I snogged him so much I almost climbed on top of him, until he laughed and I remembered to slow down. I'm sure I'll find this situation much more reconcilable once I can get into his trousers.

On that front, I can report some progress too. He seems to be really into kissing, and he likes to hold me and hug me. And when he looks at me, I don't see repulsion or anything like that. He likes to look at me. And though our crotches don't touch when we kiss, I'm pretty sure I saw him adjust himself at one point, after getting up from having snogged me on his sofa.

Wednesday, 5 May

HAD A really shitty day at work today. My computer broke, the lad who was meant to come and fix it didn't, and I spent hours on the phone trying to sort out the paperwork to apply for the deputy head position, which, from gossip, I understood I had an actual chance for.

On top of that, like an idiot, I tried to pull this book out of my bookshelf, and it wouldn't budge, so I pulled harder, until I had to prop my foot up against the shelf to get proper leverage, and the book suddenly capitulated. I smacked myself on the forehead with it. Of course, then it turned out to be the wrong book.

When I got back home, not two minutes after I put my bag down, there was a fierce pounding on my door. When I opened, there was Alex, glowing with happiness, and he took me in his arms and kissed me.

He spoke against my cheek. "I won! I'll be getting *Samurai Cop 2* for virtually nothing!" He kissed me again, then looked a little perplexed. "What happened to your head?"

"I tried to read a book."

"Oh."

He didn't question it. I don't know what that means about how he views my sanity. All the same, that movie, *Samurai Cop 2*, made him very happy, which made me happy, mostly because he kissed me a lot to express his joy. What made me less happy was his insistence that we watch it together, because, as he said, "You'll love it. It's so terrible, it's hilarious!"

"But I haven't seen the cultural colossus that is Samurai Cop 1," I hedged.

"Don't worry, it's self-explanatory."

I already allowed myself to be tortured on a regular basis—they call it physical exercise but let's be real—just to be with him.

Watching *Samurai Cop 2* couldn't be worse than that, surely. So I agreed.

Thursday, 6 May

GENERAL ELECTION.

I've never in my life voted for anyone who actually won the election, so even with the recent upsurge in popularity for the Lib Dems, I'm sceptical. All the same, I gave Alex a stern look when he said he doesn't care about elections. He told me he'd go this time and actually asked me whom to vote for, so I had to sit him down and show him party after party so he could make a choice. I didn't want him to tell me whom he'd be voting for, since that could be a shock to the system and I was enjoying having a boyfriend, but he picked the Greens, which was a relief.

"Do they stand a chance?" he asked.

"I always believe you should vote for whom you want to win and not who you think can win," I said. "The voting system in this country is fucked up that way, but I refuse to vote for anything other than what I believe in, regardless of the system."

He nodded solemnly, and earlier this evening I caught him reading up on the election in the *Guardian* online, which is really sweet, because I think he's making the effort for me.

Friday, 7 May

A LIB Dem–Conservative coalition? Is this a joke?

Sunday, 9 May

MY BIRTHDAY was yesterday. I'm now officially thirty. I'm not gonna lie—it feels good. For one, I woke up next to Alex, which was pleasant.

It all started last week, when I called Amelia to tell her that Alex and I were dating now, and that whatever they'd prepared, I'd like him to be there. She was still a little miffed that I'd chosen not to meet her one other single gay friend, Stuart, but she agreed that it made sense that I should bring Alex.

Alex meeting all my friends was sort of a big deal. But he's already met Lucy, and despite her rather forward personality, he claimed to like her. So at least half the work was done. I was sure Amelia was going to love him once she got over that whole Stuart business, and Mark would be cool about it once she was. I didn't know who else might be there.

As it turned out, there was a small crowd in the pub. Frankly I barely recognized most of the people and was sure they didn't know they'd come to a celebration of my birthday. We made for a loud party, and there was even the always-embarrassing "Happy Birthday" singing, and the even more embarrassing gifts.

Of course, as a joke I received everything from a blow-up man-doll to a creepy leather gimp mask with a zipper for a mouth.

Eventually, as we settled down, my closest friends were around me so they could get to know Alex. It went well. In fact, it went great. Alex is charming, so there really was no need to be afraid of anything.

When Amelia and I went to the bar to buy the next round for the table, she grudgingly admitted that he was gorgeous. Lucy already approved; in fact she congratulated herself for having orchestrated the whole thing, and Mark got on with Alex as though they'd known one another for years. Apparently they shared a love for rugby.

"So, how did you two meet?" Amelia asked, at some point.

"Oh, I found him vomiting in the corridor between our flats one day," Alex said without skipping a beat. He continued despite my imploring glares. "And then he came on to me."

"I did not!" I protested.

"Yeah you did," he said, to the amusement of the table.

"Well, tell us!" said Lucy. "What are his best lines?"

Alex laughed. "I do hope they're not his *best* lines!"

I sunk my head onto my arms on the table, as they all laughed and Alex patted my shoulder consolingly.

"Nah, it wasn't so bad," he said.

"No, no," I said from between my arms, "tell me what I did. It's best to know now so we have time to get therapy together and recover."

Everyone laughed, and Alex said, "Well…."

I looked up, dreading this. "What? What did I say to you?"

"Well, you'd just vomited, so you had an interesting colour in your face, and you were in a bad state and I had to ask whether you were too hot. You looked deep into my eyes," he said, barely able to keep a straight face.

"Yes?"

"And you said, 'Oh, *you're* hot!'"

"Oh my God." I sank my head back into my arms as the rest of the table roared with laughter.

"And then what?" asked Lucy, wiping a tear from her eye.

"Well, he was not really firm on his legs, but I gathered from something he mumbled that he lived right there, where we were standing," Alex said. "So I asked if he wanted me to open his door for him so he could go home. He trailed his finger along my chest"—here his voice quivered with amusement—"and said, 'I thought I spent the evening with this one lady, but you're a bloke, aren't you?'"

His impersonation of me was unnecessary and not the least bit accurate, despite the applause and laughter from his enraptured audience. Sadly, he hadn't finished.

"And so I said, 'No, I'm just your neighbour. I'll help you into your flat, because I don't think you'll make it on your own.' And then he slumped back against the wall, lifted one leg sideways, leaned his head back, spread out his arms, and said, 'Okay, take me!'"

I had my hand over my eyes.

"Oh lord!" Lucy was crying openly by now. "What did you do?"

"I took his keys, opened his door, and then picked him up and carried him into the flat. It was easy enough because he draped himself over me, crying, 'Oh yeah, baby!'"

Later, when this nightmare was over and we were walking home—and I was sober, because I will never drink again—I asked him if all he said was true.

And he laughed and said, "Of course."

"Why on earth did you want to go out with me after that display?" I asked.

"Oh?" He seemed surprised. "Well, I got to know you better, didn't I? Also, I thought you were an amusing drunk. You kept quoting Churchill at me for some reason."

"Oh God," I groaned, hanging my head.

He felt bad about having told the story then, and when we went back to mine, he tried to convince me that it really wasn't so very bad, after all.

"Did *you* ever embarrass yourself completely in front of someone you like?" I asked.

"Sure, I'll do it right now. What do you want me to do? Fart in front of you? What?"

"Forget about it," I said, slumping down onto my sofa. "And I mean that literally. If you could just forget how we first met, that would be grand."

He laughed and sat down next to me and then picked up my legs and pulled them over onto his lap and kissed me.

"I am not forgetting anything," he said. "I thought it was funny. Besides, you don't remember it, so that's not really how we met. We met on the stairs, and my hands were covered in paint, and when we shook hands, we couldn't unstick them. Remember?"

I was a little cheered by that.

Then he kissed me a lot, which helped my mood rapidly.

Sometime later into the night, he asked me if I wanted my birthday present. Before we ever left for the pub, he had given me a gift already: *Bioshock 2*, because it turns out we both played the first one and thought it was incredible. It was a good gift; I didn't think he'd give me anything more.

Then my heart jumped when from his pocket he withdrew a wrapped condom.

"Only one?" I asked with a laugh, somewhat flippantly.

That was a mistake. One glance at his face and I could see he was tense and nervous. That's not what I wanted. I wanted him all horny and excited, not fearful and jumpy. So I took the condom, put it away, kissed him, and said, "It's all right. We're tired, and it's late. Come along." I took his hand, stood up from his lap, and led him to the bedroom. We fell asleep in each other's embrace. It was very nice, even if I woke up painfully hard in the morning, without the least hope of alleviation. It was cruel of him to have taken his shirt off sometime during the night, so that when I turned to wake him up, I saw the upper half of his beautiful body.

God, he's stunning. And, I may be mistaken, but I had the feeling that when I woke him with kisses along his neck and shoulder and collarbone, he was quite relaxed and amenable to more....

But then Daria knocked on the front door with Squire, whom she'd kept overnight. She had that harassed expression that said something was up.

"Was he okay?" I asked. "He didn't chew anything, did he?"

"Oh no. I'm only mentally preparing because my grandchildren are coming. Expect the sound of china breaking and the shriek of lost souls travelling through the halls. You don't happen to have some bubble wrap lying around, do you?"

"What, for your china?"

"No, for the bodies, when I have to dispose of them later," she said in a low, ominous voice, though there was a twinkle in her eye.

"No," I said with a laugh. "But I'll do you one better. I'll deflect the police when they come, so you can make a run for it."

Once Squire was back, he needed to be walked, and then, when I returned and fed him, Alex had already gone.

He came back some minutes later, rather hectically, kissing me briefly and explaining that he was extremely late for an appointment with a client.

So he left, and I'm on my own now, with work to do. I could tackle the big pile of articles that I've been avoiding all week.

Or I can fantasize about Alex's upper body.

Evening

WELL, THIS is awkward. Alex and I were just sitting down to enjoy *Samurai Cop 2*, and he was just softening me to the prospect of sitting through that crapfest by explaining that he would hold me if I got actually scared, when there was an urgent knock on my door.

I opened and there was… Jack. To be precise, Jack with a bottle of wine and something that looked suspiciously like a birthday present.

To confirm my suspicions, he said, "Happy Birthday!"

"Jack!" I was flabbergasted. "What the—My birthday was yesterday."

"Was it?" he said, shrugging. "It's not too late to celebrate a little, is it?"

At this point, Alex came to stand next to me, one hand on my shoulder and the other on the door frame. Just at that moment, he seemed enormous.

Jack's eyebrows rose in surprise. And, infuriatingly, in amusement.

"All right, mate?" Alex said, nodding at him cheerfully, though with an undertone of something less than cheerful.

"Who's this?" Jack asked me.

"I'm his boyfriend," Alex said. "Who are you?"

"Boyfriend!" Jack said, with a startled laugh.

I had to give it to him. He knew how to mask embarrassment. By the look of him, you'd think *we* were the ones made to look ridiculous just then.

He said, "I don't believe you!"

"Oh yeah? Well, you'd better believe it, because what would I be doing in his flat, then?" Alex said.

This was getting childish, and quickly.

"Judging by that glottal stop, painting his walls?" Jack said.

"Fact is," Alex said, unconcerned, "I'm on this side of the door, and you're not."

"All right," I said, worried that they'd get into a fight soon, "Jack, thank you for remembering my birthday. It's very kind of you to come around and all, but, er, it's not a convenient time."

"Yes, I can see that," said Jack, with one eyebrow raised.

I could tell at once that I'd become twenty times more attractive to him on the spot. If I want to marry him or something, all I need to do now is add some ninja assassins to my rooftop to shoot at him any time he came near. *Weirdo.*

We said stiff, polite goodbyes, and then Alex closed and locked the door.

On the plus side, Alex is spending the night. He's in the shower now.

Wednesday, 12 May

OH MAN, what a day.

Alex slept over again last night, and as always it was really nice— he is warm, kind, and affectionate, and waking up in his arms or even to the sight of him is frankly one of those things someone should report as a lost Wonder of the World.

We've been slowly progressing along the lines of intimacy for some time, and this morning I thought it would be okay if I tried to go down on him. It started off innocently enough. We were kissing, and I was rubbing him over his boxers, and I thought we'd just go ahead with a hand job. But then I got carried away, so I interrupted the kiss and positioned myself so I could peel back his boxers. But he hurriedly pulled them back and, red in the face, stammered that he hadn't got the time, that he had to go, that he was awfully sorry, et cetera. He kissed me hurriedly and then made his escape, leaving me sitting back on my heels.

It was not a pleasant mood to go to work in, and Jack could have picked a better time to approach me—but then, my entries in this diary prove that timing is by far Jack's weakest point. So he cornered me by the coffee machine, looking coldly down at me and asking if he "could have a word" with me.

I shrugged. We went to his office, which was good, since that way I could leave whenever I wanted.

He paced the length of the room and then said, "Well, what have you to say to all this?"

"To what?" I asked, blinking at him.

"You have a boyfriend," he said, almost viciously.

"Yeah, and so what? What's it to you?"

"You've had a boyfriend all this time! All this sanctimonious business about Sasha was nonsense!"

"What?"

"I remember the bastard from that time I was over at yours! He was bringing you a cake!"

"I still don't see what any of that has to do with—well, with anything," I said.

"Oh yeah?" His eyes were hard and narrowed. "You made me break up my engagement, making it sound as though I were a cheating liar when I wanted to be with you. And you were double-crossing me all along!"

I was angry. Too angry to be surprised that that's the spin he had on the whole situation. "Now hang on," I said. "For the record, I didn't cheat on anybody. I didn't make you do anything either. You said you wanted to be with me, and when you said that, Jack, I was single. Alex was just a neighbour—a friend, nothing more. You were the one who decided you wanted to be with me and not with Sasha, and so you broke up with her. Or, at least, so you led me to believe. And then, when I wanted you to step up and be my boyfriend, you never showed up! You didn't ring or text, there was no getting hold of you. So I agreed to go out with Alex instead. That's the order of events, okay?"

I may have spoken a trifle loudly, and there may have been curse words interspersed in this, but the gist of it struck Jack dumb.

"I—I didn't know," he said. "It was a confusing time for me. Breaking up with someone who lives in your house and is dependent on you isn't easy or straightforward, you know."

"I can imagine. And I'm sorry. But you could have called, Jack. You could have texted. Anything. I would have waited if you had asked me to."

"Okay," he said. "I could have done that."

"All right. I must be going; I've got to get to Beckett Hall by three. Did you find out what happened to the projector in there?"

"Hm? No, ask Nick."

And on that rather prosaic note, we parted ways.

I was high-strung all day; during my lectures I made a tolerably effective impression of Hitler giving a speech. I had a meeting with one girl whose MA dissertation I'm supervising, and I can't say I was kind. To be fair, she's not the brightest penny in the piggybank, and she was annoying me by her insistence to compose her entire dissertation out of quotes.

Then it was raining, so I got soaked on the way home. I didn't knock on Alex's door, only went straight to mine, but he must have heard me return because I'd barely managed to get my coat off and shake the rain off it, when he knocked.

I opened and found my anger melt away at the sheepish, apologetic look on his face.

"Hey, can we talk?" he said.

"Sure," I said, letting him in.

Once I closed the door behind him, he dug his hands into his pockets and said, "Look, about this morning…."

"It's okay," I said. "You weren't ready; I shouldn't have presumed."

"No, no," he said quickly, "it's not that. It's just…."

"What? Have you got something? An infection or—or some kind of…?"

"What? No! Of course not!" he said. "I didn't mean that. Only… only what you were about to do…. I couldn't think straight, and I couldn't quite say what I wanted to say, and so I ran away, which was stupid and cowardly. And I'm so sorry, Leo, really I am."

"Well, thanks," I said. "It did make me feel like I've got the pox or something."

"Oh God!" he said, horrified. "It's just that… Leo"—he turned very earnest—"I don't want you to do anything for me that I couldn't do right back for you, you understand?"

I really didn't.

"I mean," he added, "if you were going to do that, then… then I'd have to do the same to you. It's only fair, and I wasn't sure I was ready, you see?"

I stared at him in utter bewilderment. "What are you blathering on about?" I said in irritation. "You think this is some sort of sex exchange? You think I wanted to go down on you, so that you'd go down on me?"

"It would only be fair," he repeated.

"Fair! What's *fair* to do with it? Has it ever occurred to you that I might *want* to go down on you? That I might have been thinking about it for days, and brought myself off thinking about it, and that seeing you and tasting you and hearing you would be no fucking sacrifice to me?"

I may have been a tad forceful, but frankly, I'd had it with the stupidity of my fellow humans by that point.

"I'm gay, remember?" I said irritably as his eyes widened at my speech and he turned a different shade of crimson. "I like cock! And I like you! See the connection yet?"

"Christ," he muttered.

"Look," I said, trying to rein in my temper, "if there's one thing that sure as hell is a turn-off for me, it's reluctance on your part. If you're not interested in being in a sexual relationship with a gay man, Alex, all you've got to do is say so. I won't force myself on you—I don't even blame you. You were mistaken in your preferences, you wanted to see how you liked it and you didn't, and that's okay. But let us get one thing quite clear between us: I *like* cock, I like sex, I want to have sex with my boyfriend, and I want my boyfriend to want to have sex with me. Savvy?"

"Er, yeah," he said, blinking. "I—I'm sorry, Leo."

"Don't be," I said, even as my heart was sinking. Still, I was determined not to show him that this was crushing me. I lifted my chin and was about to remind him that we'd agreed to remain friends when this didn't work out, but I didn't manage to say anything.

Because he came to me and pulled me into his arms and said, "Man, I'm as thick as a brick, huh?" into my cheek between kisses, and with a laugh in his voice.

"Oh?" I was a little shocked. "What—what are you doing?"

"Did you really bring yourself off thinking about *me*?" he asked, pressing me closer to him—and thus pressing against me the evidence that he was not unaffected by me either.

"Yes," I said unsteadily.

"Oh, Leo," he said, kissing my neck.

We sort of half walked, half he-carried-me to the bedroom, and then he asked if I wanted to get naked.

I was like Speedy Gonzales or the Tasmanian Devil, so I was entirely naked in the blink of his eye.

He laughed and said, "Whoa, that was quick," while he was still taking off his socks.

His clothes came off slowly, but frankly, with a body like his, I was happy for him to take his time. *Bloody hell.* When he pulled his T-shirt off over his head, I thought I was going to swoon. I mean, I had felt it before, and I've seen it once or twice, but the context made a difference. Now he was naked *for me*.

His entire body was beautiful. I lay back in bed, watching him, and he laughed self-consciously and then crawled over to me until he was above me. He kissed me and I pulled him down on top of me. Between kisses I asked him what he wanted to do.

"I don't know," he said. "It's nice to kiss and touch you."

"Okay. Say stop when you're uncomfortable."

He nodded agreement.

I didn't have a plan, precisely, but I thought that blow jobs and anything anal would probably be too much for him. I think this heteronormative perspective he had on things was doing great damage to what we could do for each other, but it wouldn't do to dismantle all his cherished beliefs at once. So I let our bodies rub together, listened to his breathing quicken in response to the friction, and when he looked at me helplessly, I took us both in hand. His eyes looked dazed with lust, and his lips were swollen from my assault on them. I waited for a reaction, but other than his hard breathing and responsive hip action, there was nothing. No "Stop" or anything like that.

I hooked my leg over his hip to get a better grip, and he grabbed my butt to help me get closer still. And then I lost my mind, and with my mouth open upon his and both of us helplessly looking for a rhythm that would not be found, I came all over him.

In reaction, staring at my come in amazement, he let out a helpless sound and came too, as though in retaliation, all over me.

I cleaned us up while he lay on his back, breathing hard, his hand over his eyes. I began to worry when he continued to do so after I'd binned the tissues and returned to bed. Cautiously I lay beside him and put my hand on his belly. "You all right?"

He lifted his hand then, and his eyes found mine. And then he grinned and said, "That was really good, wasn't it? Was it for you?"

"Yeah, it was great," I said with a laugh. "You were okay with it?"

"Oh man, yeah! We can do that again, right?"

"Er—" I blushed. "—if you give me a minute."

"Not now, of course. Come here."

He pulled me to him, and I lay on top of him and looked down, like a cat perched on its owner's stomach. Words started tumbling out of his mouth in some weird excitement.

"I thought… I thought that it'd be all about anal or something… I didn't know! I didn't know we could have sex without—Oh God, that's a relief! You're so clever! I would have never thought—is that how gay men have sex? I never knew!"

"Er, well, it's the way you and I had sex, which is all that matters, isn't it?"

"Yes, of course," he said. "You're so right. I'm so relieved, I can't tell you! I so wanted to go to bed with you, honest I did, but when I tried to watch some…. I don't think I found the right website because what they did was bloody frightening, and I never knew—oh God!"

"Okay, calm down," I said. "You do understand that a gay relationship is not a prison movie, right?"

He laughed. "Yes, I know."

"And anal sex can be good," I said.

"Oh, you've—you've done it?"

"Yeah, both ways."

He seemed uncomfortable, and I rolled my eyes. "You won't have to do it if you don't want to. It's not like a gay driving test, where you've to show you know all the manoeuvres."

He laughed. "You must think I'm absurd."

"No. But I think you've some weird ideas in your head."

"I've done it once," he said, wrinkling his nose. "It wasn't good."

"Oh?"

"With a girlfriend," he said. "She was uncomfortable, and then we cut it short, and I felt like an ogre."

"You weren't doing it right, then. I could show you how to do it so that it's good. Hell, I could make you come just by fucking your bum."

"You're a poet," he said dryly.

"Thank you."

"And no, I don't think you could," he said a little warily.

"You don't trust me?"

"It's not that." He blinked in surprise that I should take it that way. "It's just that I don't think I'm like that."

"How do you know? You've never tried it."

"I don't have to try everything to know I wouldn't like some things," he said. "Besides, I thought that gay men divided into tops and bottoms? I'm sure someone told me that once."

"Some do, probably," I said, shrugging. "I don't see a reason to confine myself. But if you won't let me take you from behind, you could at least take me."

"I'd be too worried I'm hurting you."

"You won't. I told you, I know how to do it so it's good. All kinds of good, as a matter of fact."

I was getting sleepy, and I leaned my head on his shoulder, feeling his arm along my back, and I let my fingers go through the tufts of dark hair he had on his chest and the trail that led downwards.

Sleepily, I added, "It feels amazing, actually. Once you're ready for it, it's the most intense thing you can share with someone. To feel you inside me, to hear how you can barely contain yourself, to feel as you angle yourself just right, every nerve ending in my body tingling to attention, me hard just from the penetration alone, waiting for your hand, receiving you...."

I heard him gasp a breath. My hand trailed down to his hips. I took hold of his cock, and it was no longer flaccid.

I kissed his nipple and then murmured against his chest, "And then to feel that moment when you can't stop yourself anymore, and you go deep and hard against me, and I meet you halfway because I want you"—by this time I was already kissing his cock, feeling it react to my lips, stiffen in my hand—"more and harder and deeper"—and I took him into my mouth and sucked until he became rigid. He sighed and reached for my head. He tasted of come, but every ridge, every vein, the texture of his skin, the smell of him was so wonderful to me that when he came with a hoarse cry and a surprisingly hard stream in my mouth, I only had time to wipe my lips briefly before leaning over him and coming on his belly with a few tugs.

When I came back to my senses, it was late, and I remembered that I hadn't yet picked up Squire from my neighbour. Alex was deeply asleep, sprawled over my rumpled sheets.

I went out quietly, collecting random clothes in the darkness and putting them on haphazardly, only to realise that the reason they were all so baggy was because they were Alex's. I knocked on Daria's door, hoping she was still up. She opened the door swiftly enough, so I hadn't woken her up or anything. Squire ran out to greet me, breathing hard, whining and licking my face.

"All right, fluffy," I said to him, and then to Daria, "Thank you. I'm so sorry I—Something came up."

"I bet," she said with a laugh in her eyes. "When I heard you declare proudly to the entire building that you liked cock, I guessed you wouldn't be remembering me soon."

"Oh God." The heat rose in my face.

"Never mind," she said with a laugh. "It's not like it was a secret."

I had to take Squire around the block before I could take him home. Now Squire's curled up on his doggy bed, Alex is fast asleep, and I should be joining him, but I feel strangely awake and alert. I might make myself something to eat.

Saturday, 15 May

WE WENT into town today, and Alex decided to take me along to a meeting with his friend, Michael.

Alex isn't exactly out to his friends and family, so I wasn't sure it was such a good idea to spring it on them by making them face "the boyfriend" all at once, but Alex had no such apprehensions, apparently sure that this was not an essentially homophobic world in which not everyone would be A-okay with him having decided to bed a man. So I was nervous.

They arranged to meet in a coffee shop, and I have to say that I wasn't any less alarmed when I saw Michael. He was built like the Hulk. He was sort of a young Bruce Willis/Jason Statham lookalike, with hair sheared closely to his skull so he looked entirely bald, and a black T-shirt stretching over his enormous muscles.

"Ah, this is Leo," Alex said after the two patted each other's shoulders and commented on their fitness regimes.

"Leo, how are you?" said Michael, pleasantly enough.

We were mid-handshake when Alex added, "He's my boyfriend," and Michael's huge hand squeezed so hard I was sure he was going to break mine.

"How's that?" he asked, when he at last let go of me.

"My boyfriend," Alex repeated with a grin.

He had been grinning all day, because I'd joined him in the shower this morning to show him yet another way two men can have sex. He seems perpetually startled by my inventiveness.

Anyway, I had the distinct feeling that Michael wasn't pleased with the news. He frowned and said, "Well, this is... unexpected. I didn't know you had, er, a boyfriend. How did this happen?"

He sounded like it was an atrocious accident, as though he wanted to add, "Is there anything that can be done?"

Alex can't have picked up on that because his grin widened. "Oh well, I moved in opposite Leo. You know, when I told you I was coming to London? And we became friends, and I helped him work out, and then—well, then we started dating!"

"Work out?" asked Michael, staring at me in absolute astonishment. I hardly knew where to look.

"Yes," said Alex. "We work out together."

The truth is that apart from sweating between the sheets together, there really isn't much "working out" going on anymore. I have attained my goal, which was Alex, and thus lost interest in fitness. The final clincher had been when Alex said he thought it was sexy that I was so "boyish and slender." He also expressed an admiration for my freckles, my smile, and the way my cock felt in his hand. It was a good couple of days, is what I'm saying, and I saw no reason to spoil them by jogging.

Michael looked appalled and changed the subject. He asked how Alex's work was going. Alex talked of his clients, his heart rate, and some gizmos he used. It turns out, Michael is a policeman, but evidently also a gym obsessive. When he asked me what I did and I told him, he let out a *pfft* sound, as though I'd suggested that I collected benefits for a living. Alex did not seem to notice, and more infuriatingly still, decided to rise and collect our drinks from the counter, which meant that I was left alone with Michael, who eyed me with suspicion and displeasure.

At first I thought the obvious: he was a homophobe, or perhaps one of those men who was okay with other people being gay, so long as it was nobody in his family or circle of friends. But then I watched him some more as he talked to Alex—how his pupils widened as he looked at him, how he reddened a little at Alex's suggestion that he'd put on muscle recently. That son of a bitch was in love with Alex! I spent the rest of the meeting glaring at him, and when we left at last, I informed Alex of my findings.

He laughed and said, "You think *everybody* fancies me!"

That was true enough: they *did* all fancy him. I'm not making that up. Honest, I'm not. For example, even at the height of my infatuation with Jack, I could tell he rubbed some people the wrong way. Granted, I thought that was because they were jealous, but still.

Alex never rubbed anybody the wrong way. He was impossible not to like. And as he is handsome, and has considerable charm and a winsome smile, we always get really good service from gay and female waiters, and the cashiers at supermarkets always giggle and redden when he wishes them a good day—man or woman. So his dismissal of my Sherlock-like abilities to tell that his so-called friend had the hots for him irritated me.

"I'm telling you, the man wants you," I said.

"Nonsense, he's not gay."

"Er, he's certainly pretty damn gay for you, my friend."

"You think everybody is gay unless proven innocent."

I was about to say something more, but he actually stopped dead in the middle of the street, mouth agape, eyes wide. "Oh! Oh, Leo! Oh, Leo, look!" He shook my arm. "There! Oh, Leo, look there! *The Room!*"

"What?"

"*The Room!* Look!"

So I looked where he was pointing. On one of the buildings a poster was plastered, rather high and somewhat oddly. It consisted of little more than the scowling face of a man with long dark hair hanging down the sides of his face. Underneath it read *The Room*. I didn't get it.

"Oh, Leo, we must see it!"

"What is it? I never heard of it."

"It's a cult classic. It's quite possibly the worst movie ever made. It's also one of the most brilliant! *Lisa, you're tearing me apart!*" This last he cried in a funny accent while holding me by my shoulders, and I guessed he was quoting the movie at me. Naturally we had to find out, through our phones, where and when the screening of this movie was held. Then we grabbed some food before heading out to make it to the showing. It was in a small indie theatre, and consequently, Alex and I were the only non-hipsters there. It was wonderfully ironic to be the only non-hipsters at a hipster convention.

Alex was so excited he could barely keep calm. He explained that he'd seen the movie once and that it must be viewed with a large audience, because otherwise it was basically creepy in an uncomfortable way.

I could see what he meant—the movie really was that. It was set in San Francisco and was clearly the product of the lurid imaginings of a subintelligent, melodramatic, derivative, intellectual dwarf. But the audience *loved* it. They cried out at the most ridiculous lines, quoting them aloud and for some reason throwing plastic spoons at the screen, altogether enjoying the thing as though it were a rock concert.

Alex was in heaven.

I can't say I enjoyed the movie, but I did enjoy seeing Alex glow with happiness afterwards and laugh heartily at my observations when we went out for a drink with the group of hipsters who'd sat next to him, whom he inevitably befriended.

Tuesday, 18 May

RECEIVED AN interesting email from a friend in Sydney. He is starting a special research project, for which he had just received the funding, and is gathering a team to work on the Eastern Bloc and secret police foreign operations. It sounds awfully exciting, but I don't think I'd be able to convince Alex to move to Australia with me for what looks like a two-year project. I can't imagine leaving him behind, though.

It was kind of strange to see the email and know I wouldn't go, even as I thought about KGB action in Afghanistan, at the back of my mind. But no, it's impossible.

Wednesday, 26 May

I RECEIVED an angry text message from Lucy demanding to know by what right I'd gone missing over the past month or so.

So I went out with her and Amelia for drinks after work. I hadn't really noticed that I spent less time with them, but when I saw them again, Lucy had a new piercing in her nose and Amelia had dyed her hair and the roots were already showing. Perhaps I had been gone a while.

"You don't see *me* disappear from the face of the earth with every new boy toy, do you?" Lucy said, irritably.

"Okay, I'm sorry," I said. "And Alex is not a 'boy toy.' He's my boyfriend—that's different."

"Cut him some slack," Amelia said to Lucy. "It's like that when you're first in love. All your friends disappear, family stops mattering… give them a couple of months to shag it out of their system."

I sputtered at "in love," but neither paid any attention to me. Lucy only grumbled that she didn't see any reason to keep everybody completely out of the loop, and then she demanded to know how big Alex was and whether he was a good lay, which made Amelia groan.

"*Obviously* he must be a good lay," she said, rolling her eyes, "or else Leo wouldn't be spending all his free time in bed with him."

Then all of the sudden, I remembered her own dry spell, and very beautifully segued into that, asking how she was getting along with Mark.

Indeed, things hadn't got better: he was busier at work than usual; business in her online shop was slow; and she was frustrated in her search for solutions. One of her sons was struggling with maths; the other struggled with bullies. She could not get the house clean, whatever her efforts, and now all three of her men demanded that they buy a puppy, which would only add stress and mess into an already overwrought situation. She unburdened herself to us liberally, and we plied her with wine and sighs of "Oh, dear" and "How about a cat? I hear they're quite independent?"

I shared my anecdote about the cat my sister had trained to assassinate me, which brought general amusement.

Here's the thing, though: as much as I loved seeing them again, I was impatient to get home. That *never* normally happens to me. The only thing that stopped me from wandering the streets of London night after night used to be Squire. Now, the only reason I didn't cut short the evening with my friends was because they were already pissed off at me for being so out of touch with them.

I was glad when the evening ended, and I could hurry home. It was a relief to let Alex in and then curl up on my sofa next to him. Going to bed with him has now hit that sweet spot where sinking into his arms is both familiar and exciting at the same time.

Shit, I think I do love him.

Thursday, 3 June

HAD TO supervise an exam today. There's nothing more boring than that. People don't generally cheat, but you have to be on the lookout. Mind you, it's pretty tough, considering the size of our sports hall. It's hard to see what people are doing. I think the exam was chemical engineering.

I had lunch with Adam and Sarah. Adam's Ancient Greece, and he came back a couple of weeks ago from his sabbatical. They've invited me to go to this conference in August, in the States. It's a big Ancient Civilisations thing, but that's not my terrain. Also, I was planning on doing nothing this summer.

That never works out—usually I catch up on the article I'm writing, start research on another one, that sort of thing.

But… this time I have a boyfriend! This time I might actually go somewhere!

I should ask Alex about that. He's out with Michael and some of his other friends tonight. He wanted me to go with them, but I've piles of work to do, and I've had a trying day.

"Not going to Sydney, eh?" Jack said when he found me standing by the kettle in the rec room. "I should have thought that was your very thing. Didn't you come up with the idea for that project? Isn't the end goal a series of popular historical books? Have you suddenly become allergic to success?"

"Shut up," I grumbled.

"Or is it your working-class boyfriend that's keeping you back?" he mused. "That's it, isn't it? Gary…."

"Alex!"

"Right, *Alex* wants to throw weights around in London, and so you have to stay in London too," he said with a sad sigh. "My dear, if you take my advice—"

"Oh yes, please," I bit out. "Go ahead and teach me how to lead a happy life. Let's see… if I want to date a man, shouldn't I first get engaged to a woman? Yes, right, there we go. I'll ask Sarah. She'd do, wouldn't she?"

Sarah was just walking past, and she startled at hearing her name. "What's that, pet?"

"I'm proposing to you," I told her. "I think you and I should get married."

"I'm already married," she told me patiently.

"Perfect! I think that makes it all the better, doesn't it, Jack? I'm not sure, but you're the expert in fucked-up relationships. Go on, enlighten us!"

He sighed condescendingly. "As someone who is older and more experienced, take it from me. Adonis comes and goes, but these kinds of career opportunities don't come around very often. This one's golden. I'd go. I think you should go. Gary can come with you, or perhaps you can try it long distance. Whatever it takes, Leo."

Then he gave me his most charming smile and left, as always with the last word, as always utterly unsinkable. *Bastard.*

Sarah watched him go and then tilted her head at me. "That Australia thing?"

"Yes," I grumbled. "I'm not going. I don't know how the hell he found out."

"Oh, you *should* go, pet! It sounds like a wonderful opportunity, and that sort of thing will put you in good stead when you apply for a professorship or anything of that kind later on, you know."

"Yes, thanks." I wish they wouldn't keep telling me this. I know it's a good opportunity. I feel bad about not going, but for heaven's sake, I can't just drop my life and move to the other end of the world. For one thing, I'm in love with Alex and I want to stay with him. And honestly, when he and I are together, I feel no regret at all.

He's fantastic. He's amazing and beautiful and everything I could wish for. Why is that less important than possibly speeding up my career a little? Maybe in a few years, when Alex and I are more settled, something like this will come up again, and then we can both move to Australia or Iceland or wherever-the-fuck. So there.

Jack can go climb the ladder all on his own, if it makes him that happy. Here's what makes me happy: discovering that Alex really likes it when I nibble the back of his neck.

Monday, 7 June

LENA CALLED today. She's expecting the baby by the end of the month and said that Mum and Dad were coming to see her, and she wondered if I'd come too to greet the baby. I said of course I would, and I started looking for flights as soon as we hung up.

It's still kind of hard to believe I'll be an uncle. I actually feel a little excited. I wonder if I'll ever have children.… I resigned myself to the unlikelihood of that scenario, and for the most part I was too young and single to think much about it, but Alex would make a great dad. He's tons of fun and has masses of energy.

I never asked him—probably should at some point. I haven't told him I love him yet, so it might seem premature to him if I start suggesting adoption agencies. Or maybe we'd use a surrogate?

It'd be funny to see Lucy pregnant, come to think of it.

Tuesday, 8 June

AMELIA RANG me today, sounding super-excited. "Oh, Leo! Leo! Leo! Leo!"

"What's up?"

"Guess where I am!"

"Crikey, must I? The moon! Reykjavik! Your mother's attic!"

"Oh shut up," she laughed. "I'm at Heathrow."

"What are you like?" I said sarcastically.

"Guess where I'm going."

"Amelia, dear, I've not the slightest clue. Where are you going?"

"Tokyo!"

"What?"

"That's right! Read it and weep! I'm going to Tokyo."

"What, why?"

"Because my darling husband has surprised me with a romantic trip! Ha!"

"You're joking!"

"No, I'm not," she said. "Isn't he a dear? Must go, the gate's just opened. I'll see you next month. Kisses to you and your bed bunny, *mwa, mwa!*"

When I hung up, it struck me that it's almost summer now and New York would be a perfect getaway for Alex and me. I mean, it's not the best place to be in hot weather, but there are great clubs, shows, and museums, and importantly, it's far away from London. I started warming up to the idea.

Alex was a bit funny about it, though, when I made the suggestion.

"Nah, that's all right," he said. "You should be with your family."

"We could take advantage of this whole baby business and use it as an opportunity to get away for a bit, you know."

"I'm sure you'll be too busy taking care of your sister."

Then he had to leave for an appointment. I tried again this evening. Told him of hotel rooms and walks in Central Park, and all the amazing things to do and see.

Finally he said, "All right, fine."

However, as soon as I told him the cost of a plane ticket, the mood changed. Suddenly he was all quiet and uncomfortable, and at last said, "That's a little steep, mate. I can't pay that."

"I'll pay for you, that's not a problem."

It was the wrong thing to say. He threw me this hurt look and said, "Nah, that's all right, thanks."

Thursday, 10 June

HEATWAVE.

I've been feeding Squire ice cubes all day. How can someone who wears such a huge amount of fur stand it? I've been sitting in front of the open window in my boxers all day, working, though when my laptop began to burn my legs, I put it away and focused on the book I'm reading.

Alex came in from his jog and asked if he could use my shower. He had a meeting with a potential client to get to. If the client saw Alex come straight from a jog, Alex would get the job at once—what with sweat beading on his muscled arms, his hair glistening, and his legs....

I need to get something to drink.

Friday, 11 June

ALEX WON'T be going to New York with me. Michael—with no ulterior motive at all!—has (miraculously) come up with some boot camp for rock climbers (aka sex retreat for repressed gay men) that just happens to coincide (was specifically designed to clash) with my having to go and see Lena.

When I raised my eyebrows at this, Alex said, "It's not like that! It's this really tough camp led by this ex-SAS captain. He teaches you…"

As can be imagined, I was not particularly interested in what an ex-SAS captain might teach you.

Seeing that, Alex said coaxingly, "Well, you know, it's better that I go while you're not here; otherwise, I might feel like taking you with me."

He had me there. Everything he said about this alleged boot camp sounded like the perfect scenario for a nightmare. I think the fact that Michael received this buy-one-get-one-free offer on this thing had played a role in Alex's decision, though Michael's inability to explain how he came by that offer makes me suspicious.

In the end Alex reconciled me to his decision pretty quickly by kissing me, asking me not to be a grouch, and then, to my surprise, popping my trousers open and making his first attempt at a blow job. For his first-ever effort, it was amazing. Actually, the fact that he did it on his own accord and so suddenly was amazing. It was kind of funny, because up to a certain point, he was quite confident, kissing me and petting me until I was hard and ready, and then he just sort of stared at my cock as though wondering which way to tackle it, and I couldn't bear it anymore and began to laugh.

"What are you doing?" I asked.

He looked up at me, distracted, and laughed self-consciously. "Okay, you have to be patient with me. I looked it up, and I know what to do in theory, but—"

"Oh my God."

"Oi!" he said, punching my thigh. "Shut up, Taylor, or I'll lose my cool."

"Oh, all right," I said, biting my lip. "Don't let me stop you. Hey, there's some bananas in my fruit bowl if you want to practice."

"Shut up." He put his hand over my laughing mouth.

"Here's what you do," I said through his fingers. "You go down there, look my dick in the eye, tip your hat to him, and say 'how do you do, sir.' Remember, he's more scared of you than you are of him."

"God, you're a wanker. I don't know why I put up with you."

And then, before I could say anything else, he just dived right in there. As ways to shut me up go, that's a pretty effective one. It was, in fact, so good that I could barely focus enough to sigh instructions. "Breathe through your nose" and "Hide your teeth."

It was as though he was on a mission. At first he didn't take me in very deeply, and his movements were sort of tentative, as if he was afraid to hurt me. But then he eased into it, wrapping his hand around my base. And the feel of his lips and tongue—God, I don't know why people do anything else with their lives. I guided him with my hand, and eventually we got a good rhythm going. The feel of him, the warmth of his mouth and tongue, and the sight of half my length disappearing in his mouth, tipped me over the edge.

He made a funny face when he swallowed, and I don't know whether it was that, or the blow job, or what, but even as I breathed heavily from having just had an orgasm, I blurted out, "I love you."

He laughed. "That's cute. You're so easy, Leo."

Friday, 18 June

GOT A text from Yi Chen today. Lena gave birth to a baby boy; they named him Francis. He kept the texts coming for most of the day, but they got scarcer as the day went on, presumably because he was busy taking care of Lena and the baby.

I was emotional all day. Lena had gone into labour yesterday evening, and Yi's texts had begun then. So all night I had a hard time sleeping, thinking of all the things that could go wrong, googling pregnancy and birthing complications. To assuage my worries about Lena, I reminded myself that she was a tough old bird, was healthy, and presumably in the care of competent doctors.

Until you have an actual loved one pregnant and about to pop out a human being, the amazing, unbelievable, near-impossible nature of the feat doesn't really occur to you. But it's dangerous! I read some scary stuff last night that made me glad I'll never marry a woman and have to see her go through that. I can easily sympathise with Yi's emotions now. When the thing was done and both came out of it safe and sound,

I felt a huge relief. I had a call from Mum, all in tears; I could barely make her out.

Alex was out last night with his mates, but when I texted him about the baby, he came back and was very excited to see the pics today. I think he likes kids. I didn't ask him if he wanted any, just because he was out most of the day and there wasn't time.

Anyway, I've got to prepare for my flight to New York.

Tuesday, 22 June. New York City

JUST REACHED my hotel. Had the longest day imaginable and am collapsing with tiredness. Am in the centre of Manhattan—Korea Town, to be precise—and God, it's loud here!

But to the beginning, since a lot has happened.

So last night I had to go to bed early, since I had an early flight this morning. Alex and I had dinner, and then we debated the wisdom of his sleeping over at my flat.

"You've an early flight," he said, giving me that knowing look.

"What's that supposed to mean?"

"Just that we never go to sleep early when I stay over," he said.

"Well, excuse me!" I felt a little offended. "I'm well able to keep it in my trousers. You're not as irresistible as you think you are."

"Okay," he said, leaning back in his seat and folding his hands on his stomach. "Let's see. Last Friday you said you wanted to hit the sheets early because of all the work you had to do the next day. I only came over because Lena had her baby and I wanted to be supportive. Yes?"

"Yes," I said a little shamefaced.

"What did we do that night?"

"Celebrate life, you bastard."

"Right. Celebrate life. And what did we do on Saturday night, even though I told you I had an early appointment on Sunday? Celebrate physical exercise? And tonight we're going to celebrate the miracle of flight, probably," he said.

Naturally, I took great offence at that and proceeded to seduce him with the firm intention of telling him, in a pure and self-sacrificial manner that was meant to show him how much self-control I had, that I needed to sleep. It ended as well as could be expected. Specifically, it ended with him laughing at me about how good I looked with his come on my chest. We did tire ourselves out eventually and fell asleep in a messy, naked tangle.

Unfortunately, in the mornings he is a) extremely attractive, with his hair ruffled, his cheeks unshaven, his body lazy with sleep, and b) horny.

Which is not a good combination when you're the guy who a) fancies him and b) should really be showering and then getting his arse to Heathrow.

Anyway, I really shouldn't be blamed for what happened.

We sort of melded from sleep into an embrace, and then we were rutting under the sheets like two adolescents, and frankly, such things as Heathrow Airport don't exist when you're in your lover's arms chasing and escaping from an orgasm.

Some physicist should get onto that. "Schrödinger's Airport," it would be called. I can't be blamed, therefore, for forgetting myself. Especially when he looked down, looming over me with his wide shoulders, and said in a hoarse whisper that he'd like to fuck me. I can't say how much I wanted to throw my phone out of the window when it began to ring just then with the alarm I'd set for myself, which I entitled "Get up you lazy slut or you'll miss your flight."

So yeah, there wasn't time. We had to scramble out of bed, I had to shower really quickly, and he was already dressed and dealing with Squire while I grabbed my bag and headed down to his car.

Then his car wouldn't start. Since having one's sexy time interrupted is never conducive to a good mood, we were both irate. I kept looking at my watch, predicting huge queues on the M25, and imagining what my parents would say when they found out I'd missed my flight. I could hear my mum in my head saying, "Tsk, typical. Lena just made a human being, and Leo can't even make it to the airport on time."

Then Alex said, "This is not going to work. Hang in there, Leo. I'm calling for help."

So he got out of the car, while I googled taxi tariffs to the airport.

Then Alex came back. "All right, Michael's going to be here in five minutes or thereabouts."

"What!"

So by "help," my boyfriend meant the chap who has the hots for him and is going to spend time sweating over some rocks in Wales with him while I was on another continent. Grand. However, it would not be wise to start an argument with Alex about this, because, let's face it, with everything going against me, I didn't want "he's a prissy bitch" added to his list of reasons to leave me.

So I determined to be gracious.

Michael arrived in his SUV—so practical for the narrow streets of London!—and took the bags from me in that manner that said he didn't think I was strong enough to haul them myself.

Even so, I thanked him for coming to my rescue.

"Anything to get you out of the country," he "joked."

Then he insisted that Alex sit up front with him. So I sat at the back, treated to Alex's occasional looks over his shoulder as he tried to include me in their discourse on climbing gear.

"So, you managed to find a helmet at last?" he asked Michael.

"They *make* helmets that small?" I grumbled to myself.

It didn't matter, since they didn't hear me. They chatted away happily, and whenever Alex made an attempt to speak to me, Michael would find a way to wean the conversation back to himself. He had the advantage over me, since in his humongous car the back seat was far away from the front ones. And just to make hearing me harder, he put on music. He listened to American R 'n' B and hip-hop, which I don't like. At all.

When we got to Heathrow, I was thoroughly pissed off. Naturally, Michael stopped at the drop-off point, which meant that Alex couldn't walk me to my gate and bid me goodbye in the traditional way, because you had to vacate the drop-off point after five minutes. So I got out, ready to just wave at him through the window, grumbling to myself, when I noticed that Alex had got out of the car and put his hand on my arm as I was about to leave.

"Hey," he said.

"I'll be late," I said. "Thank your *friend* for the ride." By this time I couldn't keep the bitterness out of my voice.

"Sure," he said. "Come here."

He pulled me into a hug. That felt nice, though I was too het up to really appreciate it. Still, he hugged me close, and then I could feel him kiss my neck, and he spoke quietly into my ear. "I'll miss you. This kind of sucks, huh?"

"Yeah."

"I love you," he said, before kissing my neck again.

That changed everything. Now I didn't give a toss about Michael sitting in his car about to take my boyfriend away. *Alex loved me.* What were a couple of days apart if you loved someone? They're nothing! I suddenly felt a complete fool about minding so much that we didn't manage to finish this morning. We'll do it when I get back. We have a lifetime of shagging ahead of us. What the hell was I even worried about?

In fact, it was sort of funny. When he emerged from the hug, looking down at me, he smiled. "If you go in there that pink in the face, Leo, they'll think you're a terrorist."

"Fuck off" was all I managed to say.

Michael called out of the window, "I can't stay here all day, you know!"

Alex gave me another hug. "Call me when you land," he said. "And call me from your hotel, all right?"

"There's a time difference. I'll be some five hours behind you."

"Doesn't matter. Call whenever. Middle of the night, I don't care. Just call me. Say hi to your sister and take lots of cute pictures with the baby."

"All right, cheeseball," I said. "Try not to kill yourself climbing with your billy goat."

It was hard to leave him, but I did it, and I made my flight.

WHEN I got to Lena's flat, after a suicide drive in a New York cab—I was sure it would end in a horrible, spectacular, daredevil death—I was exhausted, cramped, and my skin was itchy. I hate the air in planes, too dry! But all of it melted away from me when I got inside and saw Yi Chen with the baby in his arms.

I don't remember what followed, precisely, because I kind of went to pieces. I didn't cry or anything like that, but I'm sure I told the baby that he was in my will, that should something happen to Lena or Yi, I'm adopting him, and that I wasn't in the least hopeful that should happen, wink-wink.

My mum was lecturing Lena about the best schools in New York and insisted that English schools could not be beaten for quality. Lena looked tired but happy. She kept calling me Uncle Leo as she cooed to the child, which was sweet.

I did give Alex a ring when I landed, but the connection wasn't good and so I promised to call back from the hotel. I managed to connect with him through Skype once I got to my hotel room this evening, but I was and am knackered, so we didn't talk long. Alex looked adorable with Squire on his lap, trying to make him wave his paw at me through the camera.

Friday, 25 June. New York City

MY MOTHER has bought all the toys and baby clothes in New York. I kid you not. My sister's flat is literally flooded with boxes and wrapping paper. My father says he can't bring himself to look at his account anymore.

Francis is adorable, but boy does that baby have some lungs on him. We discovered that he likes it when I hold him close to my chest and walk around with him, so whenever I arrive at Lena's, someone instantly passes the baby to me to calm him down.

"I hope you're comfortable," Lena growled at me, "because you're not leaving until that boy is twenty-one and I can have a sensible discussion with him about noise levels."

Yi's parents arrived from Taiwan yesterday. I think the baby is reacting to the rising stress levels in the flat. It's quite loud there, actually, and a little messy, since they too brought gifts, not to mention packages full of food and clothing for Lena and Yi, as though they're refugees and not extremely affluent New Yorkers.

It's amusing to watch Yi keep it together under the pressure of in-laws, parents, and an irate wife, all trying not to break one another's necks as they argue how best to take care of Francis, who, frankly, hasn't done much yet in his career as a human being. He just poos and sleeps, occasionally wailing for some titty. Typical bloke, if you ask me. Anyway, to ease the pressure, I took my parents out for a walk. That way Lena and Yi Chen only had his parents to worry about.

My mum was only interested in toyshops; my dad was googling entry requirements to Ivy League universities and wasn't watching where he was going. On more than one occasion, I rescued him from being hit by one of New York's ubiquitous death cabs. I patiently led them from shop to shop, and then took them out to lunch.

Finally my mum could not stay away from the child any longer and had to go back.

I helped Lena as best I could, trying to prevent the parents from doing her head in, but it was a tough job. When women used to have children earlier in life, the interference of parents was easier to bear. But Lena is a grown, very organised, educated woman, so she has a hard time being constantly told, "not like that, honey, you're doing it wrong," and "what are you doing? Give him to me!"

Add to that each parent's differing opinion on the subject of Lena's post-pregnancy weight, the merits of the education systems of various countries, and the developmental advantages they'd already spotted in Francis despite the complete lack of empirical evidence. Currently the baby's only talents appear to be startling at the sound of his own farts and blowing spit bubbles.

Anyway, when I thought Lena was at her breaking point and Yi's hair began to turn grey in front of my eyes, I announced that I'd made a booking at a restaurant and was taking everybody over fifty out.

With Lena and Yi's help, I got everybody out of their flat.

Then I took them on a long walking tour of the city—had to tire the buggers out, after all—while surreptitiously calling this friend of mine from my clubbing days, who was kind enough to book a table in a place he recommended, where he knew the co-owner.

So that was a fluke. Naturally, as soon as we sat down to eat, all this parenting energy had nothing to focus on but—you guessed it—moi!

It was grand. First, Yi's father discovered I was gay.

My dad then sought for excuses; I'd always been a delicate, sickly boy, he explained. "No interest in sports, no interest in anything but books," he said mournfully.

"Very bad," Yi Chen's father said, shaking his head with closed eyes. "Boys need a lot of sport, a lot of running around. Ball games, boxing, running, swimming."

"Builds strength," my father agreed.

"Yes," Mr Chen said. "Character and muscle is what makes a man."

"Thank you," I said. "I'm still a man."

"Oh, nobody says you're not, dear," my mother said and then turned to Yi Chen's parents. "He was always pretty too, which you know doesn't help."

"Yes, a man should not be pretty," Mrs Chen said. "Look at Yi!" Here she laughed. "Never been pretty. Spots everywhere when he was growing up. More spots than skin! Sometimes I looked at him and said, 'Where are your eyes? I see nothing but spots!'"

This made them all laugh. Parents are evil! Yi Chen's father asked me, I think as a joke, "So, men think you're a girl?"

"No," I said. "I'm pretty sure they know I'm a man."

"My brother has a gay son," Mr Chen said to my dad, with sympathy. "Very sad. He is the only child."

"Why is that sad?" I felt immediately indignant on Yi's cousin's behalf.

"No stability," Mr Chen said. "No future! You want to see your son with wife and children, to keep him out of trouble."

"He can have that with a husband instead," I said.

"No, not in Taiwan," Mr Chen said. "Maybe in the future, someday, it will be like that. Then it would be different."

Yi Chen's mum nodded solemnly. "Right now it's not so good. You have to hide, and you're treated like a criminal. What parents want a son treated like a criminal?"

"That is indeed very sad," my dad said. "We are lucky in England, aren't we, Leo? You can have a boyfriend and get married and live together…. I suppose there's still a stigma. People from my generation, at least, have bad associations with the issue. But it's easy enough to overcome when your own son, whom you love and care about, comes out."

He put his hand on mine, and I was so startled that I didn't know what to say. I swear to God he'd never say something like this to another English person, including me. Not because he didn't feel it—I believed every word he said—but because such an earnest speech would sound weird from Englishman to Englishman. But he was speaking to a Taiwanese man, so the subtleties of "we all know what I mean" had to be put aside, and he had to say it as it was, straight.

"Thanks, Dad," I said, for want of anything better to say.

"You have a boyfriend?" Yi Chen's mother asked. "A nice boy to take care of you?"

That was a strange way to put the question, but I said yes, I did have a boyfriend. I showed them a picture of Alex and me on my phone. It was a good picture, which Lucy took when we were in the pub together. We were shoulder to shoulder, smiling, and the light had been flattering. The Chens approved of his strong physique and that he was very manly. My parents were just curious, since they've never met a boyfriend of mine before. My mum looked at him a long time and then said, "He has kind eyes. You must introduce him to us, dear. I would like to meet him."

That was strange, but I said, "Okay."

"So what does he do?" my dad asked.

I immediately deflected that landmine by saying that I needed to go to the loo, and when I came back, the conversation had shifted to how unprofitable a career in academia was, on which subject they were all in agreement. It was a tense evening, but I kept at it, taking them out for drinks afterwards and then returning them to their respective hotels, to make sure Lena and Yi had some time to themselves. I texted Yi when I got back to my room, telling him how things had gone, and he texted back.

Thanks, bro. You're a lifesaver. I thought L. was going to start knocking skulls there for a minute. All's calm on the western front atm, F. is blissfully asleep, L. nodded off and I can catch up on some work.

Had trouble connecting with Alex over the past week and tonight, too, the signal was patchy and we couldn't really talk. But he sends me emails—several a day, actually—detailing how much he's climbed and how his progress is going. I will never know what he finds so gratifying about all that stuff, but his emails are enthusiastic, and he attaches pictures of himself grinning from atop various rocks, looking more like Leonidas every day since he decided to stop shaving for some reason. He's turned brown too. Altogether, he is way too hot to be away from me at the moment.

I really want to be home right now. I've been surrounded by three couples for almost a week, and it's exhausting. His emails help.

Like this one:

I found a movie I really want us to watch. It's called Killer Klowns from Outer Space, *so technically it qualifies as science fiction and so should be right up your alley, right?*

To which I responded:

That's like Hitler saying to the Poles in 1939, "You fancied a bit of foreign culture, didn't you? Here we come!" The title sounds atrocious. If you make me sit through that, I will demand payback.

To which he sent me a load of pictures of himself on top of some rocks, shirtless and grinning at the camera. Which naturally made me wonder who held that camera.

Best not think of that.

I don't resent Alex for not being here, and his being here would obviously pose its own difficulties, but it feels wrong that he isn't. When my mum mentioned she'd like to meet him, I thought it would be nice if she did. My parents and I never discussed my love life—not that it's taboo or anything. My mum sometimes asked me if I was seeing anybody, but I always said no, since there'd never been anybody that serious before. Honestly, I couldn't imagine introducing them to my ex-boyfriend Jamie. But Alex is different. I *love* Alex. And Alex loves me. They should probably meet him.

At the moment, it's hard to think about it. I really miss him. It's pathetic—we've only been apart a couple of days. And we've only been dating… what, two months? I don't know what it is, but he drives me crazy. Maybe it's that easy, open affection. Yesterday, among his three emails, one read only *Missing your freckles.*

Monday, 28 June

I'M BACK in the UK, back in my flat, Squire's back with me, and Alex is still away. It's nice to be back home, especially nice to be away from

108

the baby drama in NY, but it's not the same without Alex here. I find it hard to sleep.

I called Lucy, and we're going out tonight, which should take my mind off things.

Tuesday, 29 June

LUCY AND I took Squire to Hyde Park today. While I was in New York, she'd been in Lisbon for a short business trip. Naturally, this being Lucy, she hooked up with someone, but this time it had been two someones! So she's had a threesome, which I think is gross, but I have to give it to her—the men she chose were not bad-looking.

She laughed at me when I wrinkled my nose at her.

"Well, *excuse me* for living my life," she said. "I remember a time when going out with you meant seeing you peel off with some random bloke halfway through the night."

"That was a long time ago," I said. "I grew up."

"Pfft! Nothing to do with growing up. It's to do with FOMO."

"The what now?"

"Fear of Missing Out," she said. "Mate, I'm a better gay guy than you ever were. You don't know what FOMO is?"

"No. It sounds like an international organisation."

"Not far off," she said with a laugh. "It's that thing were you're afraid that if you don't sleep with that chap who has a cute smile, or the one who just bought you a drink, or the one who's grinding up against you in the club, or the one—"

"Okay, I get it!"

"—It's the fear that if you don't sleep with that man, whoever he is, you'd be missing out. So you sleep with him. And that's why I can't deal with relationships. It's not that I never like a guy enough to want him to stick around… it's that I can never not like other men enough without fear of missing out on something. You know?"

"I suppose I understand you," I said grudgingly.

"Anyway," she said, "so long as nobody is getting hurt, I don't see the problem."

"I'm not judging."

"Puh-lease! Of course you're judging. Everybody judges a woman who happens to really, really like getting around."

"Hey, that's not fair. I don't judge you. I think you're amazing."

"You think some of the things I do are gross."

"Well, yeah, but I don't judge you for doing them."

"Bullshit."

"Well, I'm sorry, Luce, but when you tell me that a bloke wanted to come all over your hair and you let him…."

"Prude," she said, shoving me lovingly onto the grass.

We ended up in a pub for dinner, and she ended up picking up the waiter, though honestly, at this stage I think she only did it to prove a point.

Friday, 2 July

I WAS in my office today, since, although there are no classes to be taught at the moment, it's a good place to get work done. I have several papers on the go and things I need to read.

The department was quite empty. Most of the staff either work from home or are on holiday. Here I am, living it up, academia-style. Truth was, though, that sitting at home was depressing, since Alex was going to be away for another week. Somehow, when he first told me of the rock-climbing gig, it didn't seem like it was going to be this long.

So, after I did some work, I planned on going out—anything to keep out of the house and my thoughts away from my boyfriend. I would pop home, shower, shave, change, take Squire out, and then leave him with Daria while I have dinner with Lucy.

But when I arrived at my place I sensed something was off; something was different. I didn't know what it was until I reached my floor. Honestly, it must be a scent thing, because I was sure Alex was there. I knocked on his door.

I don't know why I was surprised that the door opened. Alex stood there, his eyes as wide as his grin. Then I fell into his arms and one of us kicked the door closed, our lips glued together as we staggered against furniture and walls all the way into his bedroom. He threw me onto his bed, straddled me, and proceeded to rip my clothes off.

We didn't exchange a word.

I didn't know how much time passed as we made love, but at last we ended, moulded together by semen and sweat, breathing hard and holding each other.

Alex had changed. His muscles had seen some extraordinary training, they were hard as rock. His normally olive skin tone was bronzed, a deep hazelnut colour that made his teeth appear blindingly white and his eyes shiny.

We rested agreeably in this manner for some time—his hand stroking my back, me kissing his chest, his neck, his cheek. It was then that I finally asked how come he was home so early.

"I missed you. I hated being away for so long. The Internet connection there was rubbish. I barely saw you."

"It's been less than two weeks, you freak," I said.

"I can go back if you want," he murmured, somewhere around that sensitive spot under my ear.

"You can try. I have enough of your DNA on me to clone you a thousand times. I don't need you anymore."

"You're cheeky for someone whose nickname is Spanky," he said with a wolfish grin.

We wrestled, and then I slipped out and escaped into the shower. He wasn't far behind, and to be fair, we both needed to wash.

I can only take so much of running my hands over his body without getting excited, so naturally it wasn't long before we were in a deep embrace, snogging wildly under the hot stream of water, his hands kneading my buttocks. I was trying to get as close to him as possible.

It was never enough.

"Wait," I said when he started stroking me. "Be right back."

I had to grab a towel and run across the hall, because of course he wasn't properly equipped, but I came back with some silicone-based lube and condoms. I wanted him inside me. He didn't appear in the least dismayed when I returned with these, but anyway, I asked whether he was okay with that.

He nodded. "What do I do?"

I kissed him, even as I spread the lube on my fingers, too revved up to teach him how to prep me. We'd do this properly some other time; right then I just desperately wanted him inside me. I slung one arm around his shoulders so I could kiss him without slipping while I used my fingers on myself. He was alternately stroking me and then himself. I was close to bringing myself off just like that, so I moved my hips away and patted my hand over to where I'd left the condoms. I ripped the little square packet open with my teeth and slid the rubber on him quickly.

I put more lube on him, stroking him at the same time. "Sit down."

I meant the edge of the tub, of course, but he looked at the bottom of the tub with alarm. I moved him by his shoulders and placed him where I wanted him.

"What do I do?"

"I'll do it, you just hold on to the edge and lean back a little."

He was good at listening to instructions. I turned around and lowered myself onto him, guiding him into me slowly.

Not going to lie, it's been a while, so I was a little stunned by the stretch for a moment and had to pause twice. But with plenty more lube, I got him in there—all of him—and bloody hell, it was good. I could feel him everywhere, from the tips of my toes all the way up to my heart.

I began to move, and with each pump of my hips, he let out a startled moan. Then I moved faster, lifting my hips higher. His hand shot out and grabbed me. He pressed his cheek against my back, his hot breath against my skin.

"Oh God, Leo," he moaned, "this is—I'm not going to last long!"

Blindly, I found his hand and guided it down my cock. He took hold of it and let out a shuddering breath.

"Christ...," he sighed.

He was right: he didn't last long. I could feel the condom filling inside me as he came, and the whole neighbourhood could probably hear him. I got off him, tossed the condom away, and he grabbed me by my hips and took me straight into his mouth.

The phone rang.

Lucy. It's a testament to my love for her that I pulled out of Alex's mouth and jumped out of the shower, hissing "Shit-shit-shit-shit" as I tried to find something on which to dry my hands.

I managed at last to pick up, my heart racing, my skin prickly hot, she said, "All right, arsehole, where are you?"

"Lucy, darling, please don't be angry," I said, breathing hard. "I was on my way to you, and it turned out Alex came back, and—honestly, I don't even know what time it is now."

"Seven!" she yelled.

Shit. Seven? We'd agreed to meet at six. This was not good.

"I'm so sorry! Please, let me make it up to you."

"All right. I want a car."

"Shut up. I'll come over, and we can—"

I caught a glimpse of Alex in the mirror and had to turn round to see better. There he was, a Roman god leaning back against the stream, his hair, overlong by now, falling back, the muscles of his chest and abdomen stretching as he lathered the shampoo onto his head…. He was like an actor in an ad, or a really, really good porno.

"Hey, arsehole! We're talking!" she yelled.

"Hm? Yes, I—I was saying something," I agreed.

"No, you were drooling. Get your head out of his arse and tell me how you will make up to me that I had to spend two hours first looking for this shithole you call a bar, in which I see nothing but snooty City twats, and then an hour standing here like a hooker, waiting for you!"

"Christ, I'm really sorry, Lucy. Honestly I am, and—and I will make it up to you. Somehow. You tell me what you want, and we'll do it. Promise. Anything."

"Okay." Her tone shifted. *Oh no.* "Yep"—she sounded positively cheerful now—"get ready, Taylor, this is going to be awesome."

"Oh, fuck me, no, Lucy. Honestly, no!"

"You owe me, arsehole, so you're going with me!"

Of course I knew exactly what she wanted. For months she's been pestering me about this club where, on certain nights, everybody had to dress kinky, and there was karaoke and amateur striptease and—well, basically everything I hate about everything!

Amelia once lost a bet and went with her, and the way she told it, it was a complete, stinky hellhole, and an hour into the evening, Lucy disappeared on her, only to reappear half an hour later with a come stain on her shirt.

It sounded awful. According to Lucy, Amelia dramatized the whole thing. She says it's a ton of fun if you just relax and get into the spirit of things.

Up until today, I'd always refused to get into the spirit of things.

"Next week, bitch!" she cried gleefully. "You can bring Alex with you, since he's more fun than you, anyway. Sucker!"

And she hung up, before I could say anything more.

Alex came out of the shower, towel round his waist as though to show me why this sacrifice was worth it. He was smiling. "Hey, lover. Who was that?"

"I stood Lucy up. I forgot—I got distracted. She waited for me for an hour."

"Oh shit, sorry," he said. "Are you hungry?"

"Starving."

But he was standing so close, and then he put his arms around my shoulders, and then I made the towel slip off his hips and onto the ground, and it was a while before we got to food. In fact, by the time we got to it, it was dark outside and my muscles were like plasticine, so I could barely move for how spent and tired I was.

Friday, 9 July

RECEIVED AN invitation to the celebration for the one hundred and fiftieth anniversary of the founding of our university. There will be a fancy reception, and pre-reception drinks at the school.

Alex said he'd come with me, which was the only reason I'd ever go. Bloody hate such things.

Lucy came over to instruct us as to what to wear for our evening out in her sex club. She tells me it's not a sex club, but I don't believe her. Her original idea was that she'd go dressed as a dominatrix, with me and Alex on leads, wearing nothing but leather trousers. When I informed her that I categorically refused any such thing, she got into a pout, from which she only recovered when Alex said he'd go with her as she wished, and he would even wear the lead, but I could just go dressed normally.

"He'll be insufferable otherwise," he told her.

I couldn't believe he would attend a party topless and in leather trousers. Though to be fair, having seen him topless, I'm not surprised he's not ashamed of his body. People pay good money to see the sort of things I see for free. Which was why I wasn't thrilled that he would be ogled by every perv in the city. But as Alex was all right with it, and as it got me off the hook, I accepted it.

We had to shop for the leather trousers since it turned out that neither he nor I possessed any. This was awkward because Alex couldn't afford an expensive pair of trousers he'd wear only once. In the shop, when he saw how much a decent pair of those things costs, he turned a little pale, so I just bought them.

It offended him, but I got away with it. "You're getting me off the hook by wearing them, so it's only fair."

He seemed okay with that. This seems to be a matter of pride with him—I need to be more careful in future.

Sunday, 12 July

YESTERDAY EVENING was Lucy's Night of Revenge. And… it wasn't so bad.

I mean, it started awful. Lucy came out of Alex's flat with him wearing nothing but leather trousers, cowboy boots, and a colourful dog collar around his neck, while she, dressed like a high-class hooker, held him at the end of a lead in her fishnet-gloved hands.

I thought I'd bust a blood vessel, since we'd agreed he'd only be in costume when we were at that disgusting club, not before. So I yelled, "You can't take him out on the street like that! What if somebody from work sees him? He'll never get another client again! Are you serious? You're not doing this! I forbid it! I'll set myself on fire like a fucking Tibetan monk, but this is not happening, nu-uh, *non, niet, nein*, no!"

Lucy and Alex, meanwhile, were trying not to laugh.

Then Lucy turned to him and said, "Told you he'd lose it."

Alex laughed and took the collar off. "We're just teasing, love."

Indeed, while I was recovering from this mini heart attack, he slipped on a T-shirt over his torso and promised to keep it on until we got to that horrid sex club.

I was dreading it every step of the way, but Alex and Lucy were cheerful. And then once we got there, it was in fact okay. A live band was playing, which I didn't expect, and they weren't crap. In fact, the guy on the electric guitar really knew what he was doing, and the lead singer was cute. People did dress kinky, that was true, but there were some people dressed normally. Besides the kinky clothing, there was really nothing to complain about. We got drinks, and we danced, and although the place was small and dingy, it was all the more intimate for that.

Of course, Lucy had to chat up all the members of the band once their gig ended and they mingled with the crowd. Eventually, she settled for the drummer. The guy seemed pretty stupefied that her fancy had fallen on him, but grateful too. He was a strange-looking guy with blond dreadlocks and a kind of parroty face, but not unattractive in a rangy, streetwise kind of way.

Alex was a hit that evening, as I suppose could be expected. I didn't find being topless in leather trousers an attractive look, and had I met him that very evening, knowing no better, I would have scoffed at the show-off with the ripped body and written him off as a gym-obsessed narcissist. Which just goes to show what a twat I can be sometimes, because all he was doing was being a good sport and, as it turned out, a good advertisement for his business.

He recruited several people to his gym and his services.

"I could look like you?" one beer-bellied bloke asked him, full of wonder.

Alex smiled and nodded. "Will need work, though, but of course you could."

He made it sound easy. Anyway, the upshot was that he'd never looked gayer, as I did not hesitate to inform him. He reddened, then laughed and kissed me.

Thursday, 15 July

DINNER WITH Amelia and Mark and co. Alex came with me, and we heard about how great Japan was. They were better at gift-giving than I was. I didn't bring anything spectacular back from New York—a T-shirt for Alex that read "I heart NY," a mug that read the same—nothing particularly original or thoughtful, since I hadn't really the time (nor am I very inventive when it comes to gifts).

Amelia and Mark brought so much stuff with them—for the kids there were all kinds of games, toys, and clothes, and for Lucy and me various quirky gadgets. We got to see lots of pictures of Japan too, which was—not gonna lie—boring. I hate other people's holiday pics. But it was good to see Amelia and Mark on good terms again. In fact, they were glowing, which makes me wistful about going away with Alex.

I'm sick of London. I mean this in a larger sense. I lived in Bristol for two years and think a place like that, or maybe Brighton, would be just the thing. But something's always in the way. When I first moved into my current flat, it was supposed to be a temporary place to stay while I made better arrangements. It's not the nicest block of flats you'd ever see, but it was relatively cheap (for London) and convenient and allowed dogs. Now that I could afford a better place, I can't find the time to look for it. Although now that I'm with Alex, maybe that's the incentive I need. He doesn't like living in London, constantly complains about how expensive everything is. He'd love to move away, and I could make that happen for him. I need to look into this.

Meanwhile, I could take him on a holiday somewhere fun.

Sunday, 18 July

LAST NIGHT I was at Alex's with Squire, and we were hanging out playing board games. It was late, midnightish; he had gone to the loo and his phone rang.

In hindsight I shouldn't have done it, but I was tired, and we'd had a couple of beers and I wasn't thinking. I just picked it up.

The voice on the other end was low, gruff, and American. "H'llo? H'llo! Who's that?"

"Oh, I—I'm sorry, just a second." My eyes adjusted to the small screen of Alex's outdated phone that read "Dad."

Not good. Not good. Mission abort. Mission abort immediately.

Alex came out of the loo, eyes wide. "What the—?" he said.

I mouthed, "It's your dad," and handed him the phone.

He was not pleased. He took the phone. "Yeah, hello? Hi, Dad! Yeah, that was—that—nobody. What?" He put a finger in his other ear, as though he were in a busy restaurant, and then walked to the corner of the kitchen, where I could still hear and see him from where I sat. He spoke in half sentences to his father.

Nobody? That stung. I mean, I knew he hadn't come out to his dad, and I don't think it's my business when he will come out to him, but still—nobody?

Anyway, when he hung up, he must have known how he'd sounded because he looked sheepish. "Sorry, freaked out there for a moment."

"Yeah," I said. "Do you want me to go?"

"What? No, no, stay. It's just that the connection was bad, so I didn't want to explain everything over the phone, and—it just came out that way. Is that really bad?"

"Well, it wasn't nice," I said, then shrugged, "but it's not like *I* wouldn't avoid saying thirty things to my parents when one would do. Besides, a short call at midnight on a Sunday doesn't seem like the right moment to drop that bombshell on someone."

He relaxed and smiled, and sank onto the sofa next to me. Then I remembered something.

"I might have outed you to my parents and to half of Taiwan while I was in New York, though. Just a heads-up."

He laughed. "Did you really?"

"Yeah, do you mind? They asked if I had a boyfriend, and I didn't feel like lying. Also, as *your* boyfriend, I felt a little bit like bragging about it."

"Flatterer," he said, putting his arm around me. "What did your parents say?"

"My mum would like to meet you. She said you had kind eyes."

"She did? Aw, that's nice," he said. "I'd like to meet your parents."

"Seriously?"

"Yeah, why not?"

"I don't know. You're the one who's not out to everybody," I said. "I wouldn't want to put you in an awkward position."

"It's just my dad. His heart isn't strong, and I worry what it'll do to him. I need to pick a good time, when he's calm and I can tell him slowly and sort of break the news in a gentle way, you know?"

"I'm sorry to hear about his heart," I said. "You don't have to tell him anything. Not on my account, anyway. But that reminds me! It's my mum's birthday next month. My parents are going to their summer house in the South of France, but we could go and see them before that. I was going to go down anyway, but you can come with me. It'd be nice, if you're up for it."

"Yeah, okay," he said.

We sat in silence for a little while, and then he asked, "When did you come out to your parents?"

"I didn't."

He frowned. "I thought they knew."

"They do know, but we don't talk about it. I suppose when I didn't bring any girls home was their first tip-off, and then at uni, Lena came to visit me once and met my very flamboyant and fabulous boyfriend, Jamie, and she sort of guessed. I asked her to run it by the parents. And she did, and so then it was out. I didn't see their faces. I don't know what they said."

He blinked at me in surprise. "That's weird. I thought coming out was all about face-to-face tears, hugs, or beatings."

"Not with my parents," I said. "In my family we don't speak of things that are important to us. I know my parents didn't hate me for being gay, because they acted like nothing had happened. In fact, I assumed we adopted an 'ask me no questions and I'll tell you no lies' policy, but in New York my dad actually said that he'd changed his mind about gay people because of me, and my mum said she'd like to meet you, so I must have underestimated them."

"Mate, you should speak to your parents," he said earnestly, looking a little disturbed by my story. "You shouldn't just bottle things up like that. Or are your parents really scary? Are you afraid of them?"

I wanted to laugh, because I don't think anybody's ever been afraid of them. I couldn't really explain how my family operates on subtle hints and subtexts.

It was that time of night—he became curious about my past and wanted to know everything.

"Have you ever slept with a woman?"

"Not in the biblical sense, no. I told you I don't like women that way. Why would I?"

"To experiment. To check if you're not even a little straight."

"I don't remember ever doubting that I wasn't even a little straight. You don't get erections watching Olympic swimmers or wrestling, without catching the drift quickly. I just didn't act on it until I was at uni, by which time I met more people who were gay, and so there wasn't that confined atmosphere like in sixth form or earlier. I did kiss girls on multiple occasions, if that helps. Didn't do anything for me. Mostly it was with women who already knew I was gay. It wasn't unpleasant—I liked them well enough—but it just didn't arouse anything in me. Not like the first time I kissed a boy, where I felt fire in my veins and my entire body came alive with interest."

"Yeah? Who was that boy?"

"Just someone I met at a club. We snogged, and then he wanted to take me home with him, but I was still a virgin and scared of casual sex. My first time was with my boyfriend, once I was comfortable with him."

"What was he like?"

I tried to remember Jamie, but there was so much of him that it was hard to put it in words. "He was camp, affectionate, and very energetic. But we were never going to work out. He was much more open than I was, which was a little scary, to be honest. He was really brave. Once, we got chased down a street in Cambridge by a band of skinheads—No, don't make that face. Nothing happened, and we managed to escape. Anyway, he had a wandering eye and I was starting my postgraduate studies, so we split up at the end of our undergrad degree. He went off to work for a big pharmaceutical corporation. I think he's doing well. We chat online sometimes."

"So, then what happened?"

"Nothing. I didn't really date anybody until you."

"You were celibate for *ten years*?"

I laughed at the incredulous look on his face. "Don't be daft, of course I wasn't. I just haven't met anybody I liked particularly to try and make it stick. When you're gay, the dating pool isn't particularly large, you know. Of the dozen or so men you meet who you think look and sound the part, one will be gay, and then probably not into you. Until a Jack Gordon comes along, I guess."

He frowned.

"But he fucked me over," I said. "And then you moved here, and I thought you were straight, and so I had a pathetic crush on you, while knowing it was perfectly hopeless. And then you asked me out, thank heaven, and...."

I wanted to say, at that point, that I was happy at last, but figured that sounded cheesy, and I didn't want to make him uncomfortable by saying something schmaltzy.

"What?" he asked.

"Nothing. That's it. Here we are."

"You should have asked me out earlier. Why didn't you?"

"I thought you were straight."

"So? What if I wasn't? Why not take the chance?"

"Er, you've not been gay for long enough to be allowed to say things like that," I said. "Hitting on a straight guy isn't fun. They never take it as a compliment."

"No? I would."

"Yeah, mate, but you're pretty gay, so I don't think that counts."

"I'm not gay! I'm bisexual," he said.

"Really?"

"Yeah. I checked on a scale. Forget what it's called, but it tells you how gay you are, and I'm somewhere in the middle."

"Okay, lay it on me. Tell me about all the women you've dated," I said.

"There was Shelley all throughout sixth form, then Lily in college, and then Becky for three whole years. We were going to get married, but it didn't work out in the end because she didn't really want to settle down. She went to live in Costa Rica. So there."

At my grumbling, he said, "No, I didn't fantasize about men the entire time. Don't be a dick. I had one crush on a guy, but I thought that it was just being so far away from women and having to constantly spend time with him that did it. I didn't know I would actually go through with it if given the chance, and he was pretty oblivious to me. And so I left. I thought I'd try to date women to get my head straight. But then I met you."

"And you had a hard-on for me."

"Shut up, no I didn't. I liked you, that's all. I liked how your hair flopped about when you ran. And I liked it when I could make you laugh, because you do generally walk around as though somebody had peed in your coffee that morning. And I liked your freckles. But I knew I was in trouble when I couldn't explain to myself why I bloody hated Jack Gordon's stupid face."

"Awww!"

"If I were less of a civilised human being," he said, "I would have punched him every time he came round to see you. What *did* you see in that creep?"

Good question. "Er, I don't know. He is hot in an intellectual sort of way, successful in his career, and very clever and witty when he uses his powers for good and not for evil."

"Pfft, forget I asked. Come here."

I know it's evil of me to be a little flattered that Jack bothered him so much. Anyway, we went to sleep really late.

Thursday, 22 July

WORKING ON a grant proposal. It's for an annual thing we used to do—a workshop on the Cold War in Europe. A collaboration between me, here in London, Stacey in Edinburgh, and Howard in Cardiff. Now we've used up all our previous grant money, and have to look for some other source of funding. We had a really good network going, so it'd be a shame if it fell through completely.

Got another email from Australia about the two-year project. I wish they'd take my no for an answer and stop pressing.

Saturday, 24 July

UGH, I feel like a dick. I was so knackered after the week I've had that I didn't feel like going out. So Alex went out with his friends without me.

Thing is, now I'm bored. I don't feel like sleeping, and the trashy sci-fi novel I'm reading isn't gripping me (although with a title like *Space*

Viking I don't know what I was hoping for). I feel bad about not going out when Alex wanted me to.

To be fair, it was a stand-up comedy gig by one of his really unfunny friends, so I'm sure I'm not missing out on much. But to be fairer: Alex does the cringeworthy things my friends make us do, and he's a good sport about it.

Tuesday, 27 July

THE ONE hundred and fiftieth anniversary reception.

I really don't like events of this kind. I don't like wearing suits. There's a reason I became an academic.

However, I have to say that I was honestly turned on when I saw Alex in his suit. He said he had to borrow it from a friend, but it fit him really well; clean-shaven, in a grey suit and white shirt, he looked like an Italian model advertising Armani. I couldn't take my eyes off him.

So I was really proud to take him with me and show him off. Everybody in my department felt sorry for me because of Jack. Well, it was time to wipe their faces in it. And to rub it into Jack's stupid face too.

There was a pre-reception in our school, where I introduced Alex to Sarah and Robert. Sarah's eyes widened a little when she saw Alex, and then she lifted her eyebrows at me in appreciation. *Yeah*, I thought to myself, *that's right.* Meanwhile, Alex and Robert found something to talk about—Robert's into trains, but apparently he knew a fair bit about RAF aircraft too. I didn't follow any of it and was glad when the talk of twin-engined turboprop monoplanes ended. Later I showed Alex my office, and he was very impressed, because he's never had an office in his life. He snogged me on my desk.

Then the whole party had to move to the Great Hall, where there was a speech by the vice chancellor and champagne glasses were handed out. I was just explaining to Alex what the colours in our banner meant when I spotted Jack. At his side, surprise surprise, was a woman who was so beautiful even *I* noticed. I mean, she really was stunning.

Alex's eyebrows rose when he saw her, and he said, "Whoa."

I couldn't blame him. Naturally, Jack came straight over to me, smug smile on his face.

"Hey, Leo," he said. And then, looking at Alex, "Oh, I see you brought your decorator with you. How nice of you."

"Alex is my boyfriend," I said. "And he's not a *decorator*."

"No?" said Jack, disbelief in his tone. "What *do* you do, Alex?"

I interrupted Alex's answer, to change the subject. "Who is this?" I stretched out a hand to Jack's date.

The woman, who looked Indian, shook my hand and introduced herself as Ava.

"Ava works for the BBC as Service Editor to South-East Asia," said Jack. "She speaks six languages."

Alex said, "That's impressive. What do you speak?"

"Arabic, Russian, Chinese, Japanese, Korean, and Spanish," she said.

"And English, clearly," said Alex, obligingly ignoring that Jack was clearly trying to rub her into my face. "So that makes it seven."

Jack smiled at me. "It does, doesn't it?"

"Why would you learn so many languages?" I asked her.

She recited a mini biography about a childhood spent with a father who worked in the Foreign Office, posted all over East Asia, and then her brief marriage to another foreign ministry official, who had been stationed worldwide. She spoke in the sort of way that you'd imagine an information leaflet would speak. It wasn't a biggie—she just spoke a lot of languages, married ambassadors, and had her schooling in Asia. Don't we all?

I didn't mind her so much, but Jack's "gotcha" attitude began to piss me off. Meanwhile, Alex was still asking her questions about what she did, and Jack was helpful in contributing.

"She was involved in making my history programme when I covered the war in Asia," he said. "And, in her free time, she does a lot of charity work."

"Clearly," I said, looking at him pointedly.

Jack and Ava laughed.

"Oh, I meant to tell you," he said then, his gaze oddly fixated on me, "I read your article in the *Journal of Modern History*."

"Yeah?"

"Brilliant piece," he said. "I disagreed with almost every page."

I said, "Well, you would, since you know barely anything about your own field, let alone mine."

He smiled. "Well, you used an interesting perspective—lovely analogies. But don't you think that comparing Poland to the Czech Republic is a little presumptuous? I mean, considering the vast historical and especially geographical differences is one thing, but even their experience of the Soviet occupation was vastly different."

"Yes, of course," I said, "but that doesn't make the comparison futile. You cannot compare like for like in history. It's just not a possible or tangible thing to do."

"Perhaps, but don't you think you should at least acknowledge your own position? I mean, your political analysis is so incredibly neorealist in approach, I can't believe they let you publish it without mentioning that."

"Well, maybe you can write to them and see what they say," I said. "Or better yet, actually write an article yourself and get it published…."

"I've published three books in the last three years."

"The last time I checked, they let anyone publish books," I said.

"They were well reviewed."

"By your friends." I laughed with triumph and looked at Alex for confirmation, but he wasn't there anymore. Neither was Ava.

"When did they leave?" I asked Jack. He looked amused.

"So, your boyfriend looks nice," he said. "Rebound?"

"Rebound from what!" I demanded indignantly.

Jack's eyes sparkled with amusement. It was infuriating because it was as if I was badly masking a lie. I wasn't lying!

"Well, he's not really your type, is he?" he said, with the sort of self-satisfaction where you don't know whether he's joking and whether to call him on it.

Then I realised I was wasting the evening on this stupid quarrel with a smug prat when I could be with my boyfriend. Alex had escorted Ava to the table with the canapés, and that's where I found him, discussing her fitness regime with her.

The rest of the night was boring, and I was glad to get home. And especially glad to strip my boyfriend out of his suit and get him into bed.

Tuesday, 3 August

I KEEP thinking about going away on holiday with Alex. Unfortunately, the places I want to go, he can't afford. Our conversations on this topic have been singularly unproductive. He won't let me pay, and I can't think of anything cheap enough to do with him. I like nice hotels, museums, castles, beaches, quaint little villages, and beautiful stretches of countryside.

But flights, hotels, and restaurants cost money. I could easily afford taking us both, but he won't hear of it. It's doing my head in.

Lucy is still dating the drummer we met that night at her sex club. That's really strange. I keep getting text messages from her every second day or so, telling me they broke up and she can't do it anymore, but when I call her, they're back together. I gather from the little information I can glean, that he worships her, and since she worships herself too, there seems to be a bond between them that she finds so hard to sever.

Amelia thinks they'll get married and divorced a bunch of times. I don't know, I really can't see Lucy staying in a relationship with that guy, or with anybody. We're going to the pub with them tomorrow, so I guess we'll see then.

Saturday, 7 August

HAD A bit of a fight with Alex. Didn't mean to, and we're made up now—more or less. I wanted him to come to Paris with me. I found a cheap hotel, discount plane tickets etc. I made a real effort to make it affordable for him, so that we could get the hell out of London even for a few days.

He said he couldn't, since he had clients lined up through the dates I'd planned, and he couldn't let them down. Honestly, I don't see what the big deal is. It's not like he's a brain surgeon or anything. Granted, I shouldn't have said that to him. I apologised, and we're okay now.

Monday, 16 August

HAD TO go and see Lucy's boyfriend perform last night. She refuses to call him *boyfriend*. He calls her "babe." They're really sweet together, especially because she's so squirmy about the handholding and the pet-naming. I wasn't as comfortable as I could be, though, because Alex had to bring Michael along. It's his ongoing effort at making the two of us friends, somehow. When I told him that it was probably futile for him to expect this, he said I'm not trying hard enough. So instead of pointing out that it takes two to dance this particular tango, I agreed for Michael to come along. After all, Alex gets on with all of my friends, and it's only fair I should try and befriend his.

It didn't go particularly well. All Michael did was hog Alex's attention, and I had to spend my time with Lucy and Kevin.

On the upside, though, Alex was grateful for my trying, and I made my failure up to him by introducing him to the joys of chocolate-sauce-on-dick.

Friday, 20 August

WE'RE PREPARING to go and see my parents this weekend. Not looking forward to it, if I'm quite honest. We're taking Squire with us, and since it seems like we're not going to get any other vacation together, we might as well make the most of this.

I did all the research on what to see and do in Sussex. Fuck the French Riviera, we have the South Downs. *There.*

So long as the weather holds, I don't even care that much. I do mind about my parents being there, though, but that can't be helped. Alex seems excited, and he showed me a range of T-shirts and shirts so I could pick out which would look most respectable for him to meet my parents in. He doesn't have that many clothes, but I went with the shirts, since they are my parents he's meeting, and they will judge him on every possible level.

127

Monday, 23 August

UGH, WHAT did I expect? Fuck my life.

Tuesday, 24 August

ALEX IS still not speaking to me. I'm not speaking to him. Fuck him, anyway. I'm not going to go begging for his forgiveness. At this stage, I don't even know if *I* forgive *him*.
   [torn page]

Thursday, 26 August

LUCY SAYS that if I don't tell her what happened between Alex and me, she'll stop talking to me. But I can't tell her because it's not easy to tell people things. So I told her that we can't see a future together.
   She called me, and I quote, "a complete cockwomble" for fucking this up, but then was obliging enough to take me out to get drunk. Which means I'm pretty drunk right now. Which means that it's really easy to feel sorry for myself.
   It was a mistake to go and see my parents. That's for sure. I mean—that shouldn't be a shocker, really, because it's my fucking parents. What the fuck did I even expect?
   Even as we arrived at the house, and Alex saw it, I began to feel uncomfortable. I made him pull into my parents' gate, and he did it, but he said apprehensively, "Mate, why are we stopping here? There's probably dogs here that will bite your arse if we get out of the car."
   "There's no dogs," I said. "We had a dog once, but he couldn't find his own arse, let alone yours, so don't worry."
   "Shit, Leo, you mean *this* is your parents' house?"
   His eyes went wide as he took it in. It's a nice house, of course. Personally, it's too far away from town and civilisation for me, but it

looked good, bathed in sunshine, and the lawns were freshly mown—which made them smell fresh and trim—and there were birds around the bird feeder. I could see Larry the gardener in the distance, and I waved at him. His son, Paul, was at the other end of the garden, way too far for me to hail him.

My mum came out, looking very stiff and formal. I could tell she wasn't sure how to behave, so she put on her professional smile, the one that said she was prepared for anything. She shook Alex's hand and then bid us enter. Alex blinked as he took in the size of the place.

"You will have your old bedroom, next to Daddy's study, Leo. Are you good with the bags?"

"Yes, Mum. We're only here for the weekend, remember?"

I took the bags up, with Alex, and showed him the bedroom. It was my old room, but now it's made into another guest bedroom for when my parents had one of those parties where their friends got drunk and stayed over. My posters and stereo and bookshelves are gone, replaced with mahogany furniture that looks like it belongs to another century, its shelves stuffed with *Master & Commander* novels and guides to Sussex and the local area. Pictures of sailboats and seagulls flying over sandy beaches adorn the walls. We had a view over the garden, which made Alex gape.

"Christ, how big is this place?" he asked.

"Er, I don't know," I said, busying myself with stashing our bags in the big wall wardrobe. Once that was done, I showed him where the loo was—it was an en suite, which made his eyes boggle.

"Your bedroom has an en suite?" he said.

I said that it did, and he repeated, disbelievingly, "You used to have your own *bathroom*?"

"Yeah. It's no big deal—it's really small. Here, do you want to put your toothbrush in there or do you want a tour of the house?"

He went with the tour of the house. It was probably the biggest he had ever been in apart from hotels, and his eyes were wide the entire time. I felt like I was walking him through Chatsworth. Once I showed him around the house, I found my mum in the kitchen with Olga, the woman who cooked for them sometimes. She also had a daughter, and together they came to clean the house three times a week. I really wished Mum hadn't asked Olga to cook, this once.

My mum made us coffee, and we sat down in the living room, and the atmosphere was, er, sort of stiff. Alex was evidently uncomfortable; Mum was uncomfortable. I wondered what had got into my head to actually think of doing this. I mean, seriously, what the hell was I thinking?

"Daddy is in town at the moment," my mum told me, her back ramrod stiff. "He's just getting a few things for the roast dinner tomorrow. I would have sent Paul out, but your dad wanted to run some errands anyway. He'll be back shortly."

"That's okay, Mum," I said. "Why don't I take Alex and walk round for a bit. There's some great walks here. We'll take Squire, so he doesn't annoy Larry and Paul."

My mum smiled gratefully, and so Alex and I went out, walking in the woods nearby.

When we returned, my dad was back, his enormous Jag standing in the driveway, looking incongruous with Alex's tiny Fiesta next to it. My dad shook Alex's hand vigorously, and I could tell he was a little uncertain how to treat him, but settled, at last, for the way he treated all my friends: a bright, friendly smile, a pat on the back, and a "Where are you from, then?"

Which was cool. At least it gave Alex something to talk about. So he told my parents about his dad, who had been in the US Marines, and his mum, who had been a teacher and later a housewife, but who had divorced his father. He spoke of his siblings: he had two sisters and two brothers.

It went well; my parents relaxed a little, apparently becoming gradually aware that Alex was just a human being. Eventually, at dinner, my parents spoke of Lena and me, and of their own professions, and we could laugh at what a nerdy kid I once was. After dinner, my father opened another bottle of wine—dessert wine, because for dinner we had red, to go with the beef—and we sat down in the sitting room, where all the walls were covered floor-to-ceiling with packed bookshelves.

And that was when my dad asked, "So, Alex, what do you do?"

I panicked. I'd known they were going to ask that, and I had a million strategies of how to deflect the criticism that would follow. I was going to take it all on myself, say something about Australia or the article I recently published, anything really, but last minute I just sort of lost it, and when Alex told them he was a personal trainer, and my mum asked whom he trained, expecting (clearly) that he'd say "Prince William" or something like that, I blurted, "It doesn't matter, Mum. It's just something he does for now."

I honestly meant for them to just drop the subject, but Alex looked at me with a surprised frown. I was nervous, so I said, "Right? I mean, you won't be doing this forever."

"I don't know," he said, visibly confused. "I like what I'm doing. And to answer your question"—here he turned to my mum—"I train people in a gym, just down the street from where we live."

"Oh," said my dad—I knew that *oh*—but he forced a smile and said, "You help people keep fit. That's great."

Great, my eye.

"Yeah," said Alex. "I get thirty to forty pounds an hour, depending on the case, but it's pretty rewarding."

"That's great," said my mum, for whom only people like Larry the gardener or Olga the housekeeper earned money by the hour. "So, you mean to remain a—a personal trainer, then? Is there a—a career ladder or—?"

"No," said Alex with a laugh, "I don't think there is. Or I don't know of one. I don't really think of it as a career."

"He won't be doing this forever," I said, irritated now with both Alex and my parents. "He used to be in the RAF, for God's sake. He's qualified to do much more than just help people lift weights."

I could see the expression on Alex's face, and I should have stopped then. But I didn't. Because Dad suggested he could show Alex the gym he was building in the spare room next to the stairs to the attic. So instead of shutting up, I said, "It's not a thing you need to make a big deal out of, Dad. It's just a thing he's doing for now. Okay? Leave it."

So yeah, it was pretty awkward after that. We slept with our backs to each other that night. Not that we would have done anything, anyway, since I was terrified of my parents hearing us.

The next day wasn't any better. My mum, maybe feeling sorry for Alex, made great efforts to be friendly to him. She decided to treat him as though he were my girlfriend, though, which wasn't cool. She asked him if he wanted to see her recipe book, by which she swore, and whether he wanted any seeds, as though we had a garden. And in between those two things, she chatted incoherently about her neighbour's back problems. Anyway, Alex played along, because he's not an ungracious prick like I am.

After the roast meal, we went back up to London. We were meant to have stayed another night, but we made some excuses about having appointments and things to do, and we left. The damage was, after all, already done.

It feels like shit to drive home knowing that there's an argument waiting there. I knew we were going to have it out, because Alex was silent, and Alex is never silent. I could tell he was pissed off, and I was pissed off too, really. Partially with him, partially with myself. Honestly, though, at that stage, if he had said the right things, or not said the wrong things, I probably would have apologised. I don't need to be right 100 per cent of the time. I'm okay with acknowledging that I was in the wrong. Maybe not always immediately, since I'm not entirely without pride, but I'm not allergic to the word sorry. And in this instance, to be fair, I *was* at fault. It had not been my finest performance, I was ready to admit.

But that's not what happened.

I thought we'd go to my flat to have it out, but he said he was tired and he would go to his. I said, "I know you're angry, Alex. You might as well tell me."

We were still in the corridor between our two flats, so he said, "Fine, but I'm tired and I want to go back soon, okay?"

"Fine."

So we went to my place, and I closed the door behind him, and then we stood there for a while, eyeing each other with obvious displeasure.

"Do you want to start?" he asked.

"Me? I'm not the one who's annoyed."

"Are you sure?" he said. "It seems like you are."

"Okay, I'm annoyed. But I think you're more annoyed."

"I'm fine, Leo. I'll just go to sleep, and then I'll be fine."

"I want to talk about this," I said.

"Well, then, speak!" he snapped. "Tell me how I'm a working-class yokel who's too poor and stupid to have anything to do with your family."

"That's nonsense. That's not what this is about."

"No, little Lord Fauntleroy? What, then? Because apparently my working in a gym is a big problem here. You should have warned me. I could have invented some other profession. I didn't know it was going to be a big deal with you."

"It's not a big deal," I said. "My parents are ambitious, that's all. They like to see me associate with—date—I don't know, someone who does something meaningful."

Alex's jaw fell open. "You think I'm not doing something meaningful?"

"Well, it's not exactly a job that gets you anywhere, Alex. Come on... this can't be news to you!"

"It's a job I enjoy. It pays me money. I don't rip anybody off, I don't hurt anybody, I help people, I make a comfortable living. What the hell is your problem with that?"

I said, "It's just not something I thought you wanted to do forever. I mean, that's ridiculous! It's a job for a twenty-something while he's supplementing his student loan, not a thing a grown man should be doing for a career. Seriously, do you want to be doing this forever?"

"Maybe not," he said. But the colour had drained from his face, and I could see that he was seriously holding back. "But *you* don't get to decide that, mate."

Those words hit me like a slap in the face. It was like the room spun and I suddenly felt queasy.

I realised then what this was about. Who was *I*, the poof he happened to be humping for a couple of months, to tell him what to do with his life? I was *nobody*, remember? *I* didn't get to have a word.

Of course he wouldn't shift his work schedule around to go on holiday with *me*. Who was *I* to do that for? Of course he wouldn't upset his dad by telling him he was gay. Why make a fuss for *me*?

I got really angry then. He was already really angry.

"Clearly," I said, "I have misread the situation. You must pardon me, I fool myself sometimes when I should know my place better."

"Are you sure *I* shouldn't know *my* place better?" he asked, his eyes narrowed. "If I'm not good enough for you, as I am, then there's nothing else to be said!"

"Then don't say anything else. I don't know why you're wasting another second of your time with me." When he frowned in incomprehension I added, deliberately slowly as though he were hard of hearing or stupid, "You can go now. I won't keep you."

"What? That's it? You've nothing more to say?"

"Nothing."

"Fine, sod this." He left, and Squire gave a yelp that echoed what was happening inside of me at that moment. I thought that perhaps if we cooled down, we could talk again, but when I came upon him next he looked so angry, I couldn't say a word. I thought he'd just find me when he was done fuming, but that didn't happen.

Right now, I feel numb. Like I'm in a soundproof chamber and there's nothing but a void. It's not as though I wasn't halfway expecting to get my heart broken. In fact, I feel pretty stupid for assuming that it wouldn't have ended this way. Jesus, when I think that I'd actually thought about having children with him! What the hell is wrong with me?

I hate leaving the flat, for fear of stumbling into him. And I get an attack of anxiety every time I come home. I've not seen him in days. I don't even know if he's in.

Sunday, 29 August

SO THIS happened.

Yesterday morning I got a hard rap on the door.

I was hung-over, so the timing wasn't exactly perfect—Lucy tried to help me heal by supplying me with copious amounts of tequila. But short of an actual transplant of heart and brain—or the application of whatever that thing was that they used in *Eternal Sunshine of the Spotless Mind*—no poison will help. Anyway, I had a miserable evening followed by a yet more miserable morning.

So I opened the door, and then my heart sank to the pit of my stomach. Michael was standing there with an unpleasant look in his face, as though I'm the scum of the earth.

"I came to give you this—" He thrust an open shoebox with some of my stuff in it at me. "—and to pick up Alex's things."

I just stared at that shoebox like an idiot and didn't say anything, so he pushed past me to get inside. Squire yapped at his heels.

"Will you get him to shut up?" Michael snapped.

"What are you doing?" My voice was hoarse and my head was splitting. I told Squire to shut up, but he still growled at the intruder. Salt of the earth, is my Squire. He knows good people from fucking wankers at a whiff.

"I'm collecting his things, since you've broken up, right?" Michael said, looking around. "Where are they?"

"I don't know. I haven't got them ready. I didn't know—I didn't think…." I didn't know whether it was the tiredness or the headache or the all-over pain, I felt as if I was talking past an enormous gulp in my throat.

Christ, don't start crying in front of that guy, I told myself. I rubbed my eyes. "Look, now's not a good time."

"Right," he said, looking around with interest. "Let's make it quick, then, eh? Don't mean to hang around."

He took the shoebox from my hand, tipped its contents onto my dining table and said, "Go on, then."

One of the things in the box was the stuff I bought Alex in New York. "That—he put that in the box?" I asked, blinking at it. There was the T-shirt, still crumpled from wear, and a mug. "Those were gifts."

"Oh," Michael said, a little chagrined. "I'll take them back."

I felt tense with anger and started to walk around the flat, looking for anything remotely belonging to Alex. There was a pan he once lent me when we were cooking together, and a wooden spoon. His fat-free milk was in my fridge. There were his boxers, a T-shirt, some socks, his shower gel, his razor, a towel, some DVDs of the worst movies ever, and the game, *Bioshock 2*, which he gave me for my birthday. That last one I was almost going to throw in there as well, but then I didn't. It was a gift; I don't see any reason to give back a gift. So I put the rest in the box, along with the mug and the T-shirt from New York. He can be immature about this, but I won't be.

"Thanks, Michael," I said, ushering him out of the flat.

He went without hesitation. Didn't try to chat or anything. Good. Fuck him too. Then I collapsed on the floor and cried like a fucking baby.

So I wasn't in exactly the best place when Alex texted me later.

Hey Leo, sorry about M. Didn't send him with your stuff. Didn't know he'd go. Can we talk? A.

To be quite precise, I was drunk again, at Lucy's. So instead of replying something reasonable like "Okay, mate, no sweat," I actually replied, *Michael is a wanker who wants to suck your cock.*

Which ranks somewhere below a child showing the middle finger to the driver of the car behind the one in which it's sitting.

He responded, *Classy, mate. Is this really how you want to end this?*

I should have said, "It was going to end eventually, better now than later." What I sent instead was a smiling poo emoticon.

So today, after having recovered from another thundering hangover—the sort that makes you feel as though someone built a barn last night using nothing but wood, nails, and your head for a hammer—I tried to text Alex again. But I couldn't come up with anything to say.

So I knocked on his door. He wasn't in, so I rang him. Michael picked up his phone. I hung up.

Oh hell.

Tuesday, 31 August

MANAGED TO get in touch with Alex at last.

My email inbox is swamped with messages, and I haven't opened one in days. I can't think about work, can barely think about eating to stay alive, because this break-up is bothering the shit out of me. I'm a mixture of angry and desperately in love that just doesn't sit well unless I'm so drunk that I can't walk in a straight line.

Anyway, I happened to be with Amelia, Mark, and Lucy when Alex got back to me. Which meant that I wasn't allowed to form my own text messages but had to have them approved by the committee first. All my suggestions were shot down.

Lucy groaned, "What? Don't say that! It makes you sound desperate!"

"You need to cut yourself off entirely if you're ever to get over him," Amelia said.

"One word, all occasions, the letter *K*" was Mark's genius suggestion.

In short, they weren't very helpful. But in the end I communicated my desire to meet Alex to talk, and he agreed. We settled on a time and a venue—today at three, in the coffee shop around the corner from our place.

I had butterflies as I approached the place, because I missed him and wanted to see him again. Perhaps this bullshit was just one big misunderstanding, and he'd light up again at the sight of me as he used to do, and then we'd just have make-up sex and never talk of this nonsense again. When I came in, the first thing I saw was not Alex, but Alex and Michael, sitting at a table by the big window facing the street. Immediately all my good feelings fled. So this wasn't a reconciliation, it was an ambush. I considered turning around and leaving, but I was angry, so I walked over to their table and said, "You need your bodyguard to meet me for coffee now?"

Alex looked startled when he looked up. Then he flushed. "No." He sounded a little wounded. "Mike's just come to—to wait with me. You can go now, Mike. I'm all right."

Michael stood, eyeing me menacingly, and then stalked off without another word.

"Seriously?" I said to Alex. I was still standing.

He lowered his head. "You can sit down now, don't make a scene."

Oh, I wanted to make a scene. I wanted to make a whole *production* of fucking *Lion King* proportions out of this. But instead I sat down in a huff.

"Don't be angry about Michael being here," he said. "He's just being a friend."

"Yes, a very helpful *friend*. Short of hammering wooden bars against my door so that I could never leave my place to contaminate yours again, he's done basically everything."

"You know how friends are after a break-up, Leo. Don't tell me I'm not the Devil in your friends' eyes right now too."

In fact, he wasn't. In their eyes I was the biggest fool ever born to have let him go. But I was in no mood to flatter him. I rubbed my eyes instead, trying to focus. It wasn't easy, since I was faced with him, and so couldn't think reasonably. I wanted to shout that Michael the Bastard was in love with him; that he, Alex, was being a blind idiot; and that I hated him for not loving me back. Which would not have been productive. In fact, it would probably have been a rather sad thing to do. So instead I tried to focus and say something reasonable. "What now?"

"I was hoping you'd tell me," he said.

"Well, you said yourself we broke up." I kept my voice emotionless. It was easy enough when I allowed the anger to take control. "You wanted to meet up again, so I'm here. What do you want from me?"

"Christ, Leo, must you be like this?" His shoulders were slumped, and he seemed miserable.

"Like what?"

"Look, I don't even know what happened! Since when did my being a trainer bother you so much? I mean, was it always such a big thing to you? Why is it now, so suddenly? I don't get it. It's so—it's unfair!"

"What's unfair? Having to think about your future, Alex? It's part of being an adult. And having to consider your partner's thoughts on the subject—part of being in a relationship. That is, if the relationship means anything to you."

"Right," he said bitterly. "Right, because unless I wear suits to grand receptions and train famous people, I'm basically not able to be in a relationship, is that it?"

"No, but if you were serious about me, you wouldn't dismiss what I want and need out of hand, and tell me that it isn't my business. Want it or not, if you get involved with someone, and if you think of a future with them—but this is beside the point, because you clearly don't."

"What?" He blinked at me in incomprehension. "What the hell, Leo! Are you giving me an ultimatum? This is so fucked up!"

"It's not an ultimatum, Alex. It's reality. Stop making me sound like a snooty bitch for wanting to live a decent life with someone. I want to be able to go on holiday together, and maybe one day buy a house together, and—" I stopped, because I was getting choked up. So I clammed my mouth shut and turned away to watch the people passing us in the street.

"And because I'm too poor to do that with, you break up with me?" he asked, sounding incredulous.

"You don't have to be too poor to do that with! That's my point!" I said, irritated. "If you were at all serious about me, or us, or whatever, you'd listen to me, and not make it sound as though I were demanding you become Prince of fucking Persia. I'm not being unreasonable."

"What is it you want, then?" he asked. "If I get a nice little cosy programme on the telly, will that be good enough for you? Of course, I'll make sure it's the BBC and not, God forbid, something so plebeian as ITV!"

"Now you're being absurd."

"Am I? Because I'm doing something I like and am good at, and you want me to stop doing it, so you won't be embarrassed by your boyfriend."

"That's not true!" I was indignant—probably because it was, partially, true.

"Yeah, it is," he said, a bitter smile on his face. "I've seen you avoid answering the question, whenever you're asked it, Leo. You don't want to be with someone who is just a personal trainer. You think you should be with someone who is either famous or rich, or in some other way traditionally successful. And not only am I none of those things, I'm not likely to ever be it."

He exhaled and shook his head. "Do you know what I do for a living, Leo? I help people. My first client in London was this bloke, thirty-something, obese. His doctor told him he has diabetes. And he tells me and I'm like, 'Fuck it, we can beat this.' He had just been diagnosed. He was obviously too fat—that was the problem. But when you get rid of the fat around his internal organs, which inhibits the production of insulin, you can get rid of the diabetes."

He was staring at the coffee cup in his hands, with a defiant expression. "So I went to his doctor with him, and we came up with this training and diet plan together. Half a year he's been at it now, and his sugar levels are at an all-time low. He looks good now, you couldn't tell that he was ever as podgy as when I first met him. His wife is happy. They've a kid on the way now."

Here he glanced up at me to see if I was listening. "Another client," he said, "this girl, she's fifteen, skinny little thing. Hates that her brothers shove her around. So I build up her strength and her muscle. Another one, spotty little bloke, wants to impress the ladies. We build up his stamina, build up his arms and shoulders. Then I find out that he has slow-twitch muscle fibres, which means he's made for endurance sports, like marathons and such. Tells me he used to run for his school, broke some county records. So I sign him up to the athletics club. He's getting married in October."

He narrowed his eyes at me. "Yeah, it's not glamorous what I do, and I'm not a doctor or a lawyer, and I won't become a millionaire. But I love what I'm doing. I want to keep doing it. I thought this was something we had in common. But it's not all right to be embarrassed about what I do, okay? I'm not embarrassed, and it sucks that you are."

I had sunk my head into my hands by now. "I'm not embarrassed, Alex. And it's great that you do those things, but if you won't accept me paying for things, and if you won't earn any more than what you do now, then how on earth do you imagine us living together?"

I really just wanted to hear him say he wanted that. It bothered me that he wouldn't say it, as though it was more important to him to defend his profession than our relationship. Which it was, of course. Because I was nobody.

"I don't know," he said. "If you can't imagine it, then who am I to make you."

I exhaled. "Right. Because if I were a woman and you had got me pregnant, you'd be sitting here telling me how important it was that you helped the diabetic lay off the cheese."

"Are you comparing your wanting to get pissed in Paris to my getting a woman in trouble for life, Leo?" he said. "Have you lost it, mate?"

"Right." I stood up. "Belittle me if you want, but I'm a grown man. And if I want to get pissed in Paris with my boyfriend, then I should be able to do so. And if you thought of me seriously at all, you wouldn't laugh at it and make it seem like I had no say about your career and future. I delayed my career for you—I did that. I had a project in Australia that could have skyrocketed my career, but I didn't go. Because of you. Because I thought one day, when we were more settled, I'd be able to do it, go there with you, or whatever. More fool me."

And I turned and left the coffee shop, only then noticing that most of the people in it had been staring at us. So I did make a scene, after all. Well, every gay milestone must be touched at some point.

Couldn't face staying at my flat, so have temporarily moved in with Lucy.

Thursday, 2 September

HAD WHOLE lot of meetings at the department, as term is about to start. It's been hard to get out of bed, shave, get dressed—I hadn't noticed these things took up so much energy before.

Friday, 3 September

MUM CALLED.

"How are you, dear?" she asked. "Are you ready for the new term? Did you approach Duncan Harrison about that book he wanted you to write? Daddy and I think it would be a marvellous opportunity, you know. We see those Andrew Davies books in Waterstones all the time. There's no reason why you shouldn't be a popular historian, and Germaine informs me that it's both lucrative and—"

"Mum," I said, the first word I managed to get in, "this is not a good time to talk. I'm rather busy."

"Oh good. What are you doing?"

I was staring at a microwaveable ready meal at that moment, trying to force myself to open it, but not quite managing. "Working," I said. "Is there a reason you called? Everything all right with you and dad?"

"Oh yes, dear, everything is fine here. We finally found out what was the matter with my camellias. Root decay! Would you believe it? Larry is heartbroken!"

Oh good, I was about to say sarcastically. *I'm glad we got to the bottom of the thrilling mystery of what was wrong with your fucking camellias.*

I was not in a good place, so I didn't say anything. Instead I listened to her go on about honey fungus.

"But I'm sure you don't want to hear about that," she said. "How is your boyfriend?"

I could tell from her tone of voice that she was trying to be natural and accepting about my having a boyfriend and not a girlfriend, but it was the last fucking thing I needed to hear. I bit my lip painfully and then made myself say, "We broke up, actually."

"Oh? That was quick."

"Yes. I can't really talk about it right now."

There was silence on the other end. She was my mother. She had that thing, like spidey senses but for mothers, which told her that her baby was in distress. Her voice changed a little as she said, "It's hard to break up with someone. You're upset, I can tell."

"It's a break-up. It's supposed to hurt, right?" My voice quivered, which was dreadful because I was trying really hard to keep it together. So hard, in fact, my stomach muscles hurt.

"Yes," she said, "when it's been good, it's supposed to hurt. Was it anything Daddy or I did?"

"What? No. We're too different. He works at a gym, for God's sake."

"So?" She sounded astonished. "This isn't the 1920s, dear, and he's not Lady Chatterley's lover. Besides, since when do you care about such things?"

That was rich, coming from her. "I don't!" I said, defensively. "Not really. It's too much to talk about right now, Mum. I'm not feeling up to having this conversation."

"All right, I won't press you." She sighed. "I thought he was a nice boy, though, and I'm sorry to hear you're upset. But you know—" She stopped for a moment and then said in a lower voice, as though she didn't want to be overheard by the help, "—before I met your father I was in love with a working-class man too. I shouldn't really be speaking of it, and of course nothing came of it then, because the times were different and my parents had such expectations…. You've no notion how lucky you are that your dad and I are so accepting of you and so tolerant about what you do with your life, because in my time—Oh, never mind. The point is that we were separated.

"Then I met Daddy, and Tommy met a nice girl from his own spheres, and I think we are quite happy as we are now. But what I mean to say is that at the time—" Here she sighed again. "—at the time it was the end of the world for me. But it all turned out well again. And it will for you too."

I didn't know what to say. I didn't know what to think. My mother had once been in love with a working-class man? That was almost so good it made me want to laugh, though it was uncomfortable to think of her with someone other than my father.

"Who was he?" I asked, because I couldn't help myself.

"His name was Tommy Brown. And he had a great mop of brown curls, and silver-grey eyes, and he was an artist. I met him because he painted your grandfather's study."

He was a decorator? Now I laughed. Because it was too much. "Oh, Mum."

"What?" she said defensively. "He was very handsome, and such a kind, sensitive soul."

"Thank you, Mum. That's—that's good to know."

"All right, dear. Do you want to talk to Daddy? He's just come in."

"No thanks. Later maybe."

We said goodbye after that. I binned the ready meal. I wasn't hungry, after all.

I'm still at Lucy's. Can't face going home.

Hooking up with my neighbour probably wasn't the wisest idea I ever came up with. Serves me right to think I might actually end up in a healthy relationship that won't blow up in my face. I feel ridiculous for ever having got my hopes up in the first place.

Lucy says I should try to be cheerful and look on the bright side—I was free again. She took it as motivation for herself and dumped Kevin once and for all. I felt bad for inspiring her to throw away a good man who liked her a lot, but I get the impression that she'd just used me as an excuse. She seems glad to be rid of him, or if not him, then the relationship, at least.

Now she wants us to go out and hook up with random people, to live up to her mantra that the best way to get over someone was to get under someone, but the thought of touching another man makes me uncomfortable right now. Then it makes me think of Alex touching another man, and I feel physically nauseated.

I called Amelia after that, because her punitive way of telling me that I'm a complete fuckwit for having fucked this up has a strangely bracing effect on me.

"You've brought it on yourself," she told me today. "So what if he doesn't want to play house with you yet? Blimey, the way you go on, Leo, you'll never stay with someone long enough to know if it could work out.

143

You're his first gay relationship, that's got to be a big deal for him, even if he seems easy-going on the outside. I mean, I don't know what that's like, but I can imagine it's not the sort of thing you get used to quickly. And then he meets you, and all you want is to tackle him to the ground and have him turn his life around for you, and if he doesn't perform up to your standard, you think this is a slight on you. It's insane! Give the boy a chance to come out and become comfortable. This way you'll never even get to the stage where he can talk to you about his career."

Then she added, "What a stupid thing to have done. Can I call someone to revoke your degrees?"

Perhaps I was overreacting. Maybe it wasn't *over* over. We just had a tiff. It happens, right?

But it never takes long after a call from Amelia for my mood to fall back into the gutter. After we hung up, I revisited my conversations with Alex, and really, what is there to salvage? He doesn't take me seriously. He blew off coming to New York with me to hang out with that creep Michael. He thinks his career is more important than a life with me.

His career! And what a career! Doctor Alex Muscleman to the rescue!

And then, of course, there's the other thing. The thing that is scarier than all the rest. Looking back, let's face it, I'm not a dream of a boyfriend either. It's possible that I opened a door for him to escape, and he took it because, hell, we both know he can do much better than me.

I'm sick of myself at this stage.

Sunday, 5 September

LUCY SAYS she's tired of me playing "I Can't Make You Love Me" by Bonnie Raitt over and over again. But then, when I switch it over to "Pictures of You" by the Cure, she rolls her eyes at me. There's no pleasing that woman.

Meanwhile, Amelia called to ask why I didn't respond to her invitation to have a barbecue at hers. Turns out she'd sent an email. She doesn't know that I don't check my emails anymore. I know I have work tomorrow, but I couldn't give a toss about that either.

I thought about calling Alex again, but I worry what I might do if Michael picks up.

Tuesday, 7 September

I'VE BEEN brooding in my office most of the day. I saw Jack around the department. He asked me if I was all right and said that I looked a trifle pale. I told him to piss off—which, in hindsight, was probably an overreaction. I was going to send him an email with an apology, but then I just decided that I don't give two fucks what he thinks.

It was harder to avoid Sarah, who came back from her holiday in Spain with her husband in an annoyingly cheerful mood. Naturally she immediately knew everything.

"You broke up with that hunk of yours, didn't you, pet!" she said, watching me closely for a reaction. "Either that or someone died, but then, if any of your family had died, there'd be an obituary in the *Times*, wouldn't there? With the Prime Minister chiming in, eh? Tell me nobody's died!"

I couldn't tell her, because that would be admitting that Alex and I broke up, and I don't want to say that. If I don't say it to many people, maybe it's less true.

Meanwhile, I'm still staying at Lucy's, but wondering if I should go back to my flat and check if there's any post I need to be aware of. Or I could ask Lucy to go and fetch it for me. That would be easier, because I don't trust myself around Alex.

The way I'm feeling at the moment, I'm liable to break down in front of him and weep, which would be pathetic, considering everything.

Friday, 10 September

WE HAD to submit our lesson plans, and I spent the day mostly on the Internet, browsing agony aunt entries on various websites around the net.

I sent Lena a text message, but she didn't get back to me.

Saturday, 11 September

MARK CAME to pick me up today, which probably means that Lucy is sick of my moping and being miserable around her place. He took me out for a drive. In the car, we sat in companionable silence, listening to blues. It was soothing in its way.

Once we were out of London, he drove me to a country pub, and we had lunch/dinner.

"I don't get it," he said at last. "Why would you break up with a fella you still like? Makes no sense to me, mate."

"Just because I like him, doesn't mean he has to like me back, you know."

"Doesn't he? I was sure you were getting on okay."

"We were." I shrugged. "It's not that simple. I'd be game if I were ten years younger and he were just a hot guy I wanted to shag. But I wanted more than that with him. I wanted what you and Amelia have."

Mark considered this. "Have you told him that?"

"Not in so many words, no. Not after what he said to me. It didn't seem appropriate."

"Well, maybe he doesn't know," he said after a few moments of staring at the TV in the corner of the pub, half distracted by Australian rugby. He dragged his attention back to me with difficulty, even though I was watching the rugby myself.

"Once, when Amelia and I were first together, we quarrelled really badly, and she broke up with me."

I remembered. "Yeah, she used to do that a lot."

"Well, yeah, she did. And it was terrible. One time she broke up with me, she saw that I was really depressed about it, and she said, 'It would have ended someday.' I asked her why. And to this day she tells me that that was the day she knew I was serious about her. And that changed everything for her, apparently, because previous to that she only thought of me as a casual boyfriend. You know?"

"Hm, yes." My heart was feeling really heavy, but I didn't know whether I should allow my hopes to get up.

"The thing is," he said, "that you've got this idea in your head of this perfect, romantic relationship—like in those books and movies—made up of grand gestures, like that run to the airport, like having boom boxes over your head playing Peter Gabriel. But that's all bullshit, mate. Pure bullshit. Here's what it's really like. You meet someone, you like them, you spend time with them, you get closer to them than to anybody else, you let them inside yourself. And then, when they leave there's this huge fucking gap, and it hurts like hell. No moment defines this. Not even your last quarrel. The moments, the good ones and the bad, are just things that happened in the history of Alex and Leo, you know?"

"Yeah, right," I said, half laughing, half sniffling.

He let out a chuckle, and we both turned to the telly to let the moment pass with minimum awkwardness. The Sydney Roosters beat the Wests Tigers in golden point extra time.

Sunday, 12 September

GOT A call from Jack this morning.

"I've got something that might interest you, assuming you haven't given up on your career entirely?"

"What do you have for me?" I asked warily.

"My editor is looking for someone who could write a book about the UK and Russia during the Cold War. He thinks this is prime time for that sort of publication, but he's looking for a unique angle, and I told him of you. You're still interested in writing a popular history book, right?"

I was stunned for a moment. "Th-thanks, Jack, that's weirdly kind of you."

"Why weird? I'm always kind to you. Will you come out and have a coffee with me to discuss it further?"

"Yes, all right." I didn't know if I wanted to write that book, but it was good to think of something other than Alex in the throes of passion with a wide array of beautiful people.

This morning I woke up and had these few seconds when I thought there was someone else in bed with me. My heart warmed with a familiar glow immediately, because for a moment those past weeks hadn't happened and I would find Alex there, sleepy and horny, and all would be well. And all that had been said had not really been said at all.

Then it all came crashing down on me as I opened my eyes and they adjusted to the light and I realised I was still at Lucy's, in her guest bedroom, and the body next to mine belonged to Squire, who had, against my explicit instructions, decided he preferred to sleep on my second pillow rather than on Lucy's hardwood floors.

I met Jack in town, and he took me to some fashionable coffee place. We sat in the corner, which made it more intimate. There were cream leather armchairs and little round tables, too low to be useful. A sepia picture—of an Italian man with a horse and cart, delivering barrels to a street corner shop—hung on the wall over Jack's head.

Jack looked good in his business-casual outfit. I wonder if he ever wears anything less elegant. I've never seen him without a suit. He smiled at me in his lazy way that I used to find so attractive.

But here's the weird part: he could have been a woman for how attracted I was to him at that meeting.

We spoke of the book proposal for a bit, but in the end, he had little more to say than he already told me on the phone. We bounced ideas around about what angle would be interesting to that editor of his, and then we talked of the department, some new project he was involved in to do with the Second World War in China. Something about the Nanjing Massacre, maybe. I didn't listen too attentively.

As Jack talked I observed him, and it was as though I saw him for the first time, stripped of the layer of sparkle that my horniness and attraction to him had bestowed for so many years. Suddenly I felt weirdly compassionate towards him.

It occurred to me that many of the men in our department have fucked-up love lives. There's John Partridge, who had relationships with several of the postgraduate students; Will Sheaver, who had an extramarital affair with a woman from the Arabic Studies department, which had almost led to violence; Jack, who's had more girlfriends and broken hearts in his wake than a film star. And there's me, attaching myself to people with wild expectations beyond anything realistic, then heartbroken when the obviously impossible doesn't happen.

What the hell was wrong with us? The women seemed to do better. Most of them are married, settled, and happy.

Randomly, and rather off-topic, I interrupted Jack mid-sentence. "Did you ever seriously think of getting married?"

"What's your dowry situation?" he said with a smirk.

"Shut up. You weren't really going to marry Sasha, were you?"

He sighed heavily, as though he were tired of the topic. "Must we go over that again?"

"No, we don't need to. I was just curious. I'd understand it if you told me you were marrying Ava—I'd marry her myself if I were 1 per cent less gay—but Sasha? Seriously?"

"She was a sweet kid," he said in that odious, condescending way he could adopt sometimes. He probably thought I was having a jealous fit.

"Did you get engaged to her because of me?"

His eyebrows rose. "That's a strange question. Where did that come from?"

"I merely wonder whether your MO is to pursue those who are unavailable to you, and turn your back the moment they become available. That's the hypothesis between my friends."

"Your friends have hypotheses about me?" he said, now much amused. "How romantic."

I laughed. "Stop being charming and tell me."

"I don't know, Leo," he said. "I don't pick my fancies apart and analyse them to death. Either you feel something or you don't. Want to go back to mine?"

"No."

His eyes laughed at me. He was tickled, I could tell. He probably thought this was a weird cat and mouse game.

"You broke up with the plumber, didn't you?"

"Personal trainer. And that's none of your business."

He sighed heavily again. "Bloody hell, Taylor," he said at last, "you really like to keep a fellow waiting. I think you make me out to be much more complicated than I am. If you came home with me today, you'd get lucky. See? It's very simple, really."

"If I agreed to go home with you today, I think you should take me to the hospital, because it would mean I'm having a brain haemorrhage."

He laughed. "Tease. What's happening with that—?" He was going to make up another profession for Alex, but the warning light in my eyes must have stopped him because his smile grew milder. "What's happening with your boyfriend?"

"We quarrelled."

"You've been walking around the department like you were about to set the whole place on fire. Doesn't sound like an ordinary quarrel to me."

"No, it wasn't an ordinary quarrel," I said. "Once, when I was still enamoured of you, I wondered if perhaps you decided to get engaged to Sasha instead of doing anything with me, because I was a man. I thought you were more delicate, less take-it-or-leave-it with the women in your life. And now I think I've got myself into the same sort of situation. I might be wrong... I really don't know anymore. So that's why I'm asking you. Why did you get engaged to Sasha and didn't try anything with me? You must have known you could have."

He smiled, waited a few seconds, as though weighing his answer, probably deciding whether to tease me or to respond seriously, but eventually he went down the kinder route. "I liked being adored by you. It was nice. You were this cute, bright kid, whose face lit up at the sight of me. Who wouldn't want that? But relationships aren't like that. If we had got together, it'd be sweet at first, and then the bubble would burst and you'd be another ex, trading cynical gossip about me with the rest of the department, who all think I'm a sexual pariah. I didn't want that light to go away from your face. It was selfish, but I managed to keep it going for a while, and it was nice... for me. I thought that eventually you'd find someone else. Until Sasha came along, I didn't know you were this serious about me. And then, when she did, I decided I liked you much better."

I blinked at him. I didn't expect that. "And then what?"

"And then the usual happened," he said. "I'm not good with melodrama. In fact, I bloody hate it. And breaking up an engagement, let me tell you, involves a lot of it. I had to help her return to her country. I had to cancel a lot of things we booked, bought, arranged. And so, when it was quickly becoming very serious between you and me—and we hadn't even slept together, for God's sake!—I panicked. I didn't want that. I thought we could just start casually, you know, have sex, see how it goes. I played my cards very badly, I know I did, but I didn't mean anything by it. It doesn't mean I didn't want you."

I stared at him, quite stunned.

Then he said, "*Now* can we go to mine?"

"Christ, no, we can't! I was just beginning to like you. Stop perving out on me."

"*Beginning* to like me!" he said, pretending to be wounded.

Nobody could wound that impregnable ego of his. Jack had no shame, knew no embarrassment. I think that's what public school does to some people—this arrogance and self-importance, but also the ability to carry oneself, so certain of one's own essential superiority. Now that I didn't find him attractive, I found this more irritating than admirable. Because if I couldn't wound him, how could I affect him in any other way? How could I make him feel really good if I couldn't make him feel really bad? He'd fuck me—I had no doubt of that. Maybe he'd fatigue himself to show me a good time too, see me a few more times maybe.

I could imagine it already. He'd grow cold and distant, too busy to chat, too tired to hug. The fact that he used my infatuation, stupid though it was, for his own self-gratification, feeding it little morsels to keep it alive, for years—the magnitude of that was only just dawning on me.

"Yes," I said. "I was beginning to like you. I'd like to be friends. Not because of the book deal—I've no mind for that right now. I'm heartbroken. I haven't even had the energy to write an email, let alone a chapter of a book. You wouldn't know what that's like, would you?"

"I've been told it's akin to being kicked in the groin," he offered helpfully.

I smiled. "Yes, it is, but worse. Maybe you're wise never letting yourself fall like that. I can't say I recommend the things I'm experiencing now."

"Bloody hell, Taylor," he said, still amused. "You have it bad. I had no idea. I thought you were using the man to rub it in my face."

"Yes, I carried on a five-month relationship just to spite you," I said acidly. "You've got the highest opinion of yourself of anyone I know."

He shrugged. "I *was* going to reward you for it."

"Thank you," I said dryly.

"I still can. You're broken up, aren't you? He couldn't blame you for what you do right now."

He waggled his eyebrows at me. Somehow he managed to pull this off, even though I'm sure it shouldn't be possible for anyone, aside from maybe Pepé Le Pew.

"Even if I were tempted—which I'm not," I said, "I wouldn't go with you. If Alex had—" I stopped, because I thought of how Michael was swarming around Alex with all his muscles and macho-Jason-Statham air, and I had that clenching, nauseating feeling in my stomach again. "If it were the other way around, I shouldn't like him to succumb."

"Noble," he said, sounding disappointed.

"No, it's the golden rule," I said. "Anyway, I must be going. Thank you for your offer—the kind one, not the sleazy one. I don't know if you intend to withdraw it now that I said I wouldn't sleep with you, but if you don't, I think I probably should accept it. My sabbatical is coming up next term. Maybe we can talk about it again then."

He smiled. "Okay."

We shook hands, as though he hadn't just been trying to get me to go home with him.

My head is spinning with thoughts. Most of them are about Alex. In fact, it borders on some sort of unhealthy fixation. Mostly I miss him, and then there is the jealousy and pain, but the rest is a question in my mind.

Jack doesn't think his romantic situation is at all his fault— the way he acts is just the way the dice fall. And now I'm starting to wonder if I'm making his mistake—am I as deluded about the consequences of my own actions as he is? Is this whole thing, this break-up, *my* fault?

Was I asking too much of Alex? Was I projecting my insecurities onto a completely innocent man? The conversations we had seem out of proportion. I look back at them in this diary, and I can't make out whether that's what really happened, or whether I distorted it.

Tuesday, 14 September

IT'S INTRO week, which means first-year undergraduates are swarming the campus, being plied with leaflets to get plastered in dodgy clubs.

It's not my favourite thing in the world. The kids are so young, and many of them won't make it to a second year. Everywhere you go you hear anxious whispers. "What did you get for your A levels?" I had to introduce myself in two meetings, talk about the modules I run, encourage people to sign up for them. I can't say I presented a very friendly demeanour, though I made an effort. But who are we kidding, anyway? It's not as if any of them will remember me. They're more interested in each other.

Looking at how young this new batch of undergrads is makes me think of myself at that age. I remember meeting Mark in the college, and not liking him very much because he was reserved and shy, and I thought he was stuck-up. We bonded eventually because he liked good music, and he was a great deal cleverer than most of the people you meet in the first year, even at Cambridge.

I remember the excitement of living away from home. I tried to remember whether I was excited about meeting men, but I couldn't; somehow I don't remember that being top of my list of priorities. I'd been sent off to uni with an earful of instructions from my dad and a list of names of people he knew from his own time in Cambridge, and I'd marched around the place with an air of purpose because of it.

What a tit I was back then.

Here's something I do remember: when I did eventually go out to meet boys, I was ashamed of myself. I felt like a fat person facing a cheesecake. I knew I shouldn't, but... one bite?

It was easier once I met Jamie, because he was more forceful, more outgoing, and I fell into pace with him.

Eventually I stopped fooling myself that I was doing it for Jamie. I was *homosexual*, but resolved that it was nobody else's business. When anybody asked, I told them; though now that I think about it, the reason I let the news spread was so that I didn't have to keep saying it. If everybody knew, then they couldn't ask about it. They'd just have to deal with it away from me and come back to me when they were done.

That is certainly what I did to my parents. Alex seemed shocked when I told him about it. Was it wrong? Why confront someone with unpleasant news, with disappointment, when you don't have to, right?

Thursday, 16 September

SARAH JUST told me off for not reading my emails. At this stage there are too many and I just can't be bothered. I told her my computer was buggered. The tech guy never comes, anyway, so I'm safe for now.

Had to take Squire to the vet, which was a nuisance, since Lucy lives half an hour from where my vet is.

I really should go back to my flat. Maybe over the weekend.

On Tuesday, Lucy brought some bloke home, and I had to leave because I knew what they were going to do. Afterwards the place smelled of him and of sex.

I really miss my own place. I feel homeless at the moment, and I'm so afraid that when I get back, I'll continue feeling like that.

Friday, 17 September

LENA CALLED. She sounded tired, so I didn't bother her with any of my own crap. I asked her about Francis and Yi, and she told me a few gross stories about chapped nipples, and then we hung up because I had the feeling she was falling asleep even as she was doing her sisterly duty.

Saturday, 18 September

I PACKED my things and was going to go back to my flat, but then at the last minute, I took Squire to Amelia and Mark's, hopped on the train, and went to see my parents. It was weird, but I felt an *urge* to see them again. Trouble is, if you don't have a car, my parents' place is a bitch to get to. Not even the taxis that line the kerb outside of the station know how to get to the little dirt lane that eventually leads to their house. I had to navigate for the taxi driver, while he muttered to himself about what this was doing to his tyres and suspension.

154

Eventually, when we got there, I found my parents weren't in. Olga was, however, and she let me in and told me they would be back later in the day.

I gave them a ring to warn them I was there, and my mum gave me a load of superfluous detail about where they were and what might possibly detain them.

I took my things to my room, which was as clean and ready as a hotel room. It was a grey, cloudy day, but even so, the garden looked spectacular from my windows. Alex must have thought he was dating one of the royal princes. Funnily enough, I never even thought we were particularly rich, because my parents associated with other rich people, many of them much, much richer than them. And they hadn't always been so well-off, anyway. Nor did they believe in spoiling Lena and me back then. I had to work for my pocket money and didn't receive cars for birthday presents, like some people I knew. But I don't think that would matter very much in the eyes of someone like Alex.

This place must have intimidated him. And then I'd made such a fuss about his job... that had been stupid of me. It was the wrong time to tackle the subject, if it needed to be tackled at all. I should have been more sensitive, should have just let him tell my parents his profession, and then let my parents look at each other in that way that said they were disappointed. And I should have let it pass. I should have handled the whole thing better.

I'm a moron, and, even worse, a snob.

Because there wasn't anything else to do, I took a nap. Lately I hadn't slept well at night and was constantly tired.

I liked falling asleep with Alex: there was something comforting and soothing about his presence. I try not to think about who's on the receiving end of it now. A part of me knows it's Michael, but I try to lie to myself.

When my parents returned, I must have looked a fright.

Mum put her hand to her lips and said, "Oh dear! What is the matter?"

"Leo?" My father came in after her. "What is it? You look, er, a trifle dishevelled. You've heard of hairbrushes, haven't you?"

I glanced in the gold-framed mirror that hangs in the hallway to see dark circles under my eyes; an unshaven, patchy beard; and my hair sticking up at all ends. I flattened it with my palm.

"You should have your hair cut," said Mum.

"Yes, thanks, I will." I hugged her in greeting and received a pat on the shoulder from my dad.

Then Olga came in, bustling and wanting instructions, and Dad took me to see his computer to sort out the software updates that kept popping up and other minor issues. It was a family tradition. Of course, once I sat down to fix one problem, a whole list of them appeared out of nowhere, and by the time I was done syncing my mum's Kindle with her laptop, and explained to my dad why the security software he chose to purchase is a complete rip-off, it was late, and smells of baked salmon and roasted almonds were wafting through the house.

At dinner I was grilled about my career. Somehow my mum had heard about the Australian project, and I was being pressed to try and chase up on it.

"Why didn't you go?" Mum said, blinking at me. "It's one thing not to pursue anything on your own accord, but to reject offers that fall into your lap seems... well, it seems reckless."

My dad said, "You're not afraid of success, are you, Leo? Your mother read this article the other day by a psychologist—"

"No," I said, quickly. "I was in a relationship at the time, and I wanted to stay here and be with my boyfriend. It wasn't the right time for me."

My parents looked surprised and not particularly pleased.

"Couldn't you go now, though?" asked Mum. "I mean, now that Alex is out of the picture."

"He's not out of the picture," I said and then sighed, because the thought occurred to me that if this were a heterosexual relationship, they'd be less eager to brush it off as nothing. Then I caught myself thinking that and decided not to give in to my hang-ups. "I mean, I'm not happy that it ended, and I—I don't know what I'll do next. I need time to regroup."

"That makes sense," Dad said. "You're still young, opportunities will come your way again. Maybe drop them an email to say you're still thinking about it."

"Yes," I said gloomily.

Then the topic changed, mercifully, to that of Lena and the baby. I had to sit through a whole gallery of pictures of Francis rolling his eyes at the camera and drooling from the corner of his mouth, his tongue between his lips. In other words, he looked like any other baby. He was as cute as a button, and I love him to bits, but spare me having to look at him for an hour at different angles. My mum couldn't get enough of it, however, and my dad seemed amused, so I sat there, letting Mum flick through her iPad and comment on the state of the child in each photograph.

Eventually I was given a glass of wine and we moved to the sitting room. Mum told me about the trip to Italy they were planning instead of their first planned trip to the South of France. They were going with Jude and Peter Richardson, friends of theirs I can't stand, and I was given a detailed itinerary, and then a pity invitation to go with them. I refused, of course, since my depression did not need more food to bolster its strength. Peter is a closet case of the least pleasant kind, if you ask me, and his wife is a nervous, put-upon little housewife, which is also hard to bear.

Finally, when there was a lull in the conversation, I said, "When did Lena tell you I was gay?"

It sort of came out of me like a cough or a sneeze; I couldn't hold it in. They both looked at me, startled, and I lowered my own gaze because I didn't want to see their expressions as they relived that horrible time in their lives.

My mum said, "I think it was when she came back from visiting you. She was doing her internship in Paris at the time, wasn't she, Harry?"

"Yes, that's right," my dad confirmed. "She had a short holiday, and she popped up to see you up in Cambridge. Then she came back to stay with us for a few days with that strange friend of hers—Sally? Shelley? The one who didn't eat meat or vegetables, unless the meat was roadkill and the plants had died of natural causes, whatever that is. What was her name again?"

"Sandra," I said. "What did she tell you?"

"She asked us if we knew you were gay," said Mum, "and we said of course we knew. And then she said that you had a boyfriend in your college. Then we asked who it was, and she told us it was John Marwood's son. Was it James, Harry? Or Thomas?"

"No, Thomas is married now," said Dad. "It was the other one."

"Yes," said Mum. "That was a little bit of a surprise to us, because John Marwood is a horrible bigot. He was up at St John's with your dad, you know, and your dad never liked him, but then we thought—" She laughed. "—we thought that it was a little funny that our son should have a... a *romance* with John Marwood's son. Life is queer like that, sometimes. It's very amusing, though, if you think about it. Of course, it wouldn't be to you, because I don't think you ever met John Marwood."

I couldn't really believe what I was hearing. They were actually *laughing* about it. "You *knew*?"

"Well, we didn't *know*, precisely," Mum said.

"You never told us," Dad said.

Mum added, "But when Julian and Heather were here over New Year's Eve with their daughter—you remember? You were sixteen at the time, and she was awfully pretty, like a young Brigitte Bardot. You didn't even blush and you were ready enough to talk to her, and then got bored with her, and left to do your own things. Well... one can't help but wonder."

I didn't even remember the pretty girl.

"And then you became awfully quiet and red-faced when we had that exchange kid here, the French one. What was his name?" Dad said.

"Christophe," I said at once.

"Yes!" Dad said. "And he was such a dimwit, he could barely keep himself from walking into walls. It wasn't like you to have the least patience with such people, and yet you seemed sad when he left."

"So you knew."

"We had our suspicions," Mum said, "and then Lena confirmed it for us. Why do you ask?"

"I didn't know you knew," I said. "I thought you would be disappointed if you found out."

"Well!" Dad looked a little offended. "What made you think we're so out of touch with the world that we'd be disappointed about something you've no control over? You think we're that backwards? Let me tell you, we're much older than you, and we've seen a hell of a lot more. We've known gay people. My secretary back in Brussels, Linda something, she was gay."

"Yes!" Mum said emphatically. "And what about your cousin George, Harry?"

"Oh yes, very, very gay, that one," Dad said.

"Yes, I know you've met gay people," I said patiently, "but that doesn't mean you'd rejoice at hearing your son was one."

"Well, no, we didn't *rejoice*," Mum said. "It doesn't seem like the sort of thing that one celebrates, although nowadays.... But at the time we just thought, 'Well, that's how it is.' You were always so clever and resilient, we assumed you'd cope. I was a little concerned about your sexual health, because in our generation that was what everybody was talking about in relation to... well, you know. But whenever we tried to speak to you about it, you rebuffed us, so we spoke to Lena and she had the talk with you for us."

Oh God, I remembered that.

"That was *you*?" I cried indignantly. "You gave this ammunition to my sister and then just told her to shoot at me at will? I had so many calls from her! She mocked me relentlessly about burst condoms!"

"Well, she may have done that," Mum said. "Your sister is a little emotionally repressed, and she must make jokes when there is something important at stake. But we hoped it made you aware of the dangers of anal—"

"Okay, okay! I get it, thank you," I said, putting my hand up. "I'd no idea I didn't mask myself very well. I didn't know I'd made such a fool out of myself with Christophe."

Dad laughed. "When I was that age and a pretty girl was in the room, you couldn't have tortured me into behaving reasonably. When I first met your mother, I'm pretty sure I recited the train timetable at her. I don't know why. Don't ask me. I can only be glad that I was as sensible as that!"

Mum laughed. "It's true! And I stood there listening to him prattle on about the trains, wondering whether he was a bit daft!"

They both laughed; I laughed too, because this was so fantastical it was absurd.

I'm in my old room again, waiting for sleep with the certainty that it won't come soon. I keep going back in my head, trying to remember things. I'm a forward-looking person; I rarely think of the past. And often, when you don't think about something for long enough, you forget it altogether. I try to think of good memories, but now I can't seem to come up with any. Any, that is, which are not connected to Alex. Those are still too raw.

I don't want to think about Jack. And before Jack? What have I there to be proud of? A number of faceless hookups. I try to remember any one of them that was memorable, but it's hard.

My head is aching. Why am I torturing myself, anyway? I should go to sleep.

Sunday, 19 September

COULDN'T FACE going back to my flat. I don't know what I'm afraid of, but I'm certainly afraid of it. I worry that I'll go to my place and find that it still smells of Alex. Or I'll accidentally stumble upon a pair of his boxers or something, and that fragile balance I've struck, where I'm basically able to keep it together, will fall apart. I've so much to do now the term has begun; I'm teaching my first class of the year tomorrow.

I miss him. I miss him painfully. I miss the scent of him, and his smile, and that light in his eyes when he stumbled upon a horrible movie that he hadn't seen yet but he'd heard about, something with a title like *Pirate Cowboys* or *Dwarf Hunters*. I miss him standing in my kitchen, laughing at me for having no useful cooking stuff in there. I miss how he smelled after a shower in the morning, freshly shaven, when he used to embrace me from behind as I was preparing my stuff for work, and when I complained, he'd squeeze me playfully.

I miss him so much.

Lucy says I should just call him, but I wouldn't know what to say. And I would lose it if Michael picked up, I know I would. Why doesn't he call me? Isn't that a sign he's trying to move on, or perhaps already has? The longer I think about it, the clearer it becomes: he's better off without me.

It's 2:00 a.m., and I'm trying to prepare my lecture tomorrow, but it's just not coming along. I feel so weary of myself... I'm a whiny bastard.

Going to sleep.

Wednesday, 22 September

HAVING RUN out of sensible clothes for the rapidly worsening weather, and not wishing to look and smell like a tramp when I go to work, forced me to go home at last. Lucy came with me for moral support. As it turns out, and perhaps not to anybody's surprise, I'm a giant baby who needs to grow some balls. Although Lucy assured me that I could make better use of ovaries.

"Balls are so fucking delicate," she said. "Grow a pair of ovaries. We make humans with those, and you can hit them if you want, and there's no way they'd get trapped in a zip."

"You're a poet," I told her lovingly.

Still, my heart was in my throat when we reached my building. I expected to see Alex and Michael coming around the corner on their way out, or hear them through the door of his flat, having mad monkey sex. But I didn't see him, didn't hear him.

I took out my keys and opened my door. There was a rustling sound as I moved the door because papers littered the floor. At first I thought it was all post, and I wanted to groan at that, but Lucy picked one up and read it. A weird look came over her face, and then she handed it to me.

"What is it?" I asked, putting my bags down after I'd walked past the litter on the floor.

"Read it," she said. When I took it, she bent down to pick up the rest and gather them in her hand.

The note was from Alex, and it was a trifle incoherent.

> *Remember when you sang "Debra" by Beck, and I*
> *told you that your falsetto was awful?*
> *I lied. I liked it.*

I looked at Lucy, who handed me a handful of other notes.

I didn't understand, so Lucy led me to the sofa and forced me to sit down while she went around hunting for any papers that the door had pushed aside. Some of them were completely random; some dated and timed. There were maybe twenty. The earliest was dated from 2 September.

> *Michael deleted your number from my phone, and I don't remember it by heart. I tried emailing you, but you're not responding. You're not at home, you're not in your office. I don't know where you are. You probably don't even want to hear from me.*
>
> *Just talk to me one more time. I'll do better. You came to the coffee shop looking so pissed off, I was scared. I didn't say what I wanted to say, and it all went pear-shaped. When you get this note, please just knock on my door. Or call me. A.*

There was another one from the next day, I think, because it read:

> *I shouldn't have mentioned Michael in my last note. It probably made you angry. I know you hate him, but he's only trying to be a friend to me. Please don't be like that. Please just come and talk to me. A.*

There were a few random ones.

> *It rained all day today. Sitting at home without you is awful. Going out without you is also awful.*

Or:

> *Remember that Chinese restaurant when we went for our first date? I went back there today. They had amazing Chinese dumplings. I wanted them again, but then when I*

162

got there, I saw the same old couple that stood in front of us in the queue, you know the one? You said the old lady thought you were my girlfriend, remember? She was there with her husband again. They sat at the same table as before. I think they must be regulars.

I want to be an old couple like that someday. Please call me. Are you still angry with me?

The one dated 9 September read:

I just had a horrible thought that you're going out with that wanker from your department. I know I have no right to tell you who you should go out with, but I'm thinking about it and it's killing me. Please, just at least tell me what's going on. Put me out of my misery.

Then, from 12 September:

Look, I'll be honest with you. I just don't think I'm very good at anything else, job-wise. I know you like men who are successful, and I would like to be that for you, I really would, but I'm just not very clever, and I'm not very good at anything.

I'm really sorry. I didn't do well at school, I quit the RAF, and this training gig is something I can do well now, and I like doing it. I got defensive when you were trying to hide it from your parents, and I shouldn't have. I should have just told you the truth. The truth is that I can't be successful at anything else, and this thing I'm doing now is not very glamorous.

I'm sorry, Leo. I really am. Please speak to me.

And from 15 September:

I know I should stop writing these. I have a feeling they're still on your floor, because I can feel them when I push a new one under your door. Either you're ignoring them or you're not at home. If you're ignoring them, then just text me or call me and tell me to stop and I will. I promise.

The last dated one was from Friday 17 September, and it said he was leaving to see his dad, he was driving himself crazy, Michael was driving him crazy, and he needed a break.

I looked up at Lucy, because as I was reading them I completely ignored her. She was standing there, one arm folded on her midriff, the other stretched out to me. In her hand was my mobile.

"If you don't ring him, I'm phoning the police," she said.

"What? Why?"

"Because I will have killed you," she said.

I took the phone. I had every intention of phoning him anyway. The first note would have done it for me. Or, to paraphrase a famous movie, "he had me at 'your falsetto doesn't suck.'" My heart was hammering against my chest, but I found his contact details, number one in my favourites, with that picture I liked: the one I'd taken while he was off guard, laughing at something Mark was saying. I pressed Call and waited.

The ringtone went for a long time. I thought he wouldn't pick up; it was too late. His last note didn't sound as warm as the others.

Then I startled when I heard a breathless "Hello?"

"Er, yes, hi, Alex. This is Leo," I said, a trifle hastily.

There was a pause and then, "Leo. You called. I mean, yes, of course, we're on the phone now."

He was still breathing hard and I wondered if he'd been jogging. "Er, yes," I said. "I just got home. I haven't been here for the past—God, I don't know, few weeks. I hadn't seen your notes and didn't check my email. I had no idea—I was surprised to find them."

"Oh. I'm sorry."

Was that "I'm sorry, ignore what I wrote?" or "I'm sorry you got swamped with all those love notes?"

I said, "No, it was… nice."

"Yeah?"

Did I make it up or did his voice pick up? "Yes. I haven't read them all yet. I thought I'd ring you instead. They're in my hand, though. M-my other hand… the one that isn't holding the phone."

Lucy rolled her eyes.

I can't say that I was far from reciting the train timetable here. I stood from the sofa, went to my bedroom, and closed the door behind me. "I was at Lucy's," I told him. "These past few weeks, I mean."

"Oh," he said again.

Another voice near him. A male voice. My spine stiffened.

"You're not alone," I said. "You're busy. I should call later."

"What? No!" he said quickly. "That's just my brother. We were out running. Hang on a second." Muffled voices, and then a scratchy sound before he came back on. "I'm here. I just sent him to run ahead. Sorry about that. I'm at home. At my dad's."

"I see. I hope he's well?"

"Er, yes. I think so."

"Look, I don't know if this is a good time to say this, but I need to apologise to you." I knew this was a terrible time to say it, but at that stage, I didn't want to wait any longer. So I said, "I think you misunderstood me. Or rather, I didn't express myself very well, and it all came out wrong. I don't mind what you do for a living. I want you to be happy and content with what you do, and I'm not ashamed of it. I was being an arse, and there's no excuse for it. My parents can be judgemental about my career, and I didn't want them to have more reason to be disappointed with me, so I panicked and I said stupid things and—and I was being a complete and utter pillock, and I'm so, so sorry. I didn't mean to hurt you, or make out that you somehow weren't good enough for me. That is certainly not true. If anything, it's the other way round. You're way too good for me. In fact—" I took a deep breath and then plunged ahead, eyes closed. "—I thought that what you were saying when we were arguing about it was that you didn't think I was important enough to you to discuss your career. I thought you weren't taking me seriously."

"Idiot," said Alex affectionately.

I could tell he was smiling. "Yes, I know," I said. "I was miserable this past month."

"Yeah, me too."

"I want to see you."

"My sister's birthday is the day after tomorrow. I promised I'd be here. Can you wait until Friday? I'll come down as quickly as I can then," he said. "I really want to see you too."

"Hm... I wish it could be earlier. I don't want to sound melodramatic, but I *really* miss you."

"Yes, I miss you too," he said eagerly. "Why don't you come up and see me?"

"Where are you at the moment?"

"Carlisle."

"Oh. That's... far."

"Yeah, sorry. I'll see you on Friday," he said.

"No," I said quickly. "It's almost five, but I'm sure there'll be trains running. I'll probably get there late. Can you find a hotel room for me? I'd like to see you today."

"What about your work?"

"I'll call in sick."

"Really?" He didn't sound as enthused as I'd hoped he would.

"I don't want to intrude," I said. "If you prefer I can wait until Friday."

"No! I do want you to come, I want to see you as soon as possible. I just worry—you've given up so much in your career for me, and I didn't want to make you—"

"Please stop quoting me when I'm at my stupidest," I said.

He laughed. "Okay. I meant I would like to see you, but I don't want to cost you your job."

"You won't," I said. "It's the first week. Anybody can take over from me. Most lectures are pure housekeeping. Honestly, I want to come up and see you. I won't if you think it will be awkward."

"No, it'll be great. I'll see about the hotels, as you said."

"Okay, thank you. I will text you when I'm on the train."

"How long will you stay?" he asked. "Can you stay for my sister's birthday?"

"Er... do you want me to?"

"Yes!" he said. "Will you come? You could meet my family."

"Oh, won't it be—as your friend, you mean?"

166

"Um, if you want to. I told them about us. They know who you are."

"Oh," I said, an odd flutter in my stomach. "You came out to your dad?"

"Yeah, I did. I was miserable, and I couldn't hide it. I told them everything. Well, not *everything*. You know what I mean."

I laughed. "Yes, okay. I would be honoured to meet your family."

"Okay! Great! Oh God, I'm so glad. I love you, Leo."

"I love you too. I'll see you later today."

"I can't wait," he said.

It was hard to hang up. But if I wanted to catch the train, I had to get going. When I emerged from the bedroom, I found Lucy sitting on my sofa with Squire. I told her what had happened.

She said, "I'll take your dog to Amelia and Mark. You pack. Oh, and shower and shave. You don't want him to change his mind when he sees you again, eh?"

"Very funny. Can you check trains to Carlisle before you go?"

She did.

It didn't take me long to pack, because it never does, and I was in a hurry to get to Alex. Part of me still didn't believe this was happening. I ended up calling Sarah from the train, asking her to find someone to fill in for me. She thought I was insane, but she agreed in the end. I had to tell her I was going to see my boyfriend's family, which softened her to the task of giving the few lectures I had over the next two days to someone else. But what completely won her over was my promise that I'd tell her all about it when I got back.

Anyway, I've got a four-hour journey ahead of me, and I expect to be in Carlisle by ten o'clock. I texted Alex, and he said he'd pick me up from the station.

Friday, 24 September

WHEN I arrived in Carlisle, the station was flooded by bright lights and an army of people spilled out onto the platform. Heavy bags fell with a thud, and friends and family greeted one another with happy chatter and hugs.

I saw Alex immediately. He was standing under one of the lights, with hands in his pockets. I waved, and then he spotted me. And he smiled, a bright, happy smile as of old. He looked somewhat thinner, but not significantly so, and the expression on his face was all that I wanted to see.

Standing in front of him, without being able to drape myself over him like the girl two doors to the left of me was doing to her boyfriend, was hard. I would have kissed him ordinarily, but a group of football fans had exited the train at the same time as me, and they'd been imbibing freely throughout the journey. It was best not to provoke them unnecessarily and ruin our reunion.

I could see in Alex's eyes that he thought the same.

He said, "My car's parked outside."

He took my bag off me. It wasn't a big bag, but it was the only mark of affection, besides the smile, the look, and the warmth in his voice, that we were allowed just now, and so I let him.

"I was to say that you were welcome to stay at ours," he said, "but I booked you a hotel room anyway, because… because I thought you'd want some privacy."

"Yes, I would. Will you come and stay with me?"

"Okay." His cheeks coloured, and I remembered that they used to do that a lot. He caught me staring, and smiled and rolled his eyes in embarrassment.

We were mostly quiet until we got into the car. Once inside, he leaned in and kissed me. It didn't matter who saw, since we were in the car and would drive off in a moment, and screw them all, anyway.

He kissed me very tenderly, and then, his face still close, said, "Hi."

"Hi." I couldn't repress a smile. It was reflected in his own.

The hotel was not far from the station. In fact, I could have walked the distance, probably. It was a red-brick Victorian building. Frankly, I didn't care if he put me up in a hovel, so long as I could have four walls and Alex to myself, but this was nice, and I was a little surprised.

When I raised my eyebrows at him, he said, "You can afford it," in a tone that suggested concession.

There was no bitterness in it that I could detect. When I looked admiringly at the entry hall, he seemed pleased. He picked up the booking,

168

and the receptionist, a young Polish woman, gave us our key with that efficient, robotic air that made the fact that two men were booking into a king-sized bedroom much less awkward. In fact, she went about it as though the hotel catered for no other type of couple.

We went upstairs, Alex still carrying my bag.

Once in the room, I had time to glance quickly round and find it to be really decent. I was enveloped in Alex's arms and we murmured sweet nothings, and then we were kissing, plucking at our clothes and assuring each other we'd never argue again, that this was so stupid, such a waste of time, that we hadn't meant anything we'd said.

Naturally we'll probably argue again. But it was good, soothing even, to know that Alex had hated this as much as I had.

Once we were naked in bed, once there was nothing between us and we were skin to skin, fevered flesh to fevered flesh, I was both relieved and excited. He was familiar and he was new. We had left the fairy-tale land of the honeymoon period, and we'd passed into new, exciting territory. I was okay, because I was there with him.

When Alex breathed his release into the base of my neck, I cradled his head, and then we lay there for a good long while, completely silent. I could feel his heartbeat, the sandpaper feel of his freshly shaved face on my chest, and the tickle of his breath on my flushed skin. We moulded together perfectly. Then his phone started ringing, and he groaned but eventually lifted off me. Naked in the faint light of the bathroom, he fished for his phone among the sea of clothes strewn all over the carpeted hotel floor. He found it just in time.

"Hey? ... Hm? No, I'm staying. ... Yeah, tomorrow. ... I don't know, tenish? ... Shut up. ... Okay, bye." When he turned back to me, he said, "My brother."

"Oh." I remembered now that there was a whole family to confront. "How did he take it? All of them. Do they all know?"

"Hm? Yes, all the ones you'll meet tomorrow, at least," he said, crawling back into bed and finding something approximating his former position, then hugging me close. "They were fine. Surprised, shocked, I don't know. Something of the sort. We're a loud family. We talked loudly."

"But they're okay? You're okay?"

"Yeah, yeah," he said tiredly and then yawned. "I wasn't worried. If they say something stupid tomorrow, you have to forgive them. They'll say twenty things and mean about half of them. Don't worry about it." Then he squeezed me a little. "Mmm, I missed you."

And then he fell asleep. Ten had been a generous hour for Alex to suggest, because we weren't out of bed until half past nine. We got up much earlier than that, but we'd not finished making up, and then the exhaustion of morning sex led to further naps, teasing wake-ups, shared showers, and breathless embraces. When we did get up, we found that we needed to shower again. Then we set about finding whose clothes were whose, and Alex had to dash out to buy a razor because I hadn't thought to bring mine and he hadn't packed because, as he said, "I didn't know what would happen and my thoughts were everywhere."

So we didn't get to his father's house for ten. We made it just before twelve. My own parents would have found that sort of tardiness rude, and I was therefore suitably stressed, adding to my existing stress of being introduced into a potentially hostile household. But Alex seemed relaxed, and assured me all would be well.

He parked his little grey Fiesta in front of a rather small red-brick terraced house. He had been calming me down all the way there, assuring me that no, they didn't expect me to bring anything; and no, we don't look as though we've rolled around the bed all morning; and yes, I can tell them we've been sightseeing if it makes me feel any better.

At last we were facing the door, its black, gloss paint chipping at the edges. Alex didn't use the bell that proclaimed in proud capital letters his surname, LANDI. He knocked instead.

The dull thud of running footsteps, and then a young man opened. Much younger than Alex or me, he was tall and gawky with spiky dark hair and wearing a hoodie. He gaped, first at Alex, then at me. And then he looked like he was going to laugh.

"Ah! The boyfriend, eh? Ha-ha, come in. I'm Damian." He stretched out his hand, laughing, clearly finding it hilarious and embarrassing all at once that his older brother had just brought back a boyfriend. But he wasn't hostile at all.

I shook his hand, and Alex told him to stop being a baby.

Damian ran off, shouting loudly, "Eh! Sandro is here!"

I heard voices as Alex led me towards the end of a narrow corridor and into a sitting room, where a large number of people were gathered. They all rose at once and a loud hubbub began, where my hand was shaken, my face was laughed into, and I was introduced to too many people to remember.

The birthday girl had not yet arrived; she was due tomorrow, but Alex's other brother, plus his wife and two children, were there, and his other sister, with her husband and three children. Damian's girlfriend was expected.

In an armchair in the centre of the room sat Alex's father, and he remained seated, apparently aware of his own importance. He waited for everybody else to sit and calm down, and then Alex led me to stand in front of him. His father was much shorter and less bulky than I imagined, especially in comparison to his sons, but he was tough-looking all the same. He was bald on the top of his head, and his eyes—though they were the same colour as Alex's—were smaller and narrowed at me. Unlike that of the rest of his family, his accent was American.

"You're the boyfriend, then?" He didn't seem pleased. He looked at Alex and then at me, as though trying to see what incubus had charmed his son away from the ways of the normals. Stupidly, I reverted to my defences.

"How do you do," I said, sounding to my own ears like my father at a reception.

"Sit down," Mr Landi said. "Bring him a chair, eh? They tower over me—I can't see anything. Damien, stop being a pest, where are your manners? Emilia, stop it! Eh? Tea? Ah, yes. Alex, go and make some tea. Want some tea, Leo?"

Another bustle began. Alex simply abandoned me as a chair was swiftly pushed under me and I was left one-to-one with the old man and the rest of the family ranged behind me, like a Greek chorus. It was like having an audience with the pope.

"Leo is a Latin name, did you know?" he said to me.

"Er, yes," I said.

"Your parents liked Latin names?"

Strange question, but I answered. "Er, no. I think they were more interested in naming their child after Tolstoy and Da Vinci. My sister's name is Lena."

"After…?"

"My aunt," I said stupidly.

He narrowed his eyes at me. "Not a Latin name, that. Swedish?"

"I don't know."

"Is she gay too?" he asked.

I didn't think he asked it maliciously. His tone was the same as when he was asking the other questions.

But Emilia, Alex's older sister, cried out, "Dad! What kind of question is that? It's not like if you have one gay child you immediately have only gay children."

Alex's dad frowned in confusion and said defensively, "It happens! Ask your uncle Emilio! Ah, there I have you. He had only gay children."

Emilia shook her head at him, as though he were a hopeless case. "Gina is a fe-mi-nist!" she said, enunciating the last word slowly to him. "Doesn't make her gay."

"Have you seen her?" he demanded as though she was being unreasonable.

Damien came back in, finding the whole situation vastly amusing. "Who, Gina? Ew!"

"What ew? What ew!" demanded Emilia. "You think all lesbians look like the women on the posters in your room?"

"What posters?" demanded his father.

"Thanks, Em!" moaned Damien.

Oscar, Emilia's husband, laughed. "You're confusing the issue entirely. Alex, your family will drive your boyfriend into mental illness!"

"What?" Alex's head popped in through the door. "What happened?" His eyes sought mine, but I was just sitting quietly in my chair. He smiled. "What have they been saying?"

"Gina, feminist or lesbian?" I said.

"Dad!" Alex said pleadingly.

"What? What me? What have I done all of a sudden? I sit here, having a civil conversation with Leonardo, and then I'm being told of

172

your brother's perversions and your cousin Gina's problems. I'm the victim here!"

"His name is Leo, as I told you," Alex said patiently. "And Gina is not gay... she's only big and strong. And stop gossiping about Uncle Emilio. Damien, come and help me with the mugs."

"See how they treat me?" his dad said to me when they left. "Where were we? Is your sister gay, or is she not?"

"Er, no," I said. "She has a boyfriend and had a child recently. She lives in New York."

That interested him. He grew up in New York and immediately wanted to know where my sister lived. When I gave their Park Avenue address, he made a long, impressed face.

"She must be very rich," he said directly. "How much does she make?"

This made the entire Greek chorus behind me give a roar of disapproval, accusing him of asking vulgar questions. It was really strange, but amusing too, in a way. Eventually, Alex came in with the tea, which made everybody sit back down, and his older brother, Phillip (or Fillipo as his father called him) told on his father. Alex shook his head in amused disapproval and pulled up a chair to sit nearby, which made this seem less like a strange job interview.

"Did you know his family was rich?" his dad asked him.

Alex coloured a little, but said, "Yes."

"You didn't tell me? I didn't know you were going to start dating rich people. Are you getting married?"

Again an uproar at the impertinence, and again his defensive "What? What?" And then, to me, he said, "If he had come with a girl he was serious with, I'd ask the same question. So I ask you, what are your intentions towards my boy here?"

I looked to Alex, who said, "Dad...."

Mr Landi shushed him. "Let him answer. This doesn't concern you."

I didn't know what to say, so I braved, "I want to stay with your son. We haven't discussed marriage, but maybe we can live together when he is ready to do that."

"Hm," said his father, contemplating this. "You want children?"

"Yes, I think so."

"Adoption? Surrogate? How many?"

Again an uproar from behind me, demanding he be reasonable. It was amazing how this family could hold several quarrels at once.

Emilia was asking her father whether he had asked such questions of Oscar when he'd first been introduced to him, and then she reacted with outrage when she was told that yes, he had in fact done so.

Damian was laughing into his sleeve. Oscar was trying to calm down his children, who came running up to their grandfather to defend him, and Phillip told his dad to be reasonable, while Phillip's wife was siding with Emilia on the issue.

At last the matter was dropped, somehow. I'm not sure how.

"Do you believe in God, son?" Alex's dad asked me finally.

Again the protests came, but it seemed that by raising his hand he could indicate to everyone that he would not be badgered into not asking the things he wanted to know. I didn't know this was going to be an issue, and wished Alex had briefed me on it. Since I couldn't ask for Alex's assistance, I responded truthfully. "I do not."

"Oh? Atheist, eh?" He narrowed his eyes at me.

"I suppose so. I don't give the matter much thought."

"You were brought up what, Anglican?"

"Yes." I waited for some form of condemnation, but it didn't come. He seemed to mull over the issue, and then shrugged.

"Your mother won't like it," he told Alex. And then to me, "She has converted to Catholicism, for me. I was never a big churchgoer, but she likes it. She will find it hard. All of it."

"I'm sorry to hear it," I said.

Alex's father shrugged in a way that said "what can you do?" and then let the matter drop.

Alex took me away shortly after that. We promised to return for dinner, and then I was out of the house and in Alex's car, and it was quiet and peaceful. I took a deep breath.

"How did I do?" I asked.

Alex laughed. "You did fine, I told you you would. How was it for you?"

"Good. They seemed to be okay with it. Were they?"

"Yeah, sure," he said, starting the car.

We went into town and then back to the hotel to recuperate.

The dinner was easier now that I knew what to expect. After all the men moved the chairs and sofas to the side in the sitting room, they took a large table from some back room and spread it out. A few moments later the table was heaving with food, mostly pasta dishes. I was seated with Alex on my one side and Oscar on the other, and though I was stared at with curiosity, I didn't feel like a freak or in any way excluded. Everybody made an effort to be friendly, and we had civil conversations about where in London we lived and what I did. This interested Mr Landi greatly. He seemed pleased to learn that I lectured in history, and he was impressed by my education and that I had authored a book. When I spoke of my family, his reaction was favourable. He told Alex that his mother would like that.

The whole was a convivial evening, hampered by the expected level of general awkwardness around having a new person at the table, but not to any marked degree. I suppose my being a man and Alex having just come out to these people added to their discomfort, but I gave them credit for trying to make the whole evening pass smoothly. In fact, it all went so much better than I expected. When we went back to the hotel afterwards, I was quite elated.

Later, when Alex was spooning me from behind, both of us flushed and breathing hard, I asked him if he had imagined it would go so well.

"No, I didn't know precisely," he said. "You never know how people will react to anything. But I hoped you would like them. Or at least not hate them at the very beginning. Later, when they have more time to get used to us, and to this, I think we will be fine."

I snuggled deeper into his chest, and he sighed against my shoulder.

"Leo?" he said, after a while.

"Hm?"

"I've been thinking."

"Hm?"

"About my job."

"Oh God, please let us forget I ever said anything," I moaned.

"No, listen. I was thinking… maybe if I save up, and when the economy improves a little, maybe I could start my own gym, you know?"

"Oh?"

"Yeah, I was thinking about it and once I save some money to invest in it, I think it could be profitable. I could run classes, I could still train people, I could hire other trainers…."

"I think that sounds wonderful, Alex. You should definitely do that. *We* should *both* save up for it."

"Yeah?"

"Certainly. Hey, you could run fat camps in the summer, what do you think?"

"Yeah, that sounds fun."

"Don't laugh. I think you could pull it off. I mean, you got *me* to work out, and that's right next to sorcery."

"I think that was just the power of your horniness, Leo. I can't harness that from everyone who pays me money to get fit."

"Oh, okay, if you say so," I said, and he laughed against the back of my neck.

"You don't think the idea is stupid?" he asked after a while.

"I think it's brilliant."

We fell asleep shortly after that.

The next morning, we prepared for Thea's birthday. Alex had waited for her to be here to tell her his gay news, and so she arrived without having the slightest knowledge of it. That was probably why she brought her mother with her. The moment Alex saw the old woman come in, he changed. He stood apart from me, at a safe, straight-man distance, and I could see that everyone was looking at me, a little disconcerted. I surmised from this that Alex's mother didn't know and would be unlikely to welcome the news.

After that, everything went a little pear-shaped. Damien's girlfriend, Tanya, arrived, and she was introduced to his mother, and hugged, and welcomed. Tanya was blonde and freckled, and so, perhaps because of that, Alex's mum seemed to assume that I had come with the girl, as her brother/chaperone or something, so she only gave me a cursory glance.

The girl herself was a charming dimwit, very pretty but a trifle vacuous. Still, she was an ally to me because she knew as little of this family as I did—in fact, probably less. So the three of us—me, Tanya, and Damian, with his arm around her waist—stood slightly to the side as the various children and grandchildren took their turn greeting Mrs Landi.

Alex's mother is a short, stout woman with short, permed hair, dyed blonde, and red nails. She laughed and talked as freely as the rest of the family, dispensing gifts for her grandchildren and talking of how her daughter's twenty-fifth birthday was such a great thing.

I saw Alex take Thea aside. When they emerged some minutes later, she sought me out with her eyes, said something to Alex, and then came to meet me.

"Hi," she said in a conspiratorial whisper. "I'm Thea. You're Leo, right?"

"Yes."

We shook hands.

"Look, I'm sorry, I had no idea," Thea said. "This is kind of awkward. Alex wanted to tell me to my face, and I didn't know, and so I brought Mum."

"So stupid," said Damian with a roll of his eyes.

"No, that's fine," I said. "Why shouldn't your mum be here?"

"Er," Thea looked from side to side, "I don't know. We'll see. Hey, I think I met you once, didn't I? I helped Alex move some of his stuff."

"Yes, in the hallway," I said. "I thought it was you who was moving across from me."

She laughed. "Yeah, I bet you're glad now that I didn't, eh?"

I smiled and acknowledged that to be true. Meanwhile, I watched Alex waiting for his mother to turn to him. I wasn't sure what to do next. To spare Alex the pain and awkwardness, I could have happily left and let him deal with this when he found the right time. But I could see from his expression that he was determined to get it out.

Seeing that, I said to Thea, "Er, I'm sorry if this is going to steal your show."

Indeed, a few moments later, the whole party descended into a quarrel. Alex had taken his mother aside, he and I exchanged wary glances, and Damian consoled his sister that at least this birthday would be memorable. And I had no doubt it would be.

Soon, Mrs Landi stormed into the room like a bullet, straight at me, grabbed me by my shirt, and shouted, "You! Seduce my boy! Devil! How dare you!"

Her sons and ex-husband pulled her back, while Emilia and Thea tried to calm her. She was nearly hysterical, though, her eyes bulging, demanding if everybody knew of this and how long had it been going on.

Alex came to stand by me; he straightened my shirt and muttered apologies, even though I was sure he was more distressed than I was.

"He only just told us," someone told her at last. "He came out to us a few days ago."

"A few days!" she cried. "A few days? Then it's nothing. Alex, come here. Get away from that man."

Alex didn't get away from me. He said, "Mum—"

But she didn't let him finish. "I say get away from that man! He is dangerous!" And then to her ex-husband, "You're allowing him into the house when there's *children* here?"

"Mum," said Alex, "please, calm down. We can talk about this."

"There is nothing to talk about!" she yelled. "You've been seduced by this—this *man* here, and you don't know what you're doing, but it's not too late. We can fix this. You will meet a nice girl, like Becky. Remember Becky? You were in love with Becky!"

"Mum, I'm with Leo now," said Alex, sounding very unhappy.

"Nonsense! You're ill! He is making you ill. You must get away from him, or else you will succumb to his seduction and—"

"Mum!" Alex said pleadingly, and the others were chiming in with their received knowledge about gay people, but nobody was listening to anybody, so I didn't know what good that was doing.

Meanwhile, I stood there quietly watching this unfold, finding that I didn't know what to do or say and would have gladly left. But I couldn't leave Alex to this alone. So I just stood there, letting her insult me, knowing better than everybody else that she wouldn't change her mind, at least not that day.

"Well, you can't tell me you were a straight, good boy for thirty years and then all of a sudden you've changed your mind!" she snapped. "He seduced you, confused you, but it's not too late!"

"*I* asked him to go out with me!" Alex said, losing his patience. "Okay? *I* asked him. He didn't do anything!"

"You asked him! Then you're more confused than I thought. Someone call Becky! Emilia, you know her number! Gio, stop pulling on my sleeve, I'm not hysterical. Alex, you will come to church with me tomorrow. We will sort this out. You need help!"

Alex tried to respond, but she wasn't listening, because she'd turned her fire onto me.

"And *you*! How dare you turn my son into one of your kind? How dare you even try? I made a good boy. I brought him up right. He wasn't gay until you made him, warped him, destroyed the good work I did. I hope you're happy now. You'll roast in hell for this, but you won't take my son with you!"

"I didn't make him gay," I said quietly.

My finally opening my mouth made everybody else go still, and so I was heard. She glared at me, and I said into the sudden silence, "I don't think you can make people gay. It doesn't work that way. I'm really sorry if you're upset, but this has nothing to do with Alex's upbringing. And he is still a good person—the best person I know, in fact. And I'm *not* happy if this makes you that unhappy, because I know Alex will be upset about it."

"Oh, you don't have to answer to me!" she cried. "You will have to answer to him!"

Here she pointed upwards. I didn't think bringing up my atheism would improve matters much, so I didn't say anything, and she went on further.

"He will know what to do with *you*! And he'll know this wasn't Alex's fault. Alex, you will come tomorrow with me, and we will help you, and fix this, and you will not see this man again, do you hear me? He is confusing you. I knew you should have married Becky when you had the chance."

She continued in this way, and probably would have gone on for much longer, but when she began insinuating that I was a danger to the children again, my cheeks began to burn and I was about to say something when Oscar stepped between us. He didn't say as much, but it became obvious that there would be no party until I left.

So I said it. I told Alex that I would go to the hotel and he could come when he was ready. He insisted on driving me, so I wished Thea a happy birthday and apologised for this, and then we went to the car and drove to the hotel. The drive was tense and silent. But once we arrived, he came up to the room with me, hugged me, and said, "I'm so sorry. I didn't know she'd be there. I was going to break it to her slowly and let you meet her once she's made peace with it. It's all my fault. This was not the ideal way to tell her. I just didn't want to spend the day with everybody pretending about who you were. I'm so sorry. Are you okay?"

I could see from his face that he was the one who was more distressed, so I assured him I was fine and told him to go and be with his family and not to worry about me. So he went.

It's near midnight now, and he still isn't back. I refrained from texting or ringing him. I don't doubt that there are some serious conversations going on at the Landi home, and I don't want to make things worse.

Sunday, 26 September

ALEX CAME back on Saturday with all his bags. He looked tired, and so I didn't bother him with questions. In fact, I was pretty sure there would be no happy answers to anything I could ask, so I let the matter lie.

Since he was knackered, I drove us down. He brooded in the passenger seat. I stopped at a nice service station, where I bought him ice cream and coffee. Sure his thoughts were tangled in confusion and a whole variety of unpleasant emotions, I didn't make him speak. Instead, I plied him with treats and held his hand when I didn't need to change gear.

When we finally reached London, he came with me to my flat, collapsed onto my sofa, and then patted the free space next to him. So I sat there and let him embrace me.

"It's good to be back," he said.

"Yes. Can I do anything for you?"

He sighed. "No, I'll be fine. It's just tough to think that someone you love is so angry and disappointed with you."

"I can imagine."

"Can I ask you something?" he said.

"Yeah?"

"She wants me to go to church with her and speak to her priest or pastor or whatever you call him."

I laughed. "How did you grow up in a religious household without knowing what to call the man who preaches at you every Sunday?"

"We weren't religious when I was growing up. My mum went to church, but she became more zealous with time." He smiled against my hair. "Would you go with me?"

"To church?"

"Yeah."

"Alex—"

"I don't mean to worship or anything like that. Just to, you know, take a step towards my mum. Maybe if we go together, then she'll be more reasonable to talk to, and when she knows you better, she will have to love you eventually."

"I don't think that's empirically true, Alex," I said. "But I will go with you, if you want me to."

"Really?" He squeezed me to him. "You're the best."

"You're worth it." After a few moments of winding down from the long drive and the very eventful last couple of days, I added, "Can I tell you something?"

"Anything, love."

"I was very proud of you, these past couple of days."

"Oh?" He perked up.

"Yes. I didn't have the guts to do what you did in my day, and I had to do it with fewer people, and without religion, culture, or anything else coming in the way of being understood. You were very brave. We'll win your mum over, somehow. I'll do my best, anyway. Even if I have to sit through a dozen sermons."

"Thank you," he said, relieved. "I don't know why you put up with me and all this mess."

"I love you," I said. "And sometimes I think you're the only thing that's keeping me sane."

"Oh," he said. Then he smiled mischievously and said, "Then this is probably the wrong moment to tell you. I'm a figment of your imagination."

This startled a laugh out of me. I had to kiss him. "Come here. I'm tired. Can we order in? I'll have to ring Amelia about Squire."

"Okay. Let's go and pick him up first, and then we'll order food."

And that's what we did.

I'm coming to the end of this notebook, which I never expected to fill this far. What a strange year it's been. And it's promising to get weirder. At least, as we were devouring a pizza for dinner this evening, Alex wanted to talk over perhaps moving in together. I would like that.

I'm not so crazy about the whole churchgoing thing, mainly because I'm not convinced it will soften his mother one bit, but I'll go with him all the same. Maybe, when she gets used to me a little more, she'll become less aggressive. I'd be satisfied if she could simply ignore me. But who knows? People do astonish you sometimes.

I texted Lucy to say that I'd brought Alex back home and all was well.

She responded with *About fucking time!*, which was as charming as usual from her.

Alex should be back any minute from his run. Then I promised to watch *Troll 2* with him, another one of his so-bad-it's-hilarious movies, which he'd watched five times.

Is it strange that I find this hobby of his so adorable? Lucy would tell me I'm being impossibly schmaltzy. Probably she's right.

Amelia would tell me to stop making her vomit.

Ah! The sound of the door. He's back.

Thursday, 30 September

POOR ALEX had to endure daily phone conversations with his mother all week. She won't give up on him no matter how much he pleads. So today, seeing as it was our six-month anniversary, I thought I'd do something to make this ordeal worth it.

I knew he had an appointment at ten, but that gave me plenty of time. He'd been sleeping over at my place every night since our return. So this morning I woke him up with kisses along his neck, until he took a deep breath in and pulled me to him.

"What are you doing?" he slurred.

"Waking you up." I lifted the cover from him and reached underneath. "And what do you know? You're up."

"You've got an unhealthy obsession."

"Mm-hm," I said, as I was tending to one nipple and then the other.

"Okay," I said. "Your choice. BJ then breakfast, or breakfast then BJ."

"Are *you* cooking?" he asked dubiously.

"Tsk. Make your choice, Landi."

"Definitely, definitely BJ."

I ignored what that said about my cooking. Let's be honest, he had grounds for concern. Anyway, I preferred that order as well, so I dived under the covers. If I do say so myself, I put years of practice to bloody good use. When I came up again, his eyes were wide and he was breathing hard.

"How did you—?"

"Shh." I kissed him. "Come along. We've little time, and I have much planned."

"Planned?"

I grabbed his hand and led him out into the kitchen. I know I'm a terrible cook, so instead of whipping up a fry-up—or anything that would burn the flat down before I could make my point—I had gone to the bakery down the street and fetched freshly baked pastries, and then I just brewed coffee. It produced the desired effect by filling the room with a wonderful aroma. And I'd put flowers in a vase, which made the table look nice.

"Oh wow," he said, looking at all this. "That's new. Did you sleep with someone else or something?"

"Sit down," I said. "Here."

When he sat down at last, I gave him his anniversary present. I was nervous, because I'm the worst gift-giver in the world, as I think I have demonstrated, and this one could go either way. It was a card—a shop-bought one, because I'm not into arts and crafts, and I was trying to impress him, not alarm him. The card had two puppies on the front and read simply "Happy Anniversary."

"Oh?" he said. "Shit. Did I forget an anniversary?"

"Yes, but never mind. Look inside."

He opened the card and then had to unfold the piece of paper that I had glued to it. On it was my actual gift. I watched him read it, trying to contain my anxiousness. He was startled at first, but then he smiled, and then the smile widened, until he got to the end and his eyes lifted to meet mine.

"I don't know what to say."

"Is it impossibly cheesy?" I asked, wincing.

"No. It's very sweet. Come here." He kissed my forehead. "Thank you."

He took my hand then and walked me back to the bedroom.

"What about breakfast?" I asked.

"I've got to give you your anniversary present first," he said.

He barely made it to his appointment, but by the time he was going out, we were both wreathed in smiles.

I haven't told him the bigger news yet: I've taken on a second job. It's not very glamorous—a position on the editorial board of the *English Historical Review*. Alex said he wanted to start his own gym, and by God I'm going to get him one. Plus, we'll need the additional money if we think of moving.

Anyway, last page.

The contents of my card to Alex.

For Alex

If we're nothing but stardust
Blown at random throughout time
My, am I glad, my love,
That your dust happened to fall in with mine

If we're nothing but avatars
For ancient, alien minds
My, am I glad, my love,
That yours played the game with mine

If there is nothing out there

And we're but a civilisation lost in the galaxy
My, am I glad, my love,
That in this vastness you're with me

If the world were to end tomorrow
Neither of us would have made history
My, am I glad, my love,
That there was a you and me

If there is nothing more to life
Than sleeping and waking with you
My, am I glad, my darling love,
That that's all I ever want to do

What are the chances?
What are the odds?
That I could have missed you
In a million different worlds.

MARINA FORD is a thirty-year-old book addict, who would, if permitted, spend all of her time in bookstores, libraries, or in her own bed with stacks and stacks of books. Luckily, she has a husband and a dog who force her to interact with humans of planet Earth from time to time. In fact, she so enjoyed falling in love with her husband that she can't resist evoking those same feelings in the love stories she creates in her head. She does not believe in love at first sight— but she does believe in Happy Ever After, though it must be earned. She likes her stories to be light and frothy, since real life can be miserable enough without making up more of it in fiction. She lives in England, loves rain (gives one an excuse to stay at home and read books, right?), long walks (when it doesn't rain), history, love stories, classical literature, pulpy literature, Jane Austen, languages, and dogs. It is her dream to one day possess an enormous country house in which each room is a library (okay, maybe except for the kitchen), and in which there are more dogs than people. A smaller and perhaps more realistic dream of hers is to make people smile with the things she writes.

Also from Dreamspinner Press

SOME ASSEMBLY REQUIRED

LEX CHASE
and
BRU BAKER

Life comes in pieces.
Some assembly
required.

www.ingramcontent.com/pod-product-compliance
Lightning Source LLC
Chambersburg PA
CBHW060100260626
47160CB00005B/1734